RACING THE REAPER

Jerrid Edgington

Master Koda Select Publishing

Racing the Reaper
Book one of *The Reaper* series

Racing the Reaper is a work of fiction. All names, characters, and incidents are
the product of the author's imagination. Any resemblance to real persons, living
or dead, is entirely coincidental.

An MKSP Book/March 2014

Published by Master Koda Select Publishing, LLC
www.masterkodaselectpublishing.com

Text copyright © 2013 Jerrid Edgington

All rights reserved. The right of Jerrid Edgington to be identified as the author
of this work has been asserted by him in accordance with the Copyright, Designs
and Patents Act 1988.

Originally published in eBook form by Master Koda Select Publishing in 2013
Master Koda Select Publishing, LLC functions only as the book publisher and as
such, the ultimate design, content, editorial accuracy, and views expressed or
implied in this work are those of the author.

No part of this publication may be reproduced, stored in a retrieval system, or
transmitted in any way by any means without the prior permission of the
copyright holder, except as provided by USA copyright law.

ISBN: 978-0-9859838-7-1

Cover Art :
        "Speeding Ambulance": © bluevis artist on Pond5.com
        "Grim Reaper": © 4@stokkete on Pond5.com
Cover design © Rebbekah White

Printed in the United States of America

DEDICATION

I dedicate this book to my wife, Jody. She's my best friend and my soul mate. I can't thank her enough for allowing me the countless hours of writing. With her support, anything is possible.

THANK YOU

First and foremost I want to thank God. Without Him, none of this would have been possible.

I also want to thank Kim and Arlene, the best editors I've ever known. They taught me so much and have helped me make my book a great novel. Thank you.

Chapter One

"Safe!" the umpire yelled. That was the last thing that rang through Jacob's ears before everything went dark. As he came to, it felt as though his arms were under his chest, but once the foggy vision cleared he could see they were outstretched over his head. He was lying there, the right side of his face pressed firmly into the dirt. Unable to feel anything, fear consumed him. The roaring cheers of the eager crowd were suddenly silenced.

"I can't move! Someone help me!" Jacob screamed. The only things visible were the feet and legs of bystanders around him.

"Are you okay? What's wrong?" the umpire asked.

"I can't move. I can't feel anything. What happened?"

"Someone call 911!" the umpire bellowed. He knelt down beside Jacob and leaned down. "You hit your head on the catcher's leg and then passed out. Someone call 911," yelled the umpire again. "Now!"

Jacob slid head first into home plate, as he had done a thousand times before, trying to score the winning run in a city league softball game. Lying there on the field, not able to move a muscle regardless of any effort, every inch of his body was numb. He wanted to get up, but couldn't. A scream escaped his lips. *God, what is happening to me?*

Despite the quickly approaching sirens of the emergency vehicles, he could hear the bystanders quietly talking as if he wasn't there. The sorrow and pity in their voices fueled his anxiety. Terror tore through him as the thought of sitting in a wheel chair for the rest of his life caused tears to well up in his eyes. He choked down the urge to cry. His lips quivered as the taste of dirt filled his mouth. Jacob's only hope was that the numbness would soon vanish.

He heard footsteps scurrying through the dirt towards him. "The paramedics are here, buddy. You're going to be okay. Hang in there," the umpire said.

"What happened?" a paramedic asked. He knelt down next to Jacob, placing a hand in the middle of his back. A look of concern crossed his face.

"He went head first into the catcher's leg and then passed out," the umpire replied.

The paramedic leaned down in front of Jacob's face. "Sir, can you hear me?"

"Yeah. I can't move anything. What's going on?"

"What's your name?"

"Jacob Myers."

"How old are you, Jacob?"

"Twenty-two."

"Where are you hurting?"

"I'm not. I can't feel anything. I tried to get up, but couldn't."

"Are you having any trouble breathing?"

"No, I just can't move. What the hell is going on with me?" His mind was commanding the muscles in his body to move, but they ignored his request. The thought of never being able to walk again was too much to handle. One minute he was sliding into home plate to score a run; the next he was lying in the dirt unable to move or feel anything.

The paramedic looked over at another firefighter. "We need to get a helicopter. Can you do that for me, captain?"

"Sure thing. The outfield is big enough. We'll use that for a landing zone." He stepped a few feet away to talk on his radio. After a few minutes, he returned to where Jacob was lying on the ground. "The helicopter's fifteen minutes out. They're coming from the trauma center in Scottsdale."

"Let's get him packaged up," the paramedic offered.

"Someone tell me what's going on!" Jacob screamed with a quiver in his voice.

The paramedic leaned down, reassuringly placing a hand on his shoulder, even though Jacob couldn't feel it. "My name is Brent and I'm a paramedic with the fire department. I'm a straight shooter and I won't lie to you. I'm afraid you may have a spinal cord injury. To what extent, I really don't know. There are several things we're going to do to take every possible precaution. I'm going to put this cervical collar around your neck to help remind you not to move your head. Lie still and let us do all of the work. I need to cut your clothes off so we can see any other potential injuries."

"You're not going to strip me naked out here in front of everyone are you?" Jacob asked nervously. He was a modest person and didn't feel comfortable around people without his clothes on. During high school he was always the last guy to shower, and didn't dare walk around without at least a towel wrapped around him. Guys on the team would ridicule him for his lack of confidence in his body.

"Don't worry. We'll keep you covered up as much as possible," Brent calmly said.

The tone in his voice was soothing and instilled a confidence in Jacob that he really needed at that moment. After the collar was secured around his neck, and with the assistance of a few other firefighters, they rolled him onto his back. This position allowed Jacob to see what was going on, not to mention removing his face from the dirt. That was a welcome change.

In the distance, the sound of the whipping helicopter blades drew closer. Jacob's condition hadn't improved in the slightest and that was unsettling. Was this going to be irreversible? He closed his eyes and silently prayed. He wasn't a devout Christian, but now was as good a time as any to fix that. *Dear God, I don't know if you're listening, but right now I need you more than anything. I'm hurt, hurt really bad. Please, dear God, help me. I'm so scared.*

The firefighters moved around briskly. It was obvious to Jacob this wasn't their first rodeo. Hearing the sounds of the Velcro pulled apart had him curious. Not being able to see what they were doing caused his frustration and tension to grow. Remembering what the paramedic had told him, he took a deep breath and slowly let the air escape, trying to calm down. A wave of nausea rolled through his stomach, threatening to empty out the pregame meal he consumed before arriving at the ballpark.

"We've got him secured to the back board," the captain said.

"What are his vital signs?" Brent asked.

Jacob could hear more Velcro tearing as a firefighter put the blood pressure cuff on his arm. Still, there was no feeling. *God, why aren't you listening to me?*

"It's 92/72 with a heart rate of 132. Pulse ox reads 99%," the firefighter stated.

"I'm going to get an IV started. We need to give him some fluid for his low blood pressure."

"The bird is on final approach. If you're going to do that, then get it done. We need to get him into the air," the captain barked. The two men glared at one another. Brent turned his attention to Jacob and prepared his arm to start an IV.

"You're going to feel a slight pinch as I...." He stopped in mid-sentence and paused for a moment. "I'm sorry. That was insensitive of me." At times, he wished he could put his foot into his mouth rather than say such foolish things.

"No need to apologize. I'll be the first patient who doesn't complain about the pain from an IV start, right?" Jacob asked.

Brent chuckled. "It's good that you have a sense of humor."

"Just my way of dealing with stress," Jacob said. The corners of his mouth tugged up weakly forming a half smile. As the needle slid into his arm, his mind said it hurt, but he didn't feel a thing.

"IV is in. Let's start the fluid bolus," Brent ordered. After the IV was secured, fluid dripped into the tubing at a rapid rate.

Dust swirled around and hung in the warm summer air as the helicopter landed. The paramedic left Jacob's side and met with the flight crew. After talking for several minutes, a woman approached Jacob, and knelt down next to him.

"Hi there. I'm Jessica and I'll be the nurse taking care of you." A man walked up behind her. She pointed over to him, "This is my partner, Nick. He'll be the flight paramedic helping me. We'll be taking you to the trauma center in Scottsdale. Has any feeling returned yet?"

"No. Nothing's changed," Jacob answered. His anxiety ran rapid through his body like a wildfire burning out of control through a dense forest. He wished he could erase the few seconds before he slid into home plate. Had he known what damage was going to be done, he wouldn't have slid head first. It wasn't worth the life altering changes that stood before him.

Jessica got up and knelt down next to Jacob's feet, took out her trauma shears, and scraped the bottom of his foot vertically to his toes. "Can you feel that?"

"No."

A concerned look crossed her face. "Let's get him over onto the flight cot. We need to get going." The firefighters picked Jacob up, and placed him on their cot. Once secured to it with various belts, they whisked him away towards the air ambulance.

"Did you see that?" Jessica asked Brent.

"Yeah. It isn't good."

As they got closer to the helicopter, the wind began to twirl the grass from the field. Jessica jogged up next to Jacob and leaned over him. "Close your eyes so you don't get anything in them."

The only thing he had control over was his eyes. He squeezed them tightly closed. Once under the rotor blades, there was a large amount of heat deflecting from the helicopter. So hot, that it burned his eyelids.

After he was loaded into the helicopter, the paramedic approached him and leaned in close to his ear.

"Remember what I said and stay calm. I'll be praying for you," Brent said and disappeared from Jacob's view.

The flight crew climbed in next to Jacob. They slammed the door shut with such force it shook the helicopter.

"Have you ever flown in a helicopter before?" Jessica asked loudly, competing with the roaring engines.

"No," he answered through gritted teeth. His vision blurred from the tears flooding his eyes.

"It's noisy and can be bumpy at times. If anything changes, and I mean anything, let me know right away. We have a fifteen minute flight to Scottsdale." She reached up and caressed his cheek. Jacob couldn't feel her touch, yet another gruesome reminder of how badly he was hurt.

The engines roared with power. As they shot straight up in the air, Jacob prayed again. *God, please tell me you're hearing my prayers. Look, I know I haven't exactly been around much. I don't blame you if you're mad at me, but I am so scared and don't know what to do. Please help me. I know you can heal me. Do it now before it's too late!*

Chapter Two

The next four days were a blur as Jacob dipped in and out of a drug-induced stupor. Unable to care for himself, he was at the mercy of the ICU staff.

As he drifted in and out of consciousness, there were times he swore he heard his father's voice. But that couldn't be. His father was hundreds of miles away. Then he would slip back into the hypnotic state that imprisoned him. He wished with everything in him that his father could be here, just like the countless times when he was a kid and had lost his way home.

On the fifth day, the nurses began to lower the dosages of his pain medications. As his eyes flickered to life, there he was: his father, Blake Myers, smiling and bathing him with a loving gaze.

"How are you doing, son?"

"I'm not sure. How long have I been here? When did you get here? Am I ever going to walk again?" His hopes teetered on his father's response.

"Not so many questions. You need to take it easy. You've been through a lot. There's plenty of time to talk later." Jacob's father reached down and caressed the side of his face. His hopes of this being a bad dream were quickly dashed when he couldn't feel his father's touch. *Don't you hear me, God? Why haven't you healed me?*

A few minutes later, a man in a white lab coat walked into the room. He was tall, slender, clean cut, and had short salt and pepper colored hair. Jacob guessed he was in his mid-fifties. He wore a bright colored bow tie that grabbed Jacob's attention.

"Mr. Myers, you've finally decided to join us. My name is Dr. Ebstein. I'm your neurologist. I bet you have a thousand questions. How are you feeling?"

"I'm not feeling anything. How long is this going to last?"

Dr. Ebstein hesitated. "In time, we will know more. As of right now, all I know is you have a spinal cord contusion."

Oh my God. That sounds bad! His heart sank at those three little words. "What does that mean?"

"In layman terms, it means that you have a bad bruise on your spinal cord. When you came into the emergency room, your spinal cord was inflamed. I placed you on a steroid medication, which should decrease the swelling. CT and the MRI revealed no tears in your spinal cord, which is good. The nervous system is a funny thing. Though you don't show any spinal cord damage, it could still be injured enough that you will suffer irreversible deficits. That's the part that only time will tell."

He walked over to the foot of the bed and lifted the sheets. Taking an ink pen out of his pocket, he scraped the bottoms of both of Jacob's feet. He could see what Dr. Ebstein was doing, but couldn't feel it.

"Did you feel anything?" Dr. Ebstein asked.

"No." Despair filled him.

Dr. Ebstein pulled the sheets over his feet. "Get some rest, Jacob. You really need it. If you begin to feel anything, let the nurse know right away." He then looked over at Jacob's dad. "May I speak to you outside for a moment, Mr. Myers?"

"Absolutely." He looked at his son. "I'll be right back."

The two men stepped into the hall, just far enough so he couldn't hear what they were saying. The one thing he noticed was Dr. Ebstein liked to talk with his hands. As he spoke, his hands were moving at a feverish pace. After a few moments, the doctor patted Jacob's father on the shoulder, and walked away. As his father returned, he appeared hopeful.

"What did he say?" Jacob asked.

"It doesn't matter. You're a fighter. You're going to be walking again. I promise."

"I would rather die than to not ever walk again."

Blake's face grew angry. "Don't talk like that. I'm not going to let you lie there and feel sorry for yourself. If you really want to walk again, you will. The only person, who has control over that, is you."

Jacob wanted nothing more than to crawl up in his dad's lap like he had as a child, and hear that everything was going to be okay. His greatest fear was being trapped in a wheelchair for the rest of his life.

An uncomfortable silence loomed in his room. There was a light knock on the door.

Peeking around the door was a young nurse. She stood just over five feet tall, had dark brown hair, and silver eyes. She walked into the room brushing a long curl out of her eyes. "Hello, Jacob. My name is Betty. I'll be your nurse for the next twelve hours. I need to do an assessment on you." She turned towards Blake. "I'll need you to leave the room, sir. You can come back in a little while."

"Sure thing. I'm hungry anyway." Jacob's father stood up, stretched, and disappeared through the door.

"How are you feeling? This is the first time I've seen you coherent."

"I'm still not feeling anything. Pain would be an improvement."

A slight chuckle slipped from her lips. "This is true. Look, you have to stay positive or you won't ever have a chance to get better. Mind over matter, I say." She walked over with a chart, and began to record vials signs from the monitor he was hooked to. "I must say, you're a pretty popular guy. I've received several phone calls from people inquiring on your condition. It's good to know you have a support system."

"Yeah, I have a pretty big family. They're very religious. I'm sure there have been a lot of prayers for me." *As for me, I'm not sure what to believe. So far, it seems God isn't hearing a thing I'm saying.*

Betty walked over next to his bed. She leaned over the rail and placed her fingers in his hands. "Can you squeeze for me?"

With all of his might and will, he tried; nothing moved. "I can't!" he exploded. "I'm sorry. I just…." His heart pounded in his chest; his pulse increased. Unable to complete the simplest of tasks sent him into a rage.

"Don't be sorry. Just keep trying. I have a few other patients I need to check on. I'll be back later to see how you're doing." The corners of Betty's lips lifted and formed a heartwarming smile.

As she left the room, his thoughts turned back to the God who wasn't listening. *God, where are you!? I'm a good person. Why have you let this happen to me? I know I haven't been on my knees in church every week, but what have I ever done to deserve this?* Hot tears stung his eyes. *Why aren't you answering me?*

After being in ICU for over a week, Jacob was transferred to the step down unit. He wasn't sure if that was a good or bad thing as he was still unable to move any muscle lower than his chin. *What if this was as good as it was going to get?*

Each morning while it was still dark, he would wake up to Dr. Ebstein holding his hands asking him to squeeze. It bewildered him being woken up in such a fashion. The doctor's exotic choices of bow ties caught Jacob's attention each morning.

The sun slipped through the blinds lighting up his room with a bright orange glow. Jacob's mouth was as dry as the Sahara Desert, a side effect of the pain medication. He was sure if he were to look inside his mouth he would see tumbleweeds rolling through. Sitting on a table next to his bed was a glass of water. Oh, how he wished he could reach over and grab it. As he was lying there staring at the water glass, the right side of his body began to tingle.

"Hey!" he yelled. Perspiration formed on his forehead. This was a drastic improvement. Maybe a sign that his body was beginning to heal? The pinky finger on his right hand moved slightly.

"Hey!" he yelled again. A newfound sense of hope slowly overtook his depression. A grin crept across his face. "Hey, somebody. Anybody!" His eyes traced around his room. There wasn't anyone to celebrate with him.

A few moments later, there was a knock on the door. "Come in," he yelled. A beautiful woman entered. She had brunette hair, hanging just above her shoulders, beautiful green eyes, and a captivating smile. He tried desperately not to stare, but it was impossible.

"Good morning, Jacob. My name is Desiree. I'll be taking care of you until the night shift comes on duty. Can I get you anything?" She bathed him with caring eyes. Since he'd been in the hospital, the nursing staff appeared to legitimately care. It helped curtail the anxiety that coursed through his veins each time he thought about his imminent future being imprisoned by a wheelchair.

Barely able to contain his excitement, Jacob sputtered, "I moved my pinky finger this morning."

She briskly walked over to the bedside and took both of his hands into hers. "Can you squeeze for me?" Her beautiful green eyes gazed into his.

Jacob concentrated for a few moments, and then his pinky finger moved, much more than a few moments ago.

"Good! This is exciting. I need to go call Dr. Ebstein. I'm sure he'll be pleased." She turned and headed toward the door.

Jacob grinned. He was a kid with a new toy: moving his pinky repeatedly. It wasn't more than several minutes until fatigue set in from the rigorous pinky activity, and he drifted off to sleep.

A few hours later, Jacob was awakened by a knock on the door. There was shuffling on the right side of his bed. It was his dad.

"Come in," Blake said. The beautiful nurse emerged from the hall with an enormous smile on her face. "Well hello, young lady. How are you today?"

"I'm doing fine, thank you. You must be Jacob's father."

"Guilty as charged. My name's Blake. You let me know if he ever gets out of line. He's not too old to get a spanking."

She laughed. "I'm going to have to ask you to step out, sir. I need to give your son a bath. Give me half an hour and I should be done."

Blake smiled at Jacob. "Son, you're one lucky man. What I wouldn't give to be in your place right now."

Want to trade places with me? You have no idea what kind of hell this is, Dad. Jacob wanted to pull the covers over his head, but couldn't. At times, his father had the manners of a junkyard dog.

"I'll be back later. Love you, son."

"Love you too, Dad."

Blake left and an uncomfortable silence filled the room. "How about them Dodgers?" blurted out of Jacob's mouth.

Desiree smiled. "I'm not much of a baseball fan, but I'm guessing you were cracking a joke."

She walked over to the sink and filled a small tub with water. After putting soap in it, she pulled the gown down to his waist, exposing his bare chest. Normally, lying half-naked in front of a beautiful woman would be embarrassing for him, but since being in the hospital, he had lost all modesty.

The nurse started by washing his face, and then down his neck. Jacob had more feeling returning to the right side of his body, but he wasn't going to tell her yet. He was self-conscious and wanted nothing more than to reach up and take the rag from her, but of course, he couldn't.

Just a few weeks ago, his life was normal. Now he was dependent on people to take care of his every need. Desiree suddenly stopped scrubbing his chest. She looked away not making eye contact with him. Jacob looked down and noticed he had an erection. His body was laughing at him hysterically. *God, is this your idea of a joke? Because it's not very funny!*

Desiree weakly smiled. "It's okay. We're professional here. It happens all of the time."

"I'm sorry." If he could get up and run away, he would have.

"Don't be. You can't control your body right now. It's quite all right. Think of it this way, at least now you know your body functions are improving."

He sighed. She had a point. Next to worrying if he would ever be able to walk again, he worried if his sexual functions would ever be the same. At his age, it was a concern. He wanted to get married someday and have a family of his own. If his present deficits remained, he didn't see that as a possibility.

Ten minutes later, the bath was over and Jacob was dressed. As he drifted off to sleep, he couldn't help but feel good about the day's events, even with this last embarrassing incident. Any improvement he made no matter how embarrassing, he was thankful for.

A week later, Jacob was transferred to the rehabilitation floor. The right side of his body had gotten quite a bit stronger, but the left side remained weak and numb. Overall he had improved dramatically, but he was frustrated with the small improvements. How could it be so hard to do the simplest things? How could it take every ounce of energy to move his hand? He could only stay excited over moving his pinky finger for so long. He wanted to walk again, not play pinky flex.

The physical therapists in charge of his rehab could be difficult. At first they were caring towards him, but now they were brutal and demanding. Jacob often reminded himself that it was their job. Without them, he would never walk again. Hell, he didn't know if he was ever going to move his left leg, let alone walk. Whom was he kidding?

Four to five times a day, the physical therapists would place a support belt around his waist and hoist him out of bed. It was a slow and painful process. As the feeling started to return to his body, he was stricken with hypersensitivity. Each time he was touched, it felt as if a million needles were being stabbed through his body. Dr. Ebstein reassured him that this was normal and a part of the healing process, but it didn't make it any less painful.

As time crawled along, Jacob began to feel his left leg come alive. A flicker of hope came with the feeling. Perhaps he would walk again. Perhaps someday he would even jog and then run. He grabbed the hope and tucked it away in his heart. He had to do this! He had to walk again. He *would* do this.

Sarah, one of the physical therapists, came and got him for his daily trudge to the dining hall at the far end of the rehab floor. She wasn't a very attractive woman, but she had a great personality that lit up a room when she walked in.

"All right, Jacob. Let's go eat. You ready?"

"I'm starving. I was about to walk down there by myself."

"How many times do we have to go over this? You can't walk anywhere without someone helping you. Are you trying to get me fired?"

"If I did that, would you be?"

"Now, that's not funny. If I didn't have this job, how could I support my shoe habit?"

"That would be a downright travesty." He gave her grief. This was his defense mechanism. It was difficult controlling the mood swings. One minute he would be blissful, and the next, he hated the world. In many ways this injury had brought the worst out of him. At times Jacob couldn't stand being around himself, much less having others deal with his difficult attitude.

Sarah placed the belt around his waist, which she used to steady him. With the left side of his body still weak, walking was a challenging task.

"Put your arm around my neck like we did yesterday."

With her assistance, and every bit of strength in his body, he lunged up to a standing position. Normally this would be an effortless feat, but for Jacob it was a full body workout. She gave him a minute to catch his breath.

"We're going to walk down the left side of the hall. I want you to use your left hand to help balance yourself," Sarah said.

"You do realize that's my weak side, right?"

"Of course I do. That's the point. I want you to start using only your left side to begin strengthening it."

"You're a real back breaker, you know that?"

She smiled. "Yes. I am. Don't you forget that, young man."

"That wasn't a compliment." Jacob was easily aggravated with her. Of course, it was her job to get him back on his feet. Still, she could be so annoying at times.

It took everything he had to raise his left hand up to the rail. This was not going to be easy. Frustration filled him. Each step sent pins and needles exploding through his body. He wanted to cry. With everything in him, he forced the tears back down. He couldn't cry. It was a sign of weakness, and he yearned to be strong again. His feet thudded onto the freshly waxed tile floor in an uneven rhythm. His coordination resembled that of a young child learning to walk for the first time.

Short of breath and sweating profusely, he finally made it to the dining hall. Sarah pointed at a table at the other end of the room. His stubbornness kicked in. He made it this far; he could make it to that seat. It's amazing how a simple task would become a profound accomplishment if he was able to complete it. With each step, his goal was a little closer. His legs burned with fatigue. Each step sent electrical shocks up his back. His legs buckled and he felt the belt around his waist jerk tight. Finally, as Jacob reached the seat, his body succumbed to the rigorous workout and he collapsed into the chair. Every muscle in his body began to twitch. Once he regained his balance, Sarah gave him a reassuring nod and headed to the kitchen to retrieve the meal. As he was trying to slow down his breathing, he thought how just a few weeks ago he was running in a softball game to make a point. Running: that was the key word. Now it was impossible to walk without assistance... if you wanted to call what he was doing "walking."

Sadness rolled through him, but he fought it off. This is how the mood swings always began. He would be sad, and then anger would take over. Dr. Ebstein told him that he not only had to heal physically, but mentally as well. This was going to be a long and painstaking road he had to travel. *Why are you doing this to me, God? I don't understand!*

Sarah returned with a tray of food. After that long walk, he was starving. "From this point on, I want you only using your left hand for daily tasks. I know it's going to be difficult and frustrating, but we need to retrain that side of your body. Unless you want to stay here with me every day for the rest of your life," Sarah said grinning.

He couldn't understand himself. One minute her humor drove him up the wall and the next minute it lifted him up from the pit of Hell. This was one of those moments where it brought him back to the living. "As much as I love you heckling me, pushing me, and being down right mean to me, if it's all the same to you I would rather get better so I can leave this place."

Sarah smiled broadly. "That's what I wanted to hear. So, what are you waiting for? Let's start easy. Pick up that roll and take a bite of it."

Looking down at his plate, the roll was a mile away. His pulse began to race and anxiety rose like a thermometer on a hot summer day. He attempted to raise his left hand. *Why is this so hard?* He wanted to give up, but his stomach was screaming for sustenance. His hand felt bound to his side with a heavy chain. Once he got his hand up to the table, it flopped down like a limp fish. He sighed. Sweat poured down his forehead, to the tip of his nose, and then dropped onto the smooth poly tabletop.

"It's okay, Jacob. You're almost there. Don't give up now. I know you can do it," Sarah whispered while nodding.

Jacob sucked in a deep breath through his pursed lips and lifted his hand again. He wasn't a quitter and wasn't going to give up. His hand slowly made it over to the top of the roll, but then fell helplessly on top of it. He was half way there. Now for the hard part: lifting the roll to take a bite. His arm started shaking and sweat rolled down his forehead. He couldn't get it more than a few inches from his plate. His hand flopped back down onto the table. Jacob grunted and shook his head.

"You can do this. Don't give up; just keep trying. I have to go check on another patient. When I return, I expect to see that roll eaten." Sarah smiled and headed out of the dining hall.

As he lifted his hand once more, the roll smashed into a ball in his hand. He had a difficult time gauging the grips in his hands. Glancing around the room, he noticed that no one was watching. He leaned forward and tried tossing the roll into his mouth. The butter glazed roll bounced off his face and fell to the floor. Butter dripped down his cheek. He couldn't stop the laughter. *Better than crying.* After all that work, all he had to show for it was butter dripping from his chin. Others in the room stared at him, yet he didn't care. It wasn't pretty, but at least he didn't give up on the ever daunting task of eating a dinner roll.

A few minutes later, Sarah returned to the dining hall. She stopped, placed her hands on her hips, and looked at Jacob quizzically. "Dare I ask?"

"What happens at this table, stays at this table," Jacob said grinning.

After lunch, Jacob looked up to see his dad enter his hospital room, the corners of his lips tugged downward. His eyes were moist and reddened. Seeing his dad sulking and unhappy tore a hole through his heart.

"I have some bad news, son. It's time for me to head home. I really wish I could be here for you, but I have to get back to Missouri. My work won't grant me anymore time off. I'm proud of you. You've come a long way."

Jacob fought off the urge to plead with him to stay. He knew that would just make his father feel worse. "I understand, Dad. I'm going to miss you."

Tears flowed down his father's cheeks as he leaned over to hug Jacob. Blake pulled his son into his arms. His father holding him was his security blanket. His dad stood up, kissed him on the forehead, and disappeared through the door. A lump formed in his throat. He could hold back no longer. A tear traced its way down his cheek. For several hours, he cried. His heart ached. He was alone, more alone than he'd ever been. *How am I going to do this without my dad? I need him now more than ever. God, if you're listening, please give me the strength to push on. I need him. I need You.*

After several weeks of grueling rehab, Jacob was being discharged. It had been a long and hard road, but he did it. The thought of leaving the hospital was both exciting and terrifying. For the past two months, there was always someone there to help him. Now he was going to have to do it all on his own. Jacob was flown in on a stretcher, but now he was going to walk out. His daydreaming was interrupted by a knock on the door.

"Hello there, Jacob. How are you feeling today?" Dr. Ebstein asked as he walked into the room. He met Jacob's gaze with soft and caring eyes.

"I can't wait to get out of here. It's crazy, doc. Two months ago I didn't think I was ever going to walk again; but now I'm running out of here," Jacob said with a beaming smile.

"You certainly have come a long way. Your road to recovery isn't completely over yet. You're going to need to continue working on your coordination. It will still take some time, but you should be completely healed within six to eight months. You're a lucky man, Jacob. You have surpassed all of my expectations," Dr. Ebstein said smiling.

"You can thank my father for that. After all, he made me to be as stubborn as he is."

Dr. Ebstein laughed. "That he did. Just do me one favor, will you?"

"What's that, doc?" Jacob asked inquisitively.

"Hang up your cleats and retire. I think your days of playing city league softball are over."

Jacob sat on his bed laughing and shaking his head. "I can do that. Thank you again for everything you've done." He walked over and gave Dr. Ebstein a hug. The doctor took a few steps back. "Take care of yourself, Jacob." He turned and left the room. In Jacob's book, he was the greatest man ever to live, next to his father.

After he tucked away his clothes in his bag, Jacob turned to see Sarah in the doorway smiling at him. He glanced down and saw a wheelchair.

"I know that's not for me," he growled. His eyes narrowed and his lips pursed. It was the last thing he wanted to do, be wheeled out of the hospital in a chair. He'd fought so hard through rehab and endured a great amount of pain. He wasn't going to allow Sarah to treat him like a helpless man.

"It's hospital policy. You have to be taken to the front door in it. Sorry. It's non-negotiable." Sarah crossed her arms and tapped a foot on the cold tile floor.

"This isn't a negotiation. I'm not going out in that thing. I worked my butt off to stay out of that chair. I'll be damned if I'm going to be wheeled out of here in it." His voice grew louder.

A smirk covered her face. "That's the fighter that I've come to love. I'll tell you what. I will just push it, and if someone from the hospital administration comes along, you can jump into it. I do have to protect my shoe habit."

Jacob laughed. He missed Sarah already. For the past few months, she was his rock. His life wouldn't be the same without her around to pester him. Then again, her constant griping was something he wasn't going to miss. He was ready for his victory lap. Slowly he walked past Sarah into the hall. Glancing down the long corridor, his feet sprung to life.

"So, what's next for you?" she asked.

"I'll go back to my boring office job selling tools and start living my life again. This whole experience has made me realize that there are greater things out there for me."

"What do you mean?"

"I'm a firm believer that things happen for a reason. This accident had a purpose. I'm not sure what it is yet. I have questioned why God let this happen to me, but I still don't have any answers."

"It has been a pleasure, and a pain to work with you, Jacob." They both laughed. "I'm glad you didn't give up. If you had, you wouldn't be walking out of here right now."

Not that long ago, Jacob wasn't allowed to walk down the halls without Sarah's assistance. He reached down and patted his waist. And he could still feel the belt wrapped tightly around it—it was no longer needed. The hall that once seemed miles long was now a short jaunt and easily navigated. The muscles in his legs twitched, but the excitement of leaving the hospital fueled him. For the first time his steps were in a rhythmic cadence. He stopped. The corners of his lips tugged towards his ears; the corners of his eyes crinkled. Sarah stopped and curiously looked at him. Jacob shook his head and continued down the hall. His footsteps were music to his ears.

Standing at the elevator, a feeling of elation overwhelmed him. This was it; he could now command his extremities to do as he wished. Reaching up to push the button to the elevator was an impossible task before. Now he was able to do it with ease.

Sarah stood next to Jacob with an empty wheelchair, a reminder of where he could've ended up had he not fought so hard to get back on his own two feet again. They stepped inside and descended to the ground floor, the final destination to his freedom. As the doors opened, he let out a victory sigh. The front doors were the finish line and he was racing towards it.

Jacob nearly lost his balance and fell to the ground. Thankfully, Sarah was next to him and he was able to use the wheelchair to steady himself. He looked at her. Tears trickled down her cheek.

"Don't cry. You should be happy you're getting rid of me."

She reached up and wiped the tears away. "It isn't sadness. They are tears of joy. I'm happy for you. You'd better learn to slow down or you're going to end up back here with me again."

Jacob laughed. "I will. Thank you for everything you've done for me. I appreciate it." He gave her one last smile, turned, and headed out the door. If he only knew what turns his life was about to take, he wouldn't have left the hospital.

Chapter Three

It had been a year since Jacob's accident. After several months of intense physical therapy, he fully recovered. The only remnant of the injury that he sustained was a slight numbness in his right leg. That was something he happily lived with. The alternative was being bound to a wheelchair. He couldn't have live that way. It drove him to work harder at regaining his coordination. After each therapy session, his body ached. His muscles were tense and strained. The fact that he could feel was a blissful reminder of how far he'd come.

During that year, he continually questioned why the accident happened. Was it because of being overly zealous in a softball game, or was that a way God had planned for him to change directions in his life? Not only did the injury change his perspective, but it also made him question God's plans. He often prayed, but felt that God never answered him. He was grateful for the recovery God bestowed upon him; however the other part of him wondered what he was supposed to do with the gift of his health.

Jacob took a strong interest in the medical field. The way the paramedics were able to help him, drove him to pursue a career at becoming an Emergency Medical Technician. He attended the EMT class at the local community college two nights a week for a semester. He looked forward to class. Jacob wasn't a stellar student during high school, but a fire burned inside of him and pushed him to study every chance he had. After successfully completing the training, he took the licensing exams. It was a difficult course, and an even more grueling testing process. He struggled through the didactic portion of the class, but excelled in the hands on portion of the training.

Four weeks passed since he completed his licensing exams. It was difficult going to the mailbox each day to walk away empty handed. Not finding the envelope that contained the results was maddening. He wished there were a more efficient way, so the test results would arrive quicker.

Jacob headed to the mailbox as he had every day for four weeks. The wind lifted his hair back as a car rushed by. He felt depression pressing in on him, weighing down his heart, constricting his lungs. Would today be like every day? A mailbox full of bills and ads, but devoid of any news from the licensing department? Standing at his mailbox, he looked around the neighborhood. Any distraction was welcome. He pulled the contents out and thumbed through several pieces of mail. Sports Illustrated, gas bill, electric bill, cable bill, National Registry of Emergency Medical Technicians, internet bi...wait! Emergency Medical Technicians! It was here. His results were finally here. His hand trembled as he held the envelope out in front of his face, staring intently. This was the moment he had been waiting for. Would it be a pass or fail? Would he be an EMT or go back to his mundane office job? His hands were shaking like leaves on a windy day. Fear clutched him and a knot grew in his stomach. He felt as if he might pass out. After several minutes of staring at it, he tore it open.

"Congratulations."

Jacob's heart skipped a beat. *Oh my God! I did it! I really did it!*

His hands trembled as he read the letter. His vision blurred as tears welled up in his eyes. He reached up and wiped them away. His facial muscles ached from the enormous smile plastered across his face. The letter explained the recertification requirements and included his first EMT patch. Could this be real? He traced his finger across the colorful stitching. The patch was round with red and gold as the dominant colors. In the center was the Arizona State flag with the letters EMT stretched across the top of the patch. His hand fumbled trying to pull his phone out of the front pocket of his blue jeans. He flipped it open and pushed the numbers on the keypad. It rang.

"Hello?" a woman answered.

Jacob pulled the phone from his ear and glanced at the screen. "I'm sorry, Ma'am. Wrong number." His shaking finger pressed the "end call button." He shook his head. Jacob pushed buttons again and once again got a wrong number. He couldn't control his fingers. Then he chuckled as he realized he had the phone number in his contacts list. He located the number and pushed the send button.

After a few rings, a familiar voice answered. "Hello?"

"Dad? I did it! Can you believe it? I passed my EMT licensing test!"

"Congratulations, son. Of course, I can believe it. After all, you're a Myers. I'm so proud of you."

His father's approval rang through his ears and he couldn't wipe the silly grin from his face. "Thank you, Dad. It's crazy. A year ago I was paralyzed and now, I'm a certified EMT." The butterflies in his stomach flew up and fluttered through his chest.

"You've come a long way."

"Yes, I have. It's so surreal."

"So, what are you going to do now?"

"That's a good question. I'm not sure, but when I do, you'll be the first person to know." A low growl resonated from Jacob's stomach. Now with his test results in hand, the knots in his stomach were replaced with hunger. "Well, I have to go. I'll talk to you later. Love you, Dad."

"Love you too, son."

Jacob shut his cell phone and slid it back into his pocket. He gripped the letter in his hand and trotted toward his house. Once inside the door, he leaned against the rough textured wall and a sigh of happiness slipped through his lips. He'd done it! Although the EMT program was challenging, with hours of studying, many nights of no sleep, he completed it, and passed the tests.

Jacob sat at the kitchen table sipping on a fresh cup of coffee. His fingers traced across the hot ceramic. Lifting up the cup, he blew across the top swirling the steam into the air. The smell of fresh coffee beans wafted through the kitchen.

Flipping through the Help Wanted Ads, an advertisement for the Gino Bend River Rescue seized his attention. His eyes narrowed and he circled the ad with a red ink pen. Fishing his cell phone out of the front pocket of his jeans, he dialed the number. He spoke with Charles Dupree, the commander. The next day he went to Charles' house, filled out a large stack of paperwork, and retrieved the uniform. The squad Charles commanded patrolled the river and lake. Anytime alcohol mixed with water sports, people suffered a variety of traumatic injuries. During the summer months, they were responsible for providing aid on the weekends.

Jacob sat in his micro fiber recliner studying the uniform he was issued. It consisted of navy blue cargo shorts and a powder blue polo that said River Rescue across the back. With the miserable Arizona summers, he was thankful they were able to wear shorts. It was a particularly hot summer. The temperatures were averaging one-hundred-seventeen degrees each day with the lows only dropping down to one-hundred-degrees at night.

Jacob had difficulty concentrating at work the rest of the week. All he could think about was the various calls he was going to be exposed to. Nagging thoughts of uncertainty took control of his mind. Could he handle it? What was it going to be like being tasked with saving someone's life? He shook off the negative thoughts and allowed his excitement to resume.

The week finally ended. After Jacob readied himself to head down to the river, he stopped to look in the mirror one last time. Pride filled him at the sight of the uniform. He was really going to make a difference in the world! But that thought was swept away by the nagging fear in the pit of his stomach. He was about to be baptized into the world of EMS. He pushed the fear away. A knot formed in his throat. He ran his hand down the front of the freshly ironed polo. For the first time, he felt accomplished.

Jacob arrived at the river at 5:30 that evening. He glanced around the dirt parking lot and noticed several people dressed in the same uniform, standing around talking to one another. It felt like his first day of school on the playground. He needed to find Charles, but was afraid to ask anyone. Jacob wasn't an outgoing person. Talking to strangers made his stomach tie up in knots, something that was going to have to change if he was going to be involved in patient care. Exiting his truck, he walked toward the group of responders. His feet crunched down small rocks and dust floated through the air.

"You the new guy?" a gruff voice behind him asked.

Jacob turned around. Standing in front of him was a tall, slender, but muscular man. He stood six-foot-one, had brown hair that was shaved short, and crystal blue eyes. His face showed a hard life with several lines etched into his skin.

"Yeah, I guess I am." Jacob answered.

"My name is Tyler. My friends call me Stitch. I used to be a combat medic in the Navy. I won't put up with any Navy jokes or I'll kick you in the head," he barked.

"I'm Jacob Myers. My entire family was in the Navy so you won't hear anything out of me." Jacob held out his hand toward Stitch. He paused for a moment and then returned the gesture. Stitch stared directly into Jacob's eyes as he firmly shook his hand. Jacob's dad always told him that if a man had a firm handshake, and looked you in the eye, he had nothing to hide and you could trust him.

"You're riding with me today. We run in two man teams. We're all basic EMT's out here except for Charles. He's our lone paramedic. Had any experience in the field yet?"

"No. This is my first time out."

Stitch sighed and shook his head. "Great! I get stuck with a damn rookie. That's just my luck."

Jacob wasn't quite sure how to take that. Wasn't Stitch once a new guy? Holding it against him because he was new to the field was ridiculous. A wave of nausea rolled through his stomach. He wiped his sweaty palms against his pant leg. After standing there for a few minutes, Charles made his way towards the two.

Stitch turned toward Charles, crossed his arms, and glared. "Seriously? Sticking me with the new guy? What did I do to you to deserve this?"

"Come on, Stitch. Be nice. I'm putting him with you because you're one of the most experienced guys I have. Quit your complaining, check off your gear, and get on the river," Charles ordered. "Jacob, come over here. I need to talk to you." Charles walked over behind his truck and pulled down the tailgate. "Have a seat."

Jacob jumped up on the tailgate. "What's up?"

"Ignore Stitch. He can be a little gruff, but he is a good EMT. He can teach you a lot. Just remember, you're like a baby and now it's time to learn how to crawl. Pay close attention to everything Stitch does during and after calls. If you have any questions, ask him. I promise you, he'll grow on ya."

"You got it. Thanks again for giving me this chance."

"I should be thanking you. You're free labor," Charles laughed.

"Come on, rookie. We need to check off our gear. Get moving," Stitch bellowed from his response truck.

Jacob jumped down from the tailgate and walked over to the truck where Stitch was standing. It was a Ford F150 that had a customized bed with several drawers. Stitch had a clipboard and was going through the drawers that were numbered one through thirteen. There were two large slots that held four backboards. The nausea in Jacob's stomach subsided, and was now replaced with excitement.

Stitch pushed the clipboard forcefully into Jacob's chest. The thud of the clipboard caught Charles' attention. He shook his head and walked away.

"That's the inventory checklist that we use at the beginning and end of each shift. If something is missing, you give the list of supplies you need to Charles and he'll fill the order. You need to go through each drawer to get familiar with where the equipment is and what it's used for.

I'm sure they didn't go over what each thing does in class, did they?" Stitch asked.

Jacob felt overwhelmed. "Not really. Occasionally the instructor would pull something out and tell us what it was, but we really didn't get to use the stuff very much."

Stitch's eyes narrowed and his lips pursed. "That's typical. I swear they get the dumbest people to teach those classes. Most of the instructors have never worked a day in the field."

"Are you always this upbeat or is today just one of those special days?"

Stitch crossed his arms over his chest and glared at Jacob. "Are you trying to be a wise guy? If so, it doesn't suit you."

"No, not at all. Just trying to crack a joke."

Stitch stared at Jacob shaking his head. "I like you. I don't know why, but I do."

"I'll sleep better at night knowing that," Jacob blurted. He had a philosophy: if you can't beat them, make them laugh. Being new in the field was terrifying. Feeling like he had to prove himself to Stitch added an element of stress, along with applying what he'd learned in the classroom out in the field.

"I've got to take a leak. Get to checking off the gear and I'll be back in a few minutes," Stitch ordered. He walked down a path toward the restroom. His weather worn leather boots kicked up dust as he stomped down the path. Jacob reached out and pulled a smooth plastic drawer open. He glanced down and noticed a few pairs of trauma sheers, a stethoscope, and three penlights. The corners of his mouth tugged upward. Being in uniform and handling the various pieces of equipment made him feel important. It was a sense of accomplishment that he had been longing for a long time.

Thirty minutes later Stitch returned. "You ready to go yet? Get it all checked off?"

"Yes, sir. We're all set." Jacob flipped the sheets of paper over and pushed the clipboard into Stitch's chest.

Stitch's eyes narrowed, and his brow furrowed. "Don't ever call me sir again. I work for a living." He grabbed the clipboard and climbed into the truck, slamming the door shut. Jacob's shoulders slumped. He opened the passenger door and sat down.

"Rule number one, rookie, always wear your seat belt while in this truck." He meaty hands pointed down to the center of the console. "And never, I mean ever, touch this radio. I'll take care of that. Got it?"

"Yes, sir." Stitch shot him a disapproving look.

You call me rookie and I'll call you sir. Eye for an eye.

Stitch started the truck. The powerful engine roared to life. With mixed emotions of fear and excitement, Jacob couldn't stop smiling.

"What are you grinning about, rookie? You think you're going to go out and save the world?"

"No, sir. I thought a pretty girl was looking at me."

"If you did, it's only because she was going to use you to get to me. Understand?"

"Yes, sir."

"What did I tell you about calling me sir, rookie?" Stitch threw the truck into drive, slammed on the gas, and made a hard left turn.

Jacob banged his head on the window, but not enough to be seriously hurt. He smiled inwardly knowing he had gotten the best of Stitch.

As they were cruising down a two-lane road adjacent to the river, Jacob curiously looked around. The hot breeze disheveled his hair and sweat traced down the back of his neck. There were several people out enjoying the hot summer day. Some were fishing off the bank while others were floating down the river in tubes. There were quite a few attractive women in bikinis and just as many that probably shouldn't be wearing one.

"There's something you're going to learn. We're like rock stars. Girls will throw themselves at you. It's because of the uniform. Cops, on the other hand, are hated out here. You get the occasional badge bunny, but for the most part, if you're law enforcement they wouldn't throw water on you if you were on fire," Stitch said.

"Have you ever met any women out here?"

"A few. Nothing meaningful, though. I think I make a better single person."

"I hate being single. It gets lonely."

"You're not going to start crying are you?"

Jacob tried to ignore Stitch. So much for divulging a few feelings. There were brief moments where he thought they could be friends and then Stitch proved him wrong.

The silence in the truck was interrupted by a voice blaring over the radio. "River Medic 3, what's your location?"

Jacob reached for the radio. With cat-like reflexes, Stitch smacked his hand. "I said never touch the radio, rookie." He keyed up the microphone. "This is River Medic 3. We're about a mile from the medical substation."

Jacob's hand stung. He rubbed it and glared at Stitch.

"I need you to go to the substation, code one, to do a blood pressure check. You have a fifty-six year old female not feeling well."

"What's code one?" Jacob asked.

"It means no lights or sirens. Code three means get there quick."

Stitch keyed up the microphone again. "River Medic 3 copies." Stitch threw the radio microphone to the floorboard. It bounced up and struck Jacob in the shin. "Damn it! What is an old woman doing at the river on a hot day like this anyway? Couldn't be a beautiful chick that needs her bikini bottoms extricated from her backside or anything cool like that." His jaw tensed as he silently cursed under his breath. "What are you grinning about? This is a bull crap call."

Regardless of how Stitch acted, Jacob was excited. This was going to be his first call in the field. Stitch pulled off the blacktop road, slammed on the brakes, and spit gravel is all directions. A thick cloud of dust rolled over the truck. Jacob got out first and headed for the door at a brisk pace, leaving Stitch behind.

"Hey, stupid! What are you going to use to check her blood pressure, your invisible cuff?" Stitch barked.

Jacob stopped and sighed. "Yeah. I better grab the bag."

"That just might help. I'm going in to see what's going on. Hurry up."

Jacob returned to the truck to retrieve the equipment. His pulse thumped forcefully in his throat. He retrieved the bag from the back of the truck and ran toward the substation. A trail of dust followed behind his scurrying feet. Twisting the knob, the door wouldn't open. *Did he lock me out?* Suddenly the door opened and Stitch glared at him in anger.

"It works if you actually turn the handle," Stitch mocked. He turned toward the elderly woman sitting on a chair fanning herself with a piece of paper. "This is Mrs. Jones. She has a history of high blood pressure, but forgot to take her medication today. Why don't you get some vital signs on this fine young lady?"

The woman weakly smiled at Stitch. An elderly man stood next to her rubbing her upper back with his hand. He gazed down at her lovingly. Jacob retrieved the blood pressure cuff, stethoscope, and then kneeled down next to her. His hands shook as he fumbled with the Velcro. As he was putting the blood pressure cuff on her arm, Stitch started to laugh.

"How about you try putting the cuff on her the right way? Gotta love rookies." Stitch bellowed out a hearty laugh. Mrs. Jones shot him an unpleasant look; he stopped laughing and cleared his throat.

"You have to start somewhere, don't you? I'm sure you were new at one time, now weren't you?" Her sour expression turned to a smile as she looked at Jacob. "You're doing fine, dear. Take your time. I don't mind having a nice looking young man taking care of me." Jacob's cheeks flushed.

He did as he was taught, pumped up the cuff until he couldn't hear the heartbeat and then slowly released the pressure. "Your blood pressure is 146/96. Is that normal for you, Ma'am?"

"That's a little high. I think I'll have my husband take me home so I can take my medicine and get some rest. Of course, just seeing your handsome face makes it rise, I'm sure."

Jacob was speechless. He felt his face flush as he took the blood pressure cuff off her arm and fiddled with the jump bag. He stowed the equipment into the bag and zipped it shut.

"That sounds like a fine plan, Ma'am. Don't forget to take your medicine and you need to hydrate as well. That's important. Beer doesn't count, okay?" Stitch said to her laughing.

Mrs. Jones eyes narrowed and crinkled her nose. "I don't drink beer, young man. I'm not an alcoholic."

Jacob didn't like Stitch's bedside manner, or lack thereof. Mrs. Jones rose from the chair with the help of her husband, got into their car, and they drove away.

Stitch faced Jacob. A sigh slipped through his lips. "You freaking suck up. Seriously? Why didn't you just ask her out on a date while you were at it? They say once you go gray, there's no other way," Stitch laughed.

Jacob's eyes narrowed. A flushed feeling washed over his face and he could feel his heartbeat in his temples. He glared at Stitch, grabbed the jump bag, went outside, and placed it in the truck. Jacob leaned against the truck and kicked a rock across the parking lot; a brown cloud of dust floated through the air. He ran his fingers through his hair and a sigh slipped through his lips. He wasn't going to allow Stitch to ruin his moment. A warm feeling glazed over his body. For the first time in his life, he felt like he made a difference; even with the simple task of taking a sick woman's vital signs. Jacob got back in the truck, put on his seat belt, and slammed the door shut. Stitch walked out and stood in front of the truck glaring at him. Stitch climbed into the truck and stared out of the windshield. "Feeling pretty good about yourself right now? Or are you day dreaming about saving the world?"

"No. I'm just enjoying the beautiful day." His heartbeat thumped in his temple, again.

"Here's rule number three, rookie. We don't save lives; we merely delay death. You can call it dark and cold if you want, but it's the harsh reality. I was green and ready to save everyone, just like you. One day it all came to me. The sooner you learn that, the better off you will be. This job is full of heartache and disappointment. You'll see." Stitch slammed down the gas pedal and sped out of the parking lot. Rocks shot from under the tires and dust filled the air.

After a few hours of driving up and down the river, a deep growl resonated from Jacob's stomach causing a wave of nausea to roll through him. "Are we ever going to eat?"

"Sure. There's a good burger barn just down the road. Let's go there, my treat."

Stitch pulled into the parking lot, calmly. There were several people sitting at picnic tables eating and talking. White paint flaked from the sparse building. Grease filled smoke bellowed from the top of the modest structure. It resembled a surf shack that could be found somewhere on a beach. Stitch went to order their food while Jacob took a seat at a table. There was a cool breeze cutting through the blistering heat. A few minutes later Stitch approached the table holding two baskets of food and sat down. "Here's rule number four. Eat, sleep, and crap when you can. Write that down."

Jacob smirked. "You sure are full of rules, aren't you?"

"I'm passing on my pearls of wisdom to you. My mentor did that for me and I appreciated it. The more you know ahead of time, the better off you'll be." As Jacob was about to thrust the burger into his mouth, he looked over and saw Stitch close his eyes and bow his head. Jacob sat the burger down and followed suit.

A few moments later, Stitch traced a cross over his chest. "You believe in God?"

"I guess. I'm not sure what to really believe in."

"I'm a firm believer in God. We don't decide who lives and dies; God does."

"I believe there is a God, but I don't understand why bad things happen to good people."

"Not our place to question."

Just as they took their first bites, the radio squelched. "River Medic 3, we have a traumatic injury for you. Twenty-one year old female that sustained a foot injury while cliff diving." The dispatcher's voice quivered and she spoke at a blistering pace.

Stitch jumped up, grabbed his radio, and ran to the truck. "River Medic 3 copies. What's the location of the patient?" he asked, short of breath.

"She's at Hangman's Beach. Reporting party is with her. They stated she's conscious, alert, and oriented. They also said the top of her foot is missing."

"Now we're talking! What are you doing, rookie? Let's go!" Stitch yelled to Jacob.

"What about our food?" Jacob glanced down at the basket of food. His mouth watered and his stomach tightened.

"Leave it. We have to go!" Stitch yelled. He keyed up his radio. "River Medic 3 copies. Get the status of a helicopter."

"Dispatch copies."

Jacob shot up and ran to the truck. He flung the door open, jumped inside, and shut the door. This was going to be his first trauma. Stitch switched on the lights and sirens. He pulled out onto the road spitting rocks and dust everywhere.

Jacob grabbed hold of the door handle. His knuckles were white from the tight grip. "Do you always drive this crazy?"

"You haven't seen crazy yet. Hold on, amigo."

Stitch weaved in and out of traffic. "Get the hell out of the way!" he screamed.

Jacob didn't understand why people wouldn't yield the right of way to their emergency vehicle. He was certain that if their family member was injured, they'd expect other motorists to pull to the right. The thought of the trauma victim filled his mind and fear crossed Jacob's face.

They drove up to a group of girls jumping up and down on the side of the road.

"Ah, the scene of the crime," Stitch blurted out. He pulled down onto the beach where there were several people standing around a girl sitting down on the ground. Two girls ran frantically towards them.

"You have to hurry. She's going to die!" one of the girls screamed. Tears streamed down her face from reddened eyes. The stench of alcohol was overpowering.

Jacob looked over and noticed a girl bent over throwing up on the beach. There were people curiously looking on. Everything was moving in fast forward. Jacob stopped, took a deep breath, and tried to keep his emotions under control. Stitch walked over to the injured girl and knelt down next to her.

"Come on, rookie. Get the bag over here." Stitch's face was blank and emotionless. "What happened?"

"Dude, it was crazy. She went to jump off the cliff, but she slipped and fell hitting rocks on her way down," a guy answered. His words slurred and slobber flung from his mouth.

Jacob froze in his tracks as he neared the girl. The top of her foot exposed muscle and bones. Blood freely flowed down the side of her foot. The air sucked out of his lungs. He tried to form words, but couldn't get them past the softball sized knot in his throat.

"Dispatch, this is River Medic 3. Do you have an ETA on the bird?" Stitch asked over the radio.

"River Medic 3, helicopter's ETA is seven minutes."

"Copy that. I will be Hangman's Beach Command. Sheriff's Department is on scene and has established a landing zone." Stitch was in automatic mode. Everything he did and said was with purpose. He was confident and sure of himself, something Jacob hoped he would be someday.

He couldn't move. There were tasks that needed to be accomplished, but he couldn't seem to get his feet out of the cement blocks that had him weighted to the ground. His legs trembled.

"Jacob, what are you doing? We need to get her packaged and ready for the chopper. Get a move on. Let's get her on a backboard and then get that foot bandaged up."

Stitch's stern tone snapped Jacob out of his daze and he approached the woman. She rocked back and forth sucking in a deep breath. A tear slid down her cheek leaving a dirt-drenched trail.

"Ma'am, are you hurting anywhere?" Stitch asked.

"My neck, back, and foot hurt. Oh my God, my foot hurts! Can you give me something?" she asked.

She was an attractive girl. Her eyes caught Jacob's attention, as they were a mix between silver and blue. Suddenly, her body started to convulse.

Jacob placed the c-collar around her neck and with Stitch's help, laid her flat on the backboard and secured her to it with spider straps. The sound of the Velcro being pulled apart forced the dreadful memories of Jacob's injury through his mind. He started to shake.

Stitch grabbed a bottle of saline and twisted off the cap. He grabbed a handful of gauze and saturated it with copious amounts of saline. He carefully placed the gauze over the woman's foot and wrapped it loosely with a cling wrap.

Jacob glanced over his shoulder and watched the helicopter land. The crew exited the air ambulance and briskly walked toward them with their flight cot. Stitch gave them a detailed report. The flight crew prepared her, loaded her into the helicopter, and were airborne in a matter of minutes.

As Jacob packed up all of the gear and headed back to the truck, he felt like a fool. He froze on the call and was sure Stitch was going to give him an earful. Stitch was speaking with a few of the woman's friends. Occasionally he glanced toward Jacob shaking his head.

A few minutes later, Stitch climbed back into the truck. Jacob sat in his seat staring out the window, avoiding eye contact with his partner. Stitch sighed and then pulled back out onto the road. Jacob was too scared to look up in fear of the verbal lashing he was sure Stitch was going to unleash on him. After building up enough courage, he looked over at Stitch.

"I'm sorry. I know I screwed up on that call." His shoulders were slumped.

Stitch took a deep breath and then pulled over to the side of the road. "You know, I really want to be a jerk to you, but I can't. I remember my first trauma as if it was yesterday. The only thing I did differently was puke."

Jacob couldn't believe his ears. Superman Stitch puked? He never would've guessed that. It eased the feeling of foolishness.

"Man, it's going to happen. You're human. No matter how long you do this, you're going to have moments when the human side is going to take over. All you can do is learn from it, and move on to the next one. Does that make sense to you?" Stitch asked.

Jacob felt a little more at ease. "Yes, it does. I appreciate it." Though he'd just met Stitch, he felt the need to impress his partner. Something he hadn't expected was the whirlwind of emotions this job created. One moment as high as a bird, the next he felt slammed against a brick wall. It was almost more than he could handle in such a short time span.

They arrived at the substation, cleaned up the truck, and headed their separate ways. Jacob had plans for the next weekend. He wasn't going to be able to go out to the river until the following weekend. On his way home, he couldn't stop thinking about the two calls they answered that day. It was amazing how much he had learned after just one day. It was surely just the tip of the iceberg for what was yet to come.

Chapter Four

Jacob tossed and turned in his cotton sheets. It was well after one in the morning before he was able to drift off to sleep. Most people his age would be out partying after work on a Friday night, but that wasn't the case with him. Instead, he spent the evening ironing his uniform and making sure everything was ready to go for the next day.

The next morning, after a quick breakfast, Jacob headed for the river. He pulled into the dirt parking lot. He noticed Stitch and Charles were deep in conversation. After locking up his truck, he headed towards them. Their body language was stiff. Stitch looked angry and despondent. Charles' face was red with light perspiration running down his forehead.

"I don't care, Stitch! What I say goes! Do you understand me? Don't forget who the paramedic here is!" Charles yelled as he turned and stomped off toward his truck.

Jacob approached Stitch cautiously. The last thing he wanted to do was send him into a tailspin of anger. "What was that all about?"

"Nothing. Mind your own damn business, rookie," Stitch growled. "Get over to our truck and check the gear off. Vacation's over."

"I know I wasn't here last weekend, but it was because…." He didn't get a chance to finish his sentence as Stitch walked away. Jacob followed his orders and checked off the gear on their truck.

Thirty minutes later, Stitch came back looking calmer. Jacob decided not to say or do anything that might set him off, so he refrained from asking any questions. He handed the checklist to Stitch. "We're all good. Everything is here."

"Good. Now it's time to have some fun."

Charles walked up. His face was relaxed. The tension between the two appeared to be resolved. "Get your stuff, Jacob. You're coming with me for today. The sheriffs take two EMT's with them when they go on lake patrol. Sometimes the best action you could get is on the lake. You interested?"

Jacob's stomach did a flip. Getting to go out on a boat is exactly what he wanted to do. This would be his first experience out on the lake since he didn't know anyone with a boat.

Stitch glared at Charles and then shook his head. "I'm glad I don't have to put up with you today, rookie. Have fun."

Charles ignored Stitch. "Have any experience out on the lake?" Charles asked.

"No. I'm curious though. What can possibly happen that could be more serious than the injuries people get on the river? It's wide open water, isn't it?"

His inexperience made Charles laugh. "You'd be surprised. Anytime you introduce alcohol and water sports together, regardless if it's a lake or a river, bad things can happen. I heard about your cliff diver. How'd that go?"

Jacob's stomach tightened; his lungs constricted; he couldn't breathe. Charles must've known that he had frozen up on the call and was going to have something to say about it. He nervously started at the ground. "It went okay, I guess."

Charles walked over and placed a hand on Jacob's shoulder. His gesture soothed Jacob's anxiety. "Don't feel bad about it. You're going to have a lot of firsts in the field. Some are going to take you by surprise, while others will just make you laugh. All you can do is learn from it and be better prepared the next time. Just remember, you're a baby now in the sense that you're learning to crawl. Next you'll learn to walk, and eventually you'll learn to run. You're also going to come across a lot of different personalities out here. Some will be good, while others will be bad. Don't let it get you down. You can learn something from each person you encounter. Someday you're going to be the one teaching a new guy."

Jacob's mouth dropped open. He couldn't imagine teaching anyone anything. "You and Stitch were arguing when I walked up. What's going on?"

Charles weakly smiled. "Stitch gets a little too big for his britches sometimes. He forgets who's in charge so I have to remind him. It's nothing for you to worry about." Charles turned and went to his truck to retrieve his gear.

Officer Gilmore was doing final preparations on the boat as Charles and Jacob arrived on the pier. It wasn't a big boat, but was large enough to seat six to seven people comfortably. Near the front, there were a couple of backboards, head blocks, and spider straps. That struck Jacob as kind of odd. *Why in the world would they need that equipment out on the water?* Jacob trotted across the wood pier. With each step the wood creaked under his feet. He looked down through the gaps and noticed murky green water. Weeds and a white film floated across the top. The sun reflected off the water and blinded Jacob. He held his hands over his eyes so he wouldn't fall into it. Jacob approached the boat and began to step inside of it when the sheriff's deputy whipped his head around, and glared at him. His eyes narrowed and his nose crinkled.

"Do you just walk into someone's house without knocking?" Officer Gilmore asked. He dropped the ropes he was bundling, walked over, and got inches from Jacob's face. "I asked you a question, boy. Do you just walk into someone's house without even knocking?"

Jacob felt his warm breath puff in his face. Nausea rolled through his stomach. "Um, no I don't." A large knot formed in his throat. He looked over at Charles for help; he just grinned and shrugged his shoulders.

Officer Gilmore stepped an inch away from Jacob's face, looked straight into his eyes, and then laughed. *Was this guy crazy?*

He grabbed Jacob's hand firmly and shook it vigorously. "I'm just messing with you, rookie. It's okay. You can come aboard." He glanced toward Charles. "Did you see the look on his face? I thought he was going to start to cry," he said heartily laughing.

Charles fought back a smile. "You got him good, Gilmore. You had me convinced that you were angry. How about you be nice to the young lad before we have to throw him in the lake to clean his britches out?"

Officer Gilmore released his grip on Jacob's hand, retrieved the ropes he was handling, and tied them into a bundle. Jacob stepped off the pier into the boat. It rocked side to side. He lost his balance and reached down to the side of the boat steadying himself. It took him a few moments to acclimate his balance. Jacob dragged his feet across the carpet and sat down on a white cushioned bench seat. Charles joined them and gracefully walked around the boat. Jacob was amazed at how easily the two men moved around effortlessly.

A few minutes later, Charles sat down next to Jacob and Officer Gilmore navigated the boat through the no wake zone. It was one-hundred-two degrees on the water with a slight breeze. Jacob glanced around the lake. It was surrounded by numerous small mountains covered in sagebrush, dirt, and rocks.

The men spent several hours driving around the lake, but it was uneventful. The radio buzzed with calls that were happening out on the river. Charles spent most of his day on his cell phone arguing with his wife. The guy just couldn't get a break today.

"Are you bored?" asked Gilmore.

Jacob stood up and walked over next to him. The warm air whipped through Jacob's hair. He reached up and brushed his bangs out of his eyes. *I should've worn a hat.* "Yes, but I'm just glad to be out here. I've never been on a boat before. You get much action out here?" Jacob asked.

Officer Gilmore continued to steer them around the lake looking at each boat they passed. "Sometimes we do. Weekends can be get crazy. It never fails though, when you have a new guy with you, nothing happens."

"Sorry to rain on your parade. The river is hopping. Wish I was out there. Don't take this wrong, but I didn't come out here to sit on the sidelines and watch everyone else get to play."

Gilmore laughed and shook his head. "Eager beaver, are you? Give it time, brother. The calls will come. I know what you mean, though. I was the same way when I first started. Couldn't wait to get into the action and maybe tussle with someone. Now, I would rather have these calm and peaceful days."

Jacob cautiously walked across the carpet back to the bench seat. The boat turned sharply to the right. He lost his balance and fell to the floor. He looked up and Officer Gilmore had a smile covering his face. Jacob chuckled. He crawled across the bristly carpet to the bench seat. Charles was still on his phone fighting with his wife. As they headed back to the dock, Jacob sat back enjoying the wind blowing in his face. They didn't have any calls, but Jacob was amazed how much fun it was out on the open water. The weekends had been wonderful since joining the River Rescue Squad. The realization of having to return to his humdrum office life saddened him. It was time to decide if he wanted to make this a full time career or not. His only hesitation was that there would be a significant cut in pay. Would he financially be able to support the career move? The thought of working in EMS fulltime sent butterflies through his stomach, but gave him a sense of purpose.

Charles slammed his phone shut and threw it into the lake. "Sometimes I don't know why I put up with that woman. All she ever does is yell at me about how many hours I'm working. I don't hear her complaining when she's cashing my pay checks."

Being single had its advantages. Sure it got lonely at times, but when he saw how unhappy others can be, it made Jacob realize how lucky he really was. Stitch told him that Charles was gone from home four to five days a week. For someone with a normal job it wouldn't be that big of a deal. For Charles, his usual workday consisted of being gone for a minimum of twenty-four hours at a time. He could understand why Charles' wife was so angry.

Charles sat down and put his face in his hands. Jacob felt such sorrow for him, but didn't have any idea how to console him.

Gilmore looked over at Charles and shook his head. "That wasn't very smart, Charles. There isn't a woman on earth worth getting so angry that you toss your phone into the lake. If it's that bad, brother, why not just get a divorce?"

Charles sulked and leaned back against the bench. "I can't do that to my kids. It would devastate them beyond repair. I love my wife, but when she starts complaining to me about being gone it angers me. I can't help that I'm gone that much. I have to work as much as I do because she wants to be a stay at home Mom. Well, in order for her to be able to do that I have to work enough for the both of us. I don't know. Sometimes I just want to give up, but then I think about the kids, and I can't do that."

Officer Gilmore glanced at a boat as they passed by. "I don't know what to tell you, man. I've always heard EMS was rough on the family life. I'm glad I don't have to deal with that kind of trouble in my house. Eight hours is long enough for me. I don't know how you guys do it."

This was a part of the job Jacob hadn't thought about yet. Right now, he was a single man so it wasn't really an issue. But what if he found the right woman to settle down with? Would she be able to handle the long hours away from home? Jacob wanted to be married and have kids someday. This was something he was going to have to think about before making a decision on a career change.

Officer Gilmore slowed down the boat to a crawl through the no wake zone. He pulled the craft in next to the pier and Charles retrieved the ropes out to tie it up to the dock. Charles jumped out, and tied them off. There were several people walking around. A few of them looked over at Gilmore and gave him dirty looks.

Once the boat was secured to the pier, Officer Gilmore jumped out of the boat onto the wooden dock. Jacob grabbed the side of the boat and cautiously climbed out. He felt more comfortable on solid ground, but still felt like he was swaying from side to side. The three men were standing around making small talk when Gilmore's attention shifted towards the water.

"That boat sure is coming through the no wake zone awfully fast. Stupid people never learn." He turned and headed towards the pier angrily. Jacob and Charles followed closely behind him. "Slow down! You're in a no wake zone!" Gilmore screamed.

The boat continued speeding frantically towards the pier. There were several people on it with terrified looks on their faces. The boat slammed into the pier bouncing off with an enormous jolt. The wood shook under Jacob's feet.

"What the hell are you doing?" Gilmore screamed.

"She's hurt. She's hurt really bad," the driver yelled. Charles and Jacob ran towards the boat to see what was going on. One of the passengers threw the ropes to Gilmore so he could tie it off to the pier. Charles jumped into the boat and approached a rather large woman thrashing around on one of the bench seats in the boat. The odor of alcohol was so strong that Jacob could smell her from six feet away.

"What happened?" asked Charles.

"We were driving around on the lake when we saw a boat speeding and cutting across other boats' wakes. They caught some serious air and when they came down on top of a wake, the boat snapped in half throwing everyone out," the driver explained.

Charles approached the portly woman. "Ma'am, are you hurt?"

Jacob stood on the dock, confused. Gilmore guided the other occupants off the boat to give Charles room to work.

"What's her name?" Charles asked the driver.

"I think it's Amber. She kept saying that all the way here so I'm guessing that's it," the driver answered.

"Amber, are you hurting anywhere?" The woman continued thrashing. "Jacob, get the back board and c-spine stuff off of the sheriff's boat. Gilmore, call this into dispatch and get me a helicopter," Charles ordered.

Jacob bolted towards the sheriff's boat to get the equipment. He tripped over a loose board, lost his balance, and fell into the lake. How could he be so clumsy?

Charles looked over his shoulder for Jacob, but didn't see him. "Jacob what are you doing? Get that gear over here!" screamed Charles.

Trying hard to hold back a laugh, Gilmore said, "Your rookie just fell into the lake."

Murky lake water filled Jacob's mouth. He spit it out and swam to the pier. As he climbed out of the lake, he saw Stitch running down the pier. Jacob pulled himself out of the water and jogged towards the sheriff's boat. Water sloshed over the top of his boots, his legs burned, and started to cramp. He felt his pulse thumping in his chest and his ears rang. After retrieving the equipment from the sheriff's boat, Jacob returned to the boat where the patient was: dripping wet and short of breath. *I am out of shape. I need to start going to the gym.*

"My neck's killing me. My arms and legs are numb. Do something. Help me!" the woman screamed as she thrashed against the bench seat.

"I saw her hit her head hard on the side of the boat when it broke in half," said the driver.

"Was anyone else hurt?" Stitch asked. Charles' eyes grew close together; his jaw tightened.

"No, the rest of them were fine and went in another boat that came to help."

Charles looked over at Stitch. "What are you doing here? Shouldn't you be on the river? I don't need you!"

Stitch's face grew red with anger. "I think you do because your rookie fell into the lake. You need some reliable hands. Let's quit this bickering and help this lady."

The two men stared at one another. The tension between them had returned. Whatever was going on between them overflowed into the patient care they were rendering. Stitch climbed into the boat. "Open that collar and put it on her," he said to Jacob.

"Who's in charge here? You don't tell anyone what to do!" yelled Charles.

Jacob's frustration grew. He climbed into the boat, tore open the collar from its packaging, and approached the patient. "Ma'am, this is going to be uncomfortable, but it will help remind you to sit still so you don't hurt your neck anymore than it is." He wrapped it around her neck and fastened it.

The woman stopped thrashing around and relaxed. Her eyes were wide as she panted.

"Okay, boss. What do you want to do next?" Stitch asked Charles snidely.

Charles' lip quivered. "Let's get her on the backboard and get her secured."

The three of them placed the backboard next to the patient, logrolled her, and then moved her back onto it.

"Now Ma'am, we're going to secure you to this backboard with some straps and tape your head down with a head block. This is to protect your spine in case you've injured it." Charles explained. He held the manual c-spine on her as Stitch and Jacob put the spider straps over her.

"I can't handle being strapped down. I'm claustrophobic!" the patient yelled. She started to thrash around and pull at the straps. Stitch pulled her hands down to her sides.

"We have to do this so we can take care of you. Try and stay calm. Breathe in through your nose and out through your mouth," Charles said.

"I said I can't handle being tied down!" she screamed. Amber tried to get up from the backboard. Charles was doing everything he could to keep her head still as they worked vigorously at trying to strap her to the backboard. He grabbed the head block and began to tape it down.

"You can't do that. The head's taped down last. You're doing it wrong," Stitch yelled.

"Shut up. I'm in charge here, Stitch. Not you. Don't worry about what I'm doing and just get her strapped down to the board."

Jacob couldn't believe what was happening. They were focusing more on their feud rather than the patient. Amber was still fighting them - trying to get off the backboard. Charles secured Amber's head to the backboard. She threw her lower body off the backboard. But her head remained taped down. Suddenly there were two loud cracking sounds, and then Amber's body went limp. She stopped breathing.

The color in Jacob's face faded to white. "What just happened?"

Stitch and Charles glared at one another. Jacob was certain they were about to start punching each other. Charles reached down and pressed on the side Amber's neck.

"She's got a pulse. She's not breathing, though. I need to tube her. Grab my intubation kit, Jacob," Charles ordered.

He stared at the patient and then he looked up at Charles and Stitch. His mouth fell open. He tried to speak, but couldn't force words past the knot in his throat.

"Get moving. She needs to be tubed!" Charles screamed.

Jacob shook off the shock, retrieved the intubation kit, and brought it to Charles. Luckily for him, it was in the boat so he didn't have to worry about falling into the lake again.

"You did this to her, Charles. You did," Stitch yelled.

"No time for that now. Grab the bag valve mask and the oxygen tank," Charles ordered.

Stitch grabbed the equipment and sat it next to him. Charles opened the intubations kit and assembled the laryngoscope. He slid the blade into Amber's mouth and had an endotracheal tube in his right hand. "I can't see her cords. I need to take off the c-collar."

"We can't do that. Her neck is probably already broken. If you do that it will kill her for certain," Stitch said.

"It won't matter if I can't get her intubated. It's a risk I'm going to have to take. Now take it off!"

Stitch reached down and grabbed Charles' hand. Stitch's facial expressions morphed from anger to a look of pleading. His body visibly relaxed.

"Charles, please don't take that collar off. Right now, she'll just be in a wheel chair. If you take it off, she'll be in a coffin. I have faith in you. I know you can do this."

Charles' face relaxed. For the first time he was listening to what Stitch was saying. He took a deep breath, relaxed and slid the laryngoscope into her mouth again.

"I can see her vocal cords." With ease, he slid the tube into her mouth. He hooked a bag valve mask to the end of the tube. From the first ventilation, there was misting in the tube. Each time he squeezed the bag Amber's chest would rise and fall. "Tube is good. Stitch, help me secure it so we don't lose it."

Stitch grabbed the securing device and handed it to Charles. With the tube secured, Charles and Stitch looked at one another.

"I knew you could do it. Good job." Stitch said as he patted Charles on the shoulder.

They finished packaging the patient and turned her over to the helicopter crew. Charles gave a report to the crew and then went and sat down next to his truck. Stitch was still talking to the flight nurse, who began to shake her head. It was obvious that he told her exactly what had happened. Jacob couldn't help but wonder what was going to come of this. From everything he had learned in class, Stitch was right. The head is the last thing you secure to the backboard. It made sense. This was a valuable lesson to learn. Unfortunately, it had been at Amber's expense.

Once the euphoria of the call had worn off, Jacob's stomach contracted. He was overcome with nausea. Growing up in athletics all of his life, he was taught you're only as strong as your weakest link. Win as a team, lose as a team. If that saying was true and correct, they were all responsible for what transpired during the call. Earlier that day, Charles said you learn from each call. This was a lesson that was learned the hard way.

Jacob blamed himself for not stepping up and halting the feud. He was the only one on scene whose judgment wasn't jaded with anger. It tore a hole through his heart thinking that he didn't do something more to help Amber. Until that moment, he respected and trusted Charles. He would carry that guilt around with him for the rest of his life.

Chapter Five

Although the heat of the day caused sweat to bead on the back of his neck, a shiver shot down his spine at the thought of the boating accident. While he was checking off the equipment on the truck, Stitch walked up.

"Good morning, rookie. Sleep good last night?"

"Not really. I couldn't stop thinking about that poor girl from yesterday. I kept hearing bones cracking in my sleep. Those horrible sounds kept waking me up most of the night."

"Well, in time you'll learn to let that stuff go. After a while it all becomes routine once you have some time under your belt."

Jacob's eyes narrowed. "You know, sometimes you sound like one cold hearted son of a gun."

Stitch laughed. "It's a little early for flattery, don't you think?"

"It wasn't meant as flattery." Stitch could be so cold and callous at times, which aggravated Jacob. Before he started working in the field, he always thought people in the medical profession were caring and compassionate. Then there was Stitch: the polar opposite. He promised himself that he would never turn that way. Jacob shook his head and picked through the trauma bag. "What were you talking to that flight nurse about?"

"I told her what happened on that call. You can't hide from your mistakes. What Charles did was a mistake, a monumental one at that. I called up to the flight service yesterday and the nurse told me the patient suffered a complete transection of her spinal cord at the C-4. You know what that means?"

"No."

"It means not only is she a quadriplegic, but also has to be on a ventilator for the rest of her life. It shouldn't have happened. There's a saying that we must live by. Basic life support before advanced life support. Don't forget it, rookie."

Jacob felt foolish for not knowing what he meant. "You've lost me."

"Let me explain. You start with your basic skills before you attempt any advanced skills. Yes, Charles did start with his basic skills, but he didn't perform them properly. Because of that, he harmed a patient. Was her neck already broken before we got to her? Possibly, but you can hurt someone just as much, if not more, when you don't do your basic skills the proper way."

"What's going to happen now? Will we be in trouble?" Jacob asked.

"It will go in front of a medical review board and they'll decide what to do next. Since we are both basic EMT's, the responsibility will fall on Charles. They may subpoena us to give our account of the events, but that's as far as that crap ball will travel downhill."

"What do you think they'll do to Charles?"

Stitch rested his arms across his chest and leaned against the truck. "It's hard to say. It can be anywhere from an official slap on the hand to losing his license. I don't think he's had any official complaints against him, so that will be in his favor."

Even though Stitch said nothing should happen, Jacob couldn't help but worry about it. Being in trouble over work related events was new to him. Keeping his nose to the grindstone had paid off over the years. Of course, this was a little different. Because of a mistake, a woman's life was changed forever.

Jacob and Stitch didn't have a single call for the rest of the day. They passed the time patrolling the river and talking. The one thing Jacob noticed was that Stitch was starting to open up more. He found that Stitch wasn't calling him rookie as much and even showed that he did have a soft side. This threw Jacob for a loop. Initially Stitch appeared to have a hard outer shell that not even a good torch could cut through. Maybe this was his defense mechanism? It was hard to say, but Jacob was beginning to enjoy being around him. Stitch was strong in his faith as well. Periodically he would try talking about religion to Jacob. This was something he wasn't sure what to think about. On one hand, he believed there was a God. On the other, Jacob couldn't understand why God allowed tragedies to occur in peoples' lives. There had been countless nights he lay in bed at the hospital questioning why God let him become injured. Yes, he healed and was without any debilitating disabilities, but he still sought the answer as to why he was injured in the first place.

After they had washed the truck and secured all of the supplies, Jacob walked over to Stitch. "Are we all done here?"

"Yeah, looks like we're good to go. You want to go have a beer or something?"

Jacob was taken aback. He never thought Stitch would want to hang out with him. Trying not to sound too eager, he tried to play it cool. "Um, sure. I've got nothing better to do. Where were you thinking of going?"

"How about the Rusty Nail? That's my favorite place to go when I want to get away. I need to go home and clean up first. Want to meet there in an hour?"

"Sounds good. I need to take a shower anyway. I smell like a dirty cat."

Stitch laughed. "Sounds good, buddy. I'll see you in a little bit. You know where it's at?"

"Yeah. See you there." He shook his head slightly as he walked away. Did he hear correctly? Did Stitch just call him "buddy"? He suppressed the urge to grin. He wasn't sure how much drinking they would be doing, but if he didn't eat it would be a long night. Jacob jumped in his truck and sped off towards his house.

Jacob arrived at the Rusty Nail. It was a small dive-looking bar on the south side of town. There were a few motorcycles parked in the front. As he made his way in, he had to stop just inside of the door so his eyes could adjust to the darkness. After a few moments, he was able to see Stitch sitting by himself at the end of the bar. The stench of stale beer and cigarette smoke hung in the air. There were only a few people there, and they all looked up as Jacob walked through the door. A tall, slender, red headed woman bumped into him. He grabbed a hold of her arms, steadying her from falling down. She had shoulder length red hair with teal colored eyes that grabbed his attention. Her beauty sucked the air out of his lungs. Her lips tugged upward forming a smile. After Jacob helped steady her, he walked over to where Stitch was sitting.

"Bout time you got here. I was starting to think you were going to stand me up." Stitch had an enormous smile on his face. It was obvious he had already consumed a few cocktails and was feeling good. Stitch reached across and patted Jacob on the shoulder. "Man, that woman is staring at you. I think she's into you."

Jacob glanced toward her and then back to Stitch. "She's beautiful, but I wouldn't have a chance." He shook his head.

"Rookie! Are you out of your mind? What are you doing in your uniform shirt?"

"Huh? Oh I guess I forgot to change."

"Well, you can't stay here in that. Get out to my truck and grab a T-shirt." Stitch tossed his keys to Jacob.

When he returned, a portly bartender with his belly hanging below a stained white t-shirt asked Jacob what he wanted to drink. He choked down a laugh at the heavy southern accent. "I'll take a light beer."

"Did you say a light beer? You want an umbrella with that?" Stitch chuckled.

"Only if it matches the one you have in your drink."

Stitch's face drew blank, but then made way to a smile. "I'm glad you could make it. I figured I've been a little rough on you lately. How about I buy you a drink?"

"You can buy me a drink, but this doesn't mean we're going to take long hot showers together and whisper sweet nothings into each other's ears."

Stitch spit his beer as he laughed. Was it the alcohol that made him laugh or did he actually have a sense of humor? This was a side of the guy Jacob had never seen. This man was all about business usually and busting his chops. Charles told him there was a rite of passage in EMS. You had to endure being hazed to see if you could take it. If they picked on you, it meant they liked you. If they ignored you, well then that meant they didn't care for you. If that was true, then Stitch must've really liked Jacob.

"So Jacob, tell me about you. What makes you tick?" Stitch asked lifting his beer and taking a large gulp.

"Not much to tell. I'm single. I have a boring office job, that as of late, I'm beginning to hate. I'm really close to my dad and I'm a spinal cord injury survivor."

Stitch stopped in mid-swig and stared at Jacob. "You had a spinal cord injury and you're still walking? That's a miracle man. How did it happen?"

"I did it during a head slide into home plate. I was playing city league softball. The funny thing was I scored the run."

"You're kidding me right? In a softball game?"

Jacob's irritation grew. How he was injured wasn't in a spectacular fashion, but it was traumatic just the same. "Yes, so?"

Stitch's eyes softened and he placed a hand on Jacob's shoulder. "Look man, I'm sorry. I shouldn't have acted that way. I apologize. How long were you in the hospital?"

"Two months. It took me a year to recover."

"Do you have any permanent damage from it?"

"The only thing is in my right leg. I can put it into a hot tub and it will just tickle, but if I put my left leg in I can tell how hot it really is. I consider myself lucky. I had family all over the country praying for me and look at me now? I'm completely recovered."

"Well, it sounds like you were pretty lucky, amigo."

"Yes, I was. So tell me about yourself. Your turn, and before you start, I believe you owe me a beer."

Stitch waved over the bartender and ordered another set of drinks. "Well, there's not much to tell. I've been in EMS for over 12 years and I've been married three times. And I like to bust the new guys' chops."

Jacob smiled. *You're damn good at it, too.* "You've been married three times? Are you going for a world record or something?"

Stitch glared at Jacob and then gulped down the remnants of his beer.

As Jacob sipped his beer, he wished he could take back what he'd said. "I'll open my mouth now and insert my foot. Sorry, Stitch. That was rude."

Stitch shook his head and sighed. "It's all right, man. No big deal. I guess I've always wanted to find a woman that would love me unconditionally. Unfortunately, I kept asking the wrong ones. They never could handle the hours. You know I work full time on the ambulance, right?"

"No, I didn't know that. Of course you have never really talked to me before, so there's a lot about you I don't know."

Stitch smiled. "I had to give you crap to see if you could take it. You seem all right. You're still green, but I see something in you and I think you could be great at this job. Have you thought about going full time on the truck?"

That's all Jacob had been thinking about since he began working the river. It was about comfort for him. The medical field was something he didn't know, and it scared him to death. Deep down inside, he felt like he was being pulled toward EMS.

"I've thought about it a lot, actually. I'm not sure if it's the right thing to do."

"What's not to be sure of?"

"Money is what I'm most afraid of. I would lose quite a bit financially if I were to quit my office job and take a job on the ambulance."

Stitch shifted in his seat and looked Jacob square in the eyes. "Listen to me, okay? It's not always about money. Sometimes you have to go with your heart. I've seen you in the field. I know that's where you want to be. All you have to do is man up and do it."

Jacob knew Stitch was right, but he wasn't going to let him know that. Since he'd been doing shifts at the river, it was all he could think about. He woke up in the morning thinking about it. And he went to sleep at night still thinking about it. Maybe it was time he followed his heart. For a long time now, it felt like he was meant for something more. Well, that something more was hitting him in the face day in and day out and he couldn't seem to muster the courage to just do it.

"So, what happened in your marriages?" Jacob asked.

"The first two were mistakes, but the last one took the cake. I came home early one night. I was sicker than a dog and I found my wife in bed with my best friend." Stitch glanced down at his hands.

Jacob couldn't believe what he was hearing. He felt sorry for asking such a personal question. "You're kidding, right?"

"I wish I were. I kind of felt like something was going on. She became so emotionally and physically detached, but I didn't want to believe it. I guess you could say I didn't want to know about it either, in a sense."

"What did you do?"

"I did exactly what any guy would do in that situation. I calmly walked over to my closet, got out my shotgun, and started to put shells in it. By the time I turned around, he was gone, and my wife was cussing me out for not calling her to let her know I was coming home. He lived around the block from me so I walked over there to have a little chat with him. By the time I arrived, the police were already there waiting for me."

Jacob's mouth fell open. He couldn't imagine how horrible that must've been. "Did you get arrested?"

"No. They just took my gun away and told me they would hold it for ten days. After that, I could come and pick it up. The officer told me if that would've been him, they would've been calling the coroner to come pick up the dead body."

The reason Stitch was so standoffish began to make sense. This man had been through a lot, and he'd built some walls to protect himself. Jacob was wrong. Stitch wasn't a cold hearted individual. He had been hurt too much. An eerie silence loomed in the air. Jacob traced his finger across the smooth oak bar top. He couldn't imagine what he would've done in that situation. After a few minutes, Stitch's cell phone rang. He reached into his blue jean pocket and fished it out.

"Hello? This is Stitch. What? You've got to be kidding me. I understand. Seriously? That's not right. Yes, yes, okay. I understand." Stitch hung up his phone gulped down his drink. He wiped his mouth off on his arm and hung his head.

"What's going on?"

"Well, I've got some bad news, and some really bad news. What do you want to hear first?"

"I guess the bad news," Jacob nervously answered.

"The bad news is they've terminated Charles from Life Flight. There will be no hearing, and the family is suing the County for medical negligence on that girl with the neck injury. The really bad news is they've officially shut down the River Rescue Squad effective immediately. The county had an emergency meeting and decided they can't afford more situations like this where they will have to sign a blank check."

Jacob sat there in disbelief. Just like that, his time in the field was gone. There weren't any other volunteer agencies in the area. He half expected something drastic to happen, but not quite this monumental. "Are they coming after us?"

Stitch shifted in his seat and let out a sigh. "No, they're not. They feel it was Charles' fault, so they won't be taking any measure against us." They sat in silence and sipped their drinks. The mood for talking was gone. "Well rookie. There's only one thing left for you to do."

"What's that?" Jacob curiously asked.

"Quit your job and come join me on the ambulance full time."

Jacob sat for a moment and stared into the smoke filled room, swigging down the last few drops of his drink, and slamming the bottle on the bar, he asked, "Where do I sign?"

Chapter Six

This was a new day, a new career, and Jacob's new life. He had completed his two-week notice, and now he faced orientation with Alliance Ambulance. Stitch had put in a good word for him. Over the last few weeks, Stitch and Jacob had forged a friendship and they were hanging out together a lot. This was the guy he was certain had the coldest heart of anyone he had ever met, and now he here he was calling him friend.

Butterflies floated through Jacob's stomach. Before receiving a station assignment, he had to complete an Emergency Vehicle Operations Course. The main responsibility of an EMT was to drive the ambulance and assist the paramedic on calls. After many long discussions about making a career change with Stitch, Jacob made the decision to move forward. Being this nervous about something was foreign to him. As he was getting ready, his cell phone rang.

"Hello?"

"Hey, man. How's it going? Are you getting nervous yet?" Stitch asked.

"You know I am. That's a stupid question."

"Don't be. You're only sitting in class learning about policies and procedures anyway. Try not to fall asleep in there like I did," Stitch said laughing.

"I don't think that's possible. I have a lot to learn so I'm pretty excited. Do I go in the uniform they gave me, or in street clothes?"

"You have to go in complete uniform. As of today, you're officially a practicing EMT. Make sure your uniform looks good, okay? Don't embarrass me. I vouched for you. If you fail, I fail."

Talk about pressure! As if it wasn't bad enough making a complete career change now, not only do I have to worry about my own image, but Stitch's reputation is on the line as well. Jacob pushed down the stomach contents that threatened to climb out of his abdomen.

"All right, man. I've got this. I need to go, though. I have to finish getting ready."

"That's cool, brother. Just remember to sit in the front row and pay attention. You don't want your first shift on the street to be a complete blunder because you didn't learn anything in orientation. Not everyone is as forgiving as me," Stitch said with a laugh.

Forgiving? Is he serious? It would be just his luck to have a preceptor as bad as Stitch.

"Yeah, right. Anyway, I've got to run. Later." After hanging up the phone, Jacob ironed his uniform. It was important to look professional, especially on his first day. Glancing nervously at the clock, there was still half an hour before he had to be at orientation. He ironed his uniform again and then once more for good measure. He stood tall in front of the mirror, running his hands down the front of his freshly pressed polo. The corners of his mouth tugged upward. The queasiness escaped his stomach, floated to his chest, and up into his head. He felt dizzy with excitement. He turned sideways, studying how the blue polo and cargo pants looked draped around him. With a final glance, he smiled.

Jacob drove down Main Street in Mesa. Early morning traffic halted his voyage to the first day of orientation. He glanced at his wristwatch, tapped his left foot on the floor, and gripped the steering wheel forcing his knuckles to turn white. Being on time was something he prided himself with. His stomach tightened at the thought of showing up late, especially on his first day. Traffic thinned out and he arrived at the main station twenty minutes later. Jacob leaped out of his truck and jogged across the freshly paved parking lot. A single stream of perspiration trailed down his forehead onto his nose. *Crap! I forgot to lock my truck.* He pointed his keychain over his shoulder and pressed the lock button. The horn on his truck echoed through the parking lot.

A single story building with white stucco walls and a red tile roof stood in front of Jacob. A neatly groomed landscape with rocks and cactus surrounded the building. He choked down the knot that stuck in his throat. Approaching the front of the main ambulance station, he stopped and sucked in a deep breath. This was it; his first paying EMS job. Ignoring the fluttering in his stomach, he stuck out his chest and briskly walked toward the front doors.

Glancing down at his watch as he walked, Jacob's eyes widened. Orientation was scheduled to start in five minutes. He rushed up the walkway and through the double glass doors. Sitting behind a large oak desk in the entrance was a petite and attractive receptionist. She glanced up from her computer and smiled.

"I'm here for the new employee orientation," Jacob told her.

"Welcome aboard. Go down the hall to your right. The class room is at the end of the hall through the double doors."

"Thank you." There were several offices with large glass windows lining both sides of the hallway. Various people were working busily at their desks, not really paying any attention as he walked by. Before going through the double doors he stopped, and took a deep breath. *Don't be scared; it's a new beginning, not the end of the world.*

Just beyond the doors was a large classroom with an enormous projection screen hanging from the ceiling. There were several tables with two chairs at each one set up around the room. As Jacob entered, everyone turned and looked at him.

Jacob's mouth dropped open as the urge to kill Stitch rushed through him. He was the only person in complete uniform. A few people were whispering quietly. He was certain they were talking about him. Feeling foolish, Jacob took a seat in the back of the room. *Just wait until the next time I see Stitch; I'm going to pummel him.*

After a few minutes, a middle-aged man wearing blue pants and a short sleeve, white button up shirt with gold bars on each collar entered. He walked with a swagger and glanced around the room at the fresh batch of new employees. Stopping at a podium erected in front of the tables, he let out a sigh.

"Everyone take your seats." He waited a few moments for everyone to sit down. All eyes were upon him as a wave of silence rolled through the room. "My name is Matthew Brady. I'm a district manager here at Alliance Ambulance. I've been a paramedic for eight years, all of which I have worked here at this company. I want to take a moment and have each one of you stand up, state your name, and certification level."

One by one, each person stood up and did as Matthew instructed. When it was Jacob's turn, everyone turned around staring at him intently. He stood up and cleared his throat.

"Hi, um...my name is Jacob Myers and I'm an EMT Basic." He plopped down in his seat and stared at the floor.

Matthew laughed. "Eager beaver are you, Jacob? I guess you didn't read your orientation manual because it specifically states attire for today is street clothes." A roar of laughter bellowed through the room.

"Settle down, settle down. Let's get started. As many of you may or may not know, we are a transport agency. We assist the fire department. They're considered first response and usually beat us on scene. The way it works here is that they're medical control on all scenes. This means what they say, goes. Now, with that being said, you may encounter some treatments you don't agree with. I suggest you find a politically correct way to get your point across, but again, they're in charge. If you don't like that, then I suggest you test with the fire department and get a job with them." Matthew leaned over the podium; his eyes narrowed. "Now, before you people think you're going to leave here and go get on a 911 ambulance, you're sadly mistaken. All of you, after completing your driver training, will go to an inter-facility unit. What is that you ask? It is a unit that is staffed with a nurse that does hospital-to-hospital transfers. You will not run 911 calls. This will afford you the opportunity to familiarize yourself with where all of the nursing homes and hospitals are located. Does anyone have questions?"

Everyone looked around the room at each other, but remained silent.

For the next two days, the employees spent their time going through policies and procedures. Jacob had a difficult time staying awake. Nonetheless, he couldn't wait to get on the ambulance and start working. This was like any other job. You had to sift through the boring and mundane stuff before you could start.

At the conclusion of the second day, Matthew asked if anyone had any questions. Jacob raised his hand.

"Yes? I can't remember your name, but go ahead," Matthew said.

Jacob stood up. "I was wondering. What if you're in the middle of taking a dump and the alarm goes off for a call? What do you do?" A few people laughed at his question. He sat down feeling pleased with himself.

Matthew chuckled. "You pinch it off and finish it later." The entire class erupted into laughter.

When Jacob arrived home, he decided to call Stitch again. He had been trying for the past few days, but all he got was voice mail and he was in no mood to leave a message. He felt like such a fool for showing up in complete uniform. The more he thought about it, the angrier he became. Grabbing a soda out of his refrigerator, he sat down in his lazy boy recliner, and dialed Stitch's phone number

"Hello?" Stitch answered.

"I've been trying to call you for the past few days. Where have you been?"

"I've been busy."

"You're an idiot. You know that?"

Stitch blurted out a laugh. "Let me guess. No one else was in uniform?"

"No, they weren't, you jerk. Except for me."

Stitch snickered. "Sorry about that. We always laugh at the new guy that comes to class all decked out in his uniform. We like to call him Ricky Rescue."

"Why's that?"

"It means that he's overly ambitious. I told you a long time ago that when we all started, we were ready to save the world. Your view on that will change over time. What did you think about Matthew?"

Jacob sighed and leaned back in his recliner. "He seems all right. I get the feeling he's strictly by the book."

"That's one way of saying it. With him, you have to be able to show him in black and white that he's wrong or he will argue with you until he turns blue in the face."

"Well, I don't plan on arguing with anyone. I don't even know what I'm doing yet. We have EVOC tomorrow. What's that like?"

"Some parts of the course are fun while others, not so much. I've got two words for you...blow out."

That sparked Jacob's curiosity and he sat up straight. "What's that supposed to mean?

"You'll see," Stitch said laughing.

The next day everyone showed up at the fairgrounds as ordered. Each person had to pass this driving training in order to be able to operate an ambulance. They had two older ambulances there, and several orange cones set up strategically around the parking lot. Matthew and a few other white shirts, as the employees called management, were standing around talking and laughing. Jacob was looking forward to this part of the training. No more books. Now they would get behind the wheel and drive like maniacs. A few minutes later, Matthew called everyone together.

"Gather around everyone. This is the fun part of the class. You get to drive an ambulance. How many of you have ever done that?" Matthew asked. No one raised his or her hand. "Okay. This should be interesting. There are several stations you have to complete in order to pass. Should you fail a portion, you'll have a chance to redo it. Now while doing the evasive course, you will have to wear a helmet. These two ambulances have, what we call, a blowout tire. The instructor will be sitting next to you. Without any prior notice, a tire will deflate. Your job is to keep control of the ambulance and not run into any cones. Any questions?"

Everyone looked at one another and didn't speak. The electricity of excitement sparked through the air. Jacob's stomach tightened. He choked down the urge to vomit.

"All right then. Let's get started."

Just as Stitch had stated, Jacob felt most of the course was boring. He performed pretty well and only had one more station to complete. Matthew walked over and handed him a helmet to put on.

"Here you go, young buck. Try not to kill me, okay?" Matthew gave him a slight smirk and then walked over to the passenger side of the ambulance.

Jacob opened the driver side door, got in, and buckled up. His palms were slick from sweat. He reached down and wiped them off on his pants leg. Matthew glanced over and raised his eyebrow.

"Listen, you have to be calm to operate this ambulance. The most important part of your job is getting your crew and the patient to the hospital safely. It's a dangerous part of your job, but not impossible. Now, take a deep breath and fire up this truck." Matthew grinned and pulled the helmet over his head.

Jacob sucked in a deep breath. . His heart was racing and noise was ringing in his ears. The ambulance was an old van type that looked like it belonged in the 1970's. *Surely this beast isn't going to go very fast.* Pulling the helmet over his sweat saturated hair, he turned on the ignition, and the engine sprang to life. He stared over the dash board at the line of orange cones in front of him. The only thing standing in the way of him starting his new career was this last driving test. His hand gripped the steering wheel; his body tensed.

"This is what you need to do. Go down the lane of those orange cones. You must be traveling 40 mph. I'm not going to tell you, but one of the tires is going to deflate to mimic a blowout. Your job is to keep from hitting any of the cones, apply your brakes, and bring the truck to a safe stop. Do you have any questions?" Matthew asked.

"Can I go 45 mph?"

Matthew's brow furrowed and a stern look took over his face. "No. I believe 40 mph will be sufficient." The tone Matthew used reminded Jacob of being scolded by his father. He sank in his seat and looked down at the floor mat like a beaten puppy.

"Don't get all sensitive on me. Shall I get you a tissue, Nancy? You need to toughen up or the streets will eat you alive," Matthew barked. He shook his head and powered up the console on his lap.

Jacob pulled up to the white line painted on the asphalt, and awaited Matthew's command. It felt like an eternity until he finally shouted, "Go!"

Jacob slammed the accelerator to the floor with enough force to punch through the floor. The ambulance picked up speed and the steering wheel shook. Exhilarating! He briefly looked over and saw Matthew with one hand on the control box and the other holding onto a handle in the door. The speedometer quickly reached 40 mph. Just as he passed the entrance to the orange cones, out of the corner of his eye, he saw Matthew flip a switch. With anticipation of the tire deflating, Jacob had a strong enough grip on the steering wheel to break it.

Suddenly the ambulance jerked hard to the left. He turned the wheel to the right and slammed on the brakes while still in between the cones. A second later, the truck jerked hard to the left, but before he could do anything to correct it, the earth turned sideways and they were staring at the ground. The ambulance then rolled three times before it came to rest on its wheels. Jacob's head fell back against the headrest. The world spun in and out of focus. In the distance, he could hear people running towards them yelling. After a few seconds, once he was able to get his bearings, Jacob realized that Matthew was with him. He unlatched his seat belt and reached over to shake Matthew.

"Are you okay?" Jacob asked. He feared the worst. Injuring himself, he could live with, but not if he hurt Matthew. That was something he wouldn't be able to handle.

"Yeah, I'm fine." Matthews's facial expressions went from confusion to anger in a flash. The smell of diesel fuel and burnt rubber rolled through the cab of the ambulance. Matthew pushed Jacob's hand away.

"Are we on fire? I don't see any smoke," Jacob asked glancing around the ambulance.

"No, I doubt it. Let's get out of the truck just in case," Matthew ordered. The doors were jammed shut on both sides so they climbed out the windows. One of the other district managers ran up with a horrified look on his face.

"Are you two okay? What happened?" the manager asked.

"I wasn't driving. Why don't you ask the idiot that just wrecked the ambulance?" His first concern was for their safety. "I don't know what happened. I corrected to the right then all of a sudden, the ambulance jerked hard to the left. The next thing I knew, we were rolling," Jacob answered. His heart pounded in his chest. His lungs constricted, making it difficult to take a deep breath.

Jim, one of the fleet supervisors who were there in case of any mechanical failure, walked over to the ambulance to look. He walked fifty yards back to where the ambulance first started flipping, and knelt down studying the asphalt. After a few minutes, he made his way back towards the wrecked vehicle.

Nausea rolled through Jacob's stomach. He'd come so far and now he was certain they were going to fire him before he was able to have one shift in the field.

Jim stood next to Matthew, his forehead crinkled. "I'm afraid to say it, but it's not this young man's fault. It appears the tire came completely off the rim and grabbed a crack in the asphalt back there causing it to flip. I'd say you two are pretty lucky. You might want to go buy a lottery ticket," the fleet supervisor said shaking his head.

Matthew sighed, rubbed the back of his neck, and stared at the ground. "We've had this blow out van for over ten years and have never had an incident until today. I don't know if I should pat you on the back or hit you in the back of the head."

He walked over to Matthew and stood in front of him. "So does this mean I pass?"

Chapter Seven

Jacob completed his driver training, and was released to work on the ambulance. Due to employee shortage, his first station assignment was on a 911 ambulance. Stitch said that was unheard of, but Jacob wasn't complaining. He didn't take a job in EMS to drive a nurse around from hospitals to nursing homes. He wanted to be in the trenches running 911 calls, testing his newly acquired lifesaving skills.

Pulling off Fig Street into the parking lot for Medic 61's station, he was distracted by a few birds flying circles above him, chirping in celebration of the cooler than usual summer morning. Squinting his eyes against the bright sun, he noticed a few people standing outside of the station talking to one another. He lifted his hand to shield his eyes, trying to search for any familiar faces. His heart sank when he realized he was the lone new person. Stitch told him that he had worked there for several months when he first started in EMS, and that it was the busiest station in Mesa. He told Jacob it was the best place to gain valuable experience, but the call volume had proved to be too daunting for Stitch while he was working the river, so he transferred to a slower station once he had enough seniority built up.

Jacob was nervous about meeting his new partner. What if they didn't get along? Twenty-four hours with someone you didn't like could be tormenting. He swallowed his nervousness, grabbed his bag, and strolled across the parking lot. The station was less than what he'd expected. The building consisted of white brick, a flat roof, and no landscape: a far cry from the main station where his training was held. Two white ambulances with red pin striping were backed up in adjacent spaces in the pot hole riddled parking lot.

As he walked up the narrow sidewalk filled with rocks and dirt, a couple of the guys standing outside laughed. He stopped and looked up and down his uniform. What were they laughing at? A knot formed in Jacob's throat.

"Look at the fresh meat, all dressed up nice and tidy." The man glanced down at Jacob's boots. "Look at the shine, Jesse. I bet he stayed up all night polishing them."

Jacob gulped hard. Was this the kind of people that worked in the medical field? The image he had of public service professionals was obviously tainted. Ignoring the rude comments, he hurried past them and walked inside. He was surprised at the homey feel as he walked through the door. There were four plush recliners on the hardwood floor in front of a big screen TV, freshly painted mint green walls, and a large oak kitchen table with four chairs in the dining room. Various firefighter and EMS related pictures were scattered across the walls. *Never judge a book by its cover.*

"I see you've met Jesse and Toby," a man sitting in a recliner reading a newspaper said.

"I guess you can say that."

The man folded his newspaper, stood up, and stretched his hand out towards Jacob. "My name is Trent. I'm your new partner."

"Hi. I'm Jacob Myers."

The two men shook hands, sizing the other up. Trent looked like he belonged in a GQ magazine. Standing over six feet tall, sandy blonde hair, strong jaw, and he had a muscular build. Jacob couldn't help but wonder if he was as twisted as the guys outside. Stitch told Jacob that Trent was a well respected paramedic. He had been in EMS for just over five years and was best known for remaining cool under pressure. This was the kind of paramedic he wanted to learn from.

"I'm sure there are a million things going through your mind right now. No matter what anyone says to you, just remember they were new at one time. Just stick by my side and we'll be fine. There are only a few rules I have. Okay?" Trent asked.

"What's that?"

"First and most important, when taking someone's vital signs, if you can't hear them don't make them up. Basic vital signs are one of the most important things a paramedic needs. The other rule is if there's something you don't know, ask. There's no such thing as a stupid question."

Jacob began to feel a little more at ease. Trent had a way of calming his nerves. "I can do that. I'm going to be up front. I have next to no experience, so I'm sure I'm going to talk your ear off."

A small smile crept across Trent's face. "I doubt that very seriously. We need to get our truck checked off. Go ahead and get started while I get the rest of my stuff ready."

As simple as this task was, it was still exciting for Jacob. As he walked past Jesse and Toby, he looked at the ground refusing to make eye contact with them. They each noticed this, and couldn't resist the chance to pick on him.

"Oh come on, rookie. Don't act like you don't see us. Come over here so we can put that chin to work."

"Leave my partner alone. He has work to do. Don't make me post the pictures I have of you two from last weekend out at Silvers Bar," Trent said. Both men stopped talking, turned around, and walked away. Trent winked at Jacob.

Jacob climbed into the back of the ambulance and sat down on the bench seat. He glanced around at the cabinets holding various pieces of equipment and medications. He couldn't believe he was working on an ambulance. His excitement ignited into fear. There were so many things he didn't know how to do. What if he made a mistake? Was Trent going to tolerate training a new guy? What if a mistake he made led to the death of someone who needed their help? His head swirled and he felt dizzy. Leaning back against the wall, he sucked in a deep breath.

"It's overwhelming, isn't it?" Trent asked from the back doors.

You have no idea how terrified I am right now. "Maybe a little."

Trent climbed into the back of the ambulance and sat down. He glanced around the cabinets and sighed. "I remember my first day. I was a snot nose kid that didn't have a clue what I was getting into, kind of like you. It takes time, but it will all come to you. Keep an open mind and learn as much as you can." He reached over and placed his hand on Jacob's shoulder. "One thing at a time. Let's go through all the equipment and ask as many questions as you like."

Jacob choked down a wave of nausea. "Where's the ambulance?"

Trent laughed.

The men spent two hours going through each piece of equipment. Several of the things Trent showed him, he'd never seen. He was thankful that Trent took the time to teach him. Stitch spent more time picking on him than he did showing him the ropes. That was his personality, and Jacob didn't hold a grudge. All the same, he was grateful to have a mentor teaching him vital information.

With the truck check complete, Jacob and Trent leaned against the ambulance. "Are you hungry?" Trent asked.

Jacob held his hand over his stomach in an attempt to muffle the low growls. "I could use something to eat. What do you have in mind?"

"I'm going to introduce you to the wonderful world of Felipe's Burritos. They have the best Mexican food in town. Plus, we get fifty percent off."

"Sounds good to me. I'm starving."

Jacob and Trent got into the ambulance. Rush hour traffic had subsided so it only took a few minutes to arrive at Felipe's. It was colorful and vibrant. There were piñatas hanging from the ceiling and sombreros strategically placed on the walls. Jacob couldn't help but notice they were the only white people in the restaurant. He inhaled deeply as the smell of salsa and refried beans drifted toward him. Spanish music echoed through the speakers, and employees were busy taking care of their customers.

"Feeling a little out of place, are ya?" Trent asked.

"Yes, very much so. I guess this means that they have great food if half of Mexico is here." Trent flashed Jacob a slight smile and nodded his head.

After they retrieved their food, they went back to the ambulance. Not that long ago, Jacob sat cooped up in an office, working feverishly on a computer. Now he was working in EMS enjoying some great Mexican food with, what seemed to be, a great partner.

Jacob devoured his tacos. By the time he was finished there was lettuce, cheese, and salsa all over his lap. He had never had such delicious tacos in all of his life. *Why haven't I eaten here before now?*

"I scarfed that food down so fast I didn't realize I was making such a mess," he said, taking a bite of his last taco.

"What did I tell you? Isn't this food the greatest?" Trent asked.

Jacob tried to swallow the mouthful of food he had before answering. "Yes it is. I can't believe it tastes this great. I've driven by these places a hundred times. To be honest, they looked a little crappy so I never stopped." He reached up and dabbed the corners of his mouth with a napkin.

"Ever heard "Don't judge a book by its cover"?"

Trent smiled. This made the second time today he had passed judgment before knowing everything. "So true. I'll be sure not to do that again, because I've been missing out on some great grub."

They shared a laugh as they finished their food. Jacob leaned back in the driver's seat, his full stomach threatened to shoot the button on his pants off into the windshield. The silence in the ambulance was interrupted by the frantic voice of a dispatcher over the radio.

"Medic 61, we have a pediatric arrest at 1420 Sheppard Place. You have a three-month-old female not breathing. Downtime unknown."

Trent leaned down, picked up the radio and calmly said, "Medic 61 copies. Show us en-route to this call." He replaced the microphone on its rocker and looked over at Jacob. "Are you ready, amigo?"

Jacob couldn't form words. His mind raced; he didn't know what to do. A child not breathing! His arms shook, mouth went dry, and he panted uncontrollably.

Trent reached over and placed a hand on Jacob's shoulder. "Calm down and take a deep breath. It'll be okay. I need you on this one, big guy. Remember, it's not our emergency. Now, if you don't mind, we need to get to this address. I'm sure the parents would appreciate the help," he said in a calm tone.

Jacob took a deep breath, and then shifted the ambulance into drive. As they pulled out into traffic, Jacob flipped the siren and lights on. People pulled onto the side of the road and out of their way. As they sped towards the house, a hundred scenarios raced through his mind. He shot a quick glance over at Trent who looked calm and collected. *If only I can be that calm*!

As they pulled up in front of the house, a man ran toward the ambulance holding a blue and listless baby. Jacob slammed the ambulance into park before the truck had come to a complete stop. Trent wasn't ready for that and he struck his head on the windshield. He had already unfastened his seat belt and was leaning forward. A small trickle of blood raced down Trent's forehead. His eyes narrowed; his brow furrowed. Jacob stared at him, his bottom lip quivering.

The man holding the baby pounded on the window of the ambulance. "What are you doing? Get out here and save my baby!" he screamed.

Directly behind him was a woman on her hands and knees in their front yard, crying uncontrollably. Everything was moving in slow motion.

In all of the chaos, Jacob's muscles seized. He sat frozen to his seat. Trent wiped his forehead with his arm and jumped out of the ambulance. He grabbed the baby and whisked her into the back of the unit. A fire truck pulled up next to their ambulance and four men jumped out. Three of them rushed to the back of the ambulance to assist Trent. One of the firefighters went over to the parents. A moment later, the mother was sitting in the passenger seat next to Jacob in the cab. Tears were streaming down her face. The father ran over to his truck, got in, and sped off.

"Code three to the hospital and don't kill us," Trent called. The urgency in his voice snapped Jacob out of his catatonic state. He put the ambulance into drive, and sped down the street, trying desperately to stop the trembling of his hands.

"Please save my baby. I'm begging you," the mother sobbed. Tears streamed down her cheeks from her reddened eyes. Jacob's heart sank. He wanted to help her, but didn't know how. He had to stay focused on what he was taught in EVOC; get the patient and crew to the hospital safely. What they hadn't covered, was dealing with frantic family member in the passenger seat. "Please, Ma'am. Try to stay calm. They're doing everything they can for your baby, but I need to concentrate on getting us to the hospital," Jacob pleaded with her. *Dear God, I'm begging you. Save this baby's life. This isn't right. Please bring her back to life!*

The woman tried to gain her composure, but Jacob could tell she was battling. He didn't have any children, and couldn't imagine the pain she was going through. As they got closer to the hospital, he could see in the rear view mirror they were frantically working on the small child. One of the firefighters was busy doing chest compressions, while the others were handing Trent various medications and equipment.

Traffic was heavy, which required Jacob to go in the lane against traffic. Cars bolted over to the other lane avoiding the oncoming ambulance.

"What are you doing? You're going to kill us!" the woman screamed. She gripped the door handle, terror etched over her face.

Jacob pushed a breath through his pursed lips, concentrating on navigating the traffic. The woman's screams sounded a thousand miles away. His heart thumped in his chest. He pulled the ambulance into the parking lot of the hospital, and for just a moment, he had a sense of relief. That was short lived because the firefighters and Trent were still working on the child. Jacob put the ambulance in park, the back doors swung open, and the crew rushed the child into the ER. The baby's mother jumped out of the truck and followed. Just a few moments ago, it was uncontrolled chaos. Now it was eerily quiet in the ambulance. Sitting while trying to collect his thoughts, he couldn't get over the fact he had frozen up on the call. Getting everyone safely to the hospital was his lone accomplishment.

Jacob attempted to suffocate the urge to cry, but couldn't control the tidal wave of emotions. His eyes welled up with tears and low bellows forced through his gritted teeth. His fists pounded into the dashboard. For several minutes, he sat in the ambulance. He reached up and wiped away his tears with his reddened hands.

Jacob climbed into the back of the ambulance. He glanced around the floor. Empty medication boxes, tubes, IV tubing, bag valve mask, and other remnants of medical supplies cluttered the floor. With tears flowing, he grabbed a biohazard bag and slammed the clutter inside.

"Hey," a voice came from the back of the truck.

Jacob jumped and twirled around to face Matthew.

"I'm sorry, Jacob. I didn't mean to scare you."

"It's okay. I guess I'm just a little jumpy right now."

"It's understandable. Are you doing okay?"

He wasn't sure how to answer that question. There was a myriad of emotions running through his mind. It was difficult trying to appear strong when he still had tears on his face. "I'm not sure how I'm doing. I don't know how to feel about all of this. I'm sad and angry at the same time." *How could God allow this child to die?*

"I'm here to take you back to your station. Any time a crew has a pediatric arrest, they're sent home for the remainder of their shift. Trent is going to be here a little while completing his chart and receiving some medical attention."

With all of the emotions he was dealing with, Jacob forgot about Trent hitting his head on the windshield. Was he going to be fired? It was an accident and now he was worried what was going to happen. "Is he okay?"

"Yeah, he'll be fine. After a head CT, he'll get a couple of stitches. Since he's going to be tied up, I'm going to take you back to the station so you can go home."

Jacob felt a wave of relief.

When he arrived back at his house, while he was walking up to the front door, he stopped and turned around to face his truck. Puzzled, he wondered how he got there. He felt numb. He couldn't remember the drive home. He glanced down and saw his uniform. A tsunami of emotions unleashed its unforgiving fury on him. He collapsed to the ground in tears. "No! How could You let this happen?" He yelled at God and slammed his fist against the driveway. The thought of the pain the baby's parents must be going through was a burden too heavy to bear. *Why, God, why did you have to take that baby away from her parents?* He didn't understand how such a loving God could be so merciless. It always seemed like bad things happened to good people. What had the parents done that was so awful they deserved to lose their child?

Chapter Eight

Jacob's first thought as he awoke the next morning, was to call his dad. He needed to make sense of the pediatric arrest. His roller coaster moods were uncontrollable. One minute he felt at peace and the next, he burst into tears. This couldn't be normal. It wasn't bad enough that the baby died, but knowing he didn't do his job was eating away at his soul.

The phone rang a few times. "Hello, son. How's the new job?"

Jacob's bottom lip quivered. "It's okay, I guess."

"Son, what's wrong? You don't sound like yourself."

He wasn't. A piece of him died with that small and innocent child. "I had my first pediatric arrest yesterday, Dad. The baby died." Jacob fought back the sobs. His father taught him to be strong. He was trying, but everything inside of him wanted to spew out.

There was a moment of silence.

"Oh. I'm sorry, Jacob. That's horrible, but it was that baby's time to go and there's nothing you could do about it. You have to let it go."

How could he let it go? The terror in the mother's face would forever haunt him. "Dad, I froze up. When we arrived on scene I sat in the driver's seat and couldn't move. Everything was happening so fast, I didn't know what to do."

His father sighed. "I don't think there is any way to be prepared for something like this, Jacob. Most people would react exactly as you did. There is no shame in it. You just need to coach yourself on what you will do in the future. Give yourself scenarios and then list the actions you will take. I'm not sure there's anything I can say to you to make you feel better. I'm here for you, son. You know that, right?"

The distance between them tugged at his heart. "I know Dad, but I don't think I can do this. I think I made a mistake quitting my other job."

"I can't imagine how hard this is. I'm not sure I could do it, to be honest with you. But I think God put you in the medical field for a reason. I believe your spinal cord injury wasn't an accident. It was God's way of steering you into the career path he wanted you in."

"I don't know, Dad. That just sounds like a fairy tale."

"Look. We need people like you out there fighting the good fight. Without guys like you, who would save people's lives? What if they hadn't been there for you? You could've been paralyzed, or even died."

Jacob grew silent and stared at the clock as the seconds ticked by.

"I'm going to go, Dad. I need some time to think. I miss you and love you."

"I love you too, son. Call me anytime you need to talk."

"I will." Jacob clicked his phone shut. His dad had a point. Without the emergency workers, who would be there to answer the call and save their lives? He had to find a way to deal with the baby's death, learn from it, and keep moving forward. Jacob felt drawn to the medical field; he felt that is where he belonged. If he didn't find a way to deal with death, his career was going to be full of heartache and pain that would eat away at his soul and break him, eventually.

As Jacob drove the long voyage to work, he couldn't help wonder what Trent was going to say. He was expecting the worst, but hoping for a miracle. It reminded him of the times when his father would say, "When we get home, you're getting a spanking." It was those times he wished his father would take the long way home. As he pulled into the parking lot, the previous shifts crews were outside socializing. He glanced in his rearview mirror and noticed everyone staring at him. Jacob sighed, climbed out of his truck, grabbed his bags, and slowly walked toward the station. He tried to swallow the knot that formed in his throat. With each step his stomach twisted tighter. Jacob hated the feeling of impending doom, but he had to face the music sooner or later. The conversations of him came to a grinding halt.

As he cautiously walked through the front door, Jacob caught a glimpse of Trent doing his usual morning duty - reading the newspaper. A wave of nausea rolled through his stomach. Trent continued to read his paper, not acknowledging that he'd come into the room. Finally he put down the paper, and Jacob caught a glimpse of the small bandage on his forehead.

He sat down in a recliner next to Trent and tried to figure out how to apologize. On his way to work, he had it all figured out. Now his mind was blank.

Trent leaned over in his recliner, facing Jacob. "First of all, how are you doing with the pediatric arrest?"

Jacob's shoulders slumped. He had difficulty swallowing and even more trouble breathing. It felt as if the weight of the world was sitting on his chest, mocking him. "Okay, I guess. I'm having trouble making sense of it." He turned toward Trent. "Before you say anything, I know I messed up on that call."

Trent sat back in the recliner, looking up at the ceiling. "I'm glad you had the composure to get us to the hospital safely. I'm not sure who put the mother in the front seat with you, but that shouldn't have happened. It puts a great deal of unnecessary stress on you." Trent glanced over at Jacob. His eyes bore a hole into Jacob's soul. "But I was disappointed in you."

The words crushed his brittle confidence and the air in his lungs escaped in a loud swoosh. His body grew numb. He'd rather Trent slug him in the stomach than lose his trust. "I know. I can say I'm sorry one hundred times and it will never be enough."

Trent put his hands behind his head and rocked in his recliner. "We were all new at one time. I understand that was the worst possible call you could get on your first day. The thing is you need to ask yourself if this is the career path that you want. I need you to be ready and capable to help me. I can't do this job alone."

With each word, Jacob's confidence crumbled into fine bits of dust. A lump, the size of a softball, formed in his throat. Maybe he was right. After all of the training he had been through, nothing prepared him for this.

"Trent, I'm sorry I failed you. Everything was moving so fast. All I can do is apologize and try to do better the next time."

Trent let out a sigh and had a puzzled look on his face. Jacob wasn't sure what exactly he was thinking. He wished the call had never happened, but wishing wasn't going to take it away.

"I forgive you. Make a mistake once, you're human. Make the same mistake twice... well then, you're just plain stupid." Trent stood up and held out his hand to shake Jacob's. What a relief! Jacob grasped his hand and firmly shook it.

The first twelve hours of their shift was busy. They had already run eleven calls with no relief in sight. As they were taking a patient into Mount Prospect ER, Jacob stopped dead in his tracks by the sight of the most beautiful woman he had ever seen. She stood five-foot-two with long brunette hair and a perfect figure. Time stood still. The sounds of the alarms, staff chattering, and the squeak of nurse's tennis shoes running across the freshly waxed tile floor, silenced.

"Jacob, we need to get this patient into a bed. Roll it up, buddy," Trent said laughing.

"Oh, okay. Sorry." As they walked by, she was busy talking with a doctor and didn't take notice. Jacob glanced, but didn't see a ring on her finger. Of course, that didn't mean she wasn't with someone, but it was a promising sign. After the patient was moved to the bed, Jacob joined Trent at the nurses' station. He was disappointed to see that she was gone. While Trent worked on his paperwork, Jacob took the cot out to the ambulance to put a clean set of sheets on it. Trent walked outside with an enormous smile plastered across his face.

"Her name is Bridgette Nelson. She's a travel nurse from Idaho. Today was her first day. Guess what else I found out?" Trent asked.

Jacob perked up with anticipation. "Well, spit it out."

"She's not married, no kids, and is single."

How in the world does he find out so much information on someone? Jacob shrugged his shoulders and smoothed out the linens on the cot. He suppressed his excitement. He was attracted to her, but didn't want Trent to know. "That's cool. I may holler at her later or something. We'll see," Jacob said.

Trent's eyes narrowed and a half smile tugged at his lips. "Oh you will, will you? What if I wanted to talk to her? Would you object?"

"You can do what you want, Trent. You're a big boy. I doubt she would be interested in me anyway. I probably won't talk to her." Jacob was stung by a bit of jealousy, which was ridiculous! He didn't know her. Why should he be feeling this way? Why would she be interested in him anyway? A paramedic was more enticing.

Trent blurted out a laugh. "I'm just teasing you, kid. You should talk to her. I have enough women. I don't need another one. You can have her."

"Gee, thanks." Jacob shook his head. He lifted up the cot and pushed it into the back of the ambulance. Before they stepped back inside of their truck, the portable radio chirped.

"Medic 61, I need you to go to 103 Broadway Street for an assault. Police are not on scene so please stage," the dispatcher said.

Jacob climbed into the driver's side, reached down, and grabbed the radio. "Medic 61 copies." As he went to turn the lights on, Trent stopped him.

"We don't go code three to a call we stage on. There's no sense in it. We'll go code one. If the police arrive on scene before we get do, and they need us urgently, we'll upgrade to code three," Trent said.

That made perfect sense to Jacob. On calls that were deemed dangerous, the paramedics would stage away from the scene until law enforcement arrived to make sure it was safe for them to enter. There was no need to go screaming to a call that they had to stage on. Dispatch never gave a detailed report as to what they were going to and it was annoying. Jacob liked to mentally prepare for what he needed to accomplish on a call before they arrived on scene. Of course, they can only tell you what the reporting party had told them. On the other hand, it was a little exciting not knowing exactly what they were heading into.

Jacob pulled into traffic and headed towards Broadway. In the short time he had been working in the area, it was becoming easier to navigate. Traffic was mild; it didn't take long to get near the address of the call.

"The house is just down the block from here. Let's pull in behind this business and wait. It's better if they don't see you, or else they may run up to us and that wouldn't be good, especially if the police haven't made it there yet. Remember, it's not our emergency; it's theirs."

Jacob pulled down an alleyway behind the business as instructed and shifted the ambulance into park. It was a taco shop, and directly in front of the ambulance was a dumpster. Trent surveyed the area, which was quiet, and then suddenly the dumpster lid flung open. Standing up in the middle of it was a Hispanic man holding an ice pick. He was covered in blood and was standing with both of his arms straight up in the air. He must've thought they were the police. Jacob looked over and saw Trent staring at the man in disbelief.

Trent reached down and grabbed the microphone without taking his eyes off the man. "Dispatch, this is Medic 61."

"Go ahead Medic 61."

"Tell the police I believe we have the subject standing right in front of us in a dumpster behind Julio's Taco Shop." He looked over at Jacob. "Back up and get us out of here before this guy decides to start stabbing us."

Jacob shifted the ambulance in reverse, and slowly backed up from behind the building. His hands were trembling, and all he could think about was this maniac running after them. The beeps from their back up alarm echoed off the stone walls of the businesses that surrounded them. Four police cars sped up from behind their ambulance. Jacob pulled off to one side of the alleyway to give them room to navigate around their truck. The police slammed on their brakes, jumped out of their cars with guns drawn, and were shouting orders to the man in Spanish. Jacob was in awe of the scene unfolding in front of him, even though the Hispanic man climbed out of the dumpster and complied with their orders. Two officers slammed him face first into the ground, removed the ice pick from his hand, and then cuffed him.

"Dispatch to Medic 61."

"This is Medic 61. Go ahead," Trent answered.

"The scene is code four. Police on scene state you have a thirty-two year old female with several stabs wounds all over her back and chest. They're requesting you to expedite."

"What does code four mean?" Jacob asked.

"It means the scene is safe and secure by the police."

As they pulled around the corner, there were several police cars in front of the address. The neighborhood was illuminated with red and blue pulsing lights. There were several curious on-lookers standing in their yards and in the street. As Jacob placed the ambulance into park, two firefighters exited the house shaking their heads.

"He stabbed her all over. I hope they catch him," one firefighter said.

"They did," Jacob answered. The firefighter smiled.

"Where's she at?" Trent asked.

"Sitting in a chair in the kitchen with the police officers."

"Jacob, grab the jump bag and the firefighters will bring in the cot." Trent walked towards the house as Jacob and the firefighters retrieved the equipment.

Jacob's stomach did a flip as he headed toward the house. Dust and dying grass floated through the air kicked up by his boots as he traipsed through the yard, stepping over a barrage of empty beer cans. Going into the unknown was exhilarating. Once he entered the home, he saw furniture over turned in the living room. There were several police officers standing around talking to one another with disgusted looks on their faces. Just inside the kitchen, an obese woman sat on a chair crying. She had several small puncture wounds all over her back and chest. The bleeding was minimal, which shocked Jacob.

"Are you hurting anywhere, Ma'am?" Trent asked as he knelt down in front of the woman.

She looked up at him, eyes reddened and moist with tears. "Of course I'm hurting. That crazy man tried to kill me!" the woman screamed in a thick Hispanic accent.

"Are you having any difficulty breathing?" asked Trent.

In between sobs, the woman answered. "No. I am in so much pain. Are you going to do something to help me?"

"Hand me the stethoscope. I need to listen to her lung sounds," Trent said.

One of the firefighters pulled a stethoscope from around his neck and handed it Trent. He listened to her breathing from the front of her chest. With each palpation, she grimaced in pain.

A detective stepped in front of Trent. "What happened, Ma'am?"

"What the hell do you think happened? He tried to kill me. He got angry at me because I was accusing him of sleeping with my friend. The next thing I knew, he stabbed me over and over again."

The detective's eyes narrowed. "We have him in custody. You'll need to come down to the station to give an official statement. Let these paramedics take care of you first, and then come see me later."

"Lung sounds are clear and equal bilaterally," Trent said. "We'll need to get her going to the trauma center. I don't think any vital organs were damaged, but she'll need to be checked out by a doctor to confirm that."

With all of the distractions, Jacob was finally able to obtain her vital signs. "Blood pressure is 136/84, pulse rate 126 and her room air pulse ox is 98%," he told Trent.

"Sounds good. Let's get her loaded onto the cot. We need to hit the road."

The woman stood five foot three and weighed close to two-hundred-seventy-five pounds. This actually played in her favor. With more fat tissue, the stab wounds didn't hit vital organs. Once she was seated on the cot. Jacob and Trent headed for the front door. The officers moved out of the way, but were still talking amongst themselves. Everyone in the house couldn't help but feel sorry for this poor woman. She was at her weakest moment, a spectacle, and the man she loved had just tried to kill her. *How could a man hurt the woman he loves?*

As they arrived at the hospital, Jacob's day got better. They rounded the corner and there she was. Bridgette. Amazingly beautiful. He was terrified to talk to her. Trent shot him a quick smile.

"What you boys got?" the charge nurse, Alice, asked from behind the nurses station. She stood barely five foot tall, had short spiked gray hair, and piercing blue eyes. Jacob noticed a panther tattoo on her left forearm.

"She sustained multiple stab wounds from an ice pick. Vitals are stable with clear and equal lung sounds, bilaterally," Trent answered.

Alice grinned. "Take her to trauma two. A nurse will be with you shortly," she said looking over the rim of her glasses on the end of her nose.

Be with us shortly? Who was she kidding? They've waited as long as half an hour for a nurse before. Mount Prospect had a seventy-two bed emergency room. They were one of the busiest in the city. The rule was that EMS couldn't leave until a nurse signed for the patient. If the nurses were busy, they had to sit and wait. That wasn't always a bad thing because that meant they weren't available for another call. Dispatch would page them repeatedly with calls, but unfortunately, no signature meant the unit couldn't leave.

Twenty minutes, and six status checks from dispatch, the nurse finally arrived to take report. Jacob stood with his back to the curtain. Trent's smile caught his attention. He turned around and there she was. Bridgette. His heart stopped.

"Jacob has the report for you," Trent said smiling.

Jacob couldn't form any words, and didn't want to in fear of sounding idiotic. This was his chance to talk to her. He sucked in a deep breath. "She was stabbed...a bunch."

A small smile cracked her beautiful face. "A bunch, huh? Well that certainly is a lot, don't you think?" Bridgette teased.

Trent shook his head as Jacob stood in front of her with his mouth hanging open. Doing the walk of shame, he pushed the cot into the hall and placed clean linens onto it.

After giving the nurse a full report, Trent walked over to the nurses' station and sat down his paperwork. He glanced over to Jacob and smiled.

Alice took off her glasses. "Got another new guy, Trent?"

Trent sighed. "Yeah, you could say that." He leaned on the counter. "I don't know if he's going to be able to cut it."

Not going to be able to cut it? I can hear everything you're saying!

Alice smiled. "I remember you when you were wet behind the ears. I'm sure your partner thought the same thing about you."

"I don't think I was that bad," Trent said as-a-matter-of-fact.

Alice suppressed a laugh. She leaned over the counter, inches from Trent's face. "Really? We were all that bad when we first started." She leaned back, picking up a patients chart. "You're a great paramedic. You just need to find a way to teach him. I have faith in you."

I'm glad someone has faith in me!

"If you say so. I'll see you later." He turned and walked toward the ambulance entrance.

"I hope not," Alice said grinning.

Jacob pulled the sheets tight. He dashed through the ambulance entrance doors out to their unit ahead of Trent. Once he stowed the cot, he sat down on the bumper hanging his head. He never knew Trent felt that way about him. He wasn't sure if he should tell him he heard the conversation or not.

Trent walked out of the hospital, grinning broadly. "Jacob, you're dumb. I served you up a meat ball to hit out of the park, and you struck out without even taking a swing."

Jacob couldn't look up from the ground. "I froze up. I didn't want to sound stupid." *And you think I'm hopeless. I'm going to prove you wrong.*

"Well, I'm afraid to tell you this, but you failed that mission miserably. I will say you're pretty good at freezing up."

Jacob met Trent's gaze. "Kick a man while he's down, why don't ya?" *How could he be so brutal?*

"Sorry, but you know how I am. I speak the truth. I do have some good news for you. She said my partner was cute as I was walking out."

Jacob stood up and slipped his hands into his pants pockets. "She said I was cute?"

"I'm just kidding. She didn't say anything."

Jacob shook his head and sighed. "I hate you, Trent."

Chapter Nine

Bridgette was so stunningly beautiful that he felt intimidated around her. Of course, right now it was just a physical attraction. For all he knew, she could be unstable or temperamental or spoiled. But there was something about her that drew him in. For the next two days, Jacob couldn't stop thinking about how foolish he must've appeared to Bridgette. This was crazy. Why was he so worried about what a woman thought that he didn't even know? As he was lying on his couch contemplating his next move, the phone rang. He reached into his pants pocket and fished his cell phone out. He flipped it open.

"Hello?"

"What's up, my brother from another mother?" Stitch asked.

"Nothing much. Just sitting here contemplating the meaning of life."

Stitch chuckled. "Wow, that's gay. Speaking of gay, I heard you did a face plant in front of the new nurse at Mount Prospect."

"I wouldn't call it a face plant. I prefer to think of it as gracefully falling."

"If that makes you sleep better at night. I really wish I could've been there to see it."

"You're an idiot sometimes. Only you would gain comfort from someone else's misery."

"You know me too well. Still, I wish I could've seen it. Going to be hard to face her again after that I bet."

"I'm trying not to think about it. I didn't want to sound stupid. You see how that worked out for me."

"How's it going with Trent?"

Jacob was thankful for the subject change. "Pretty good. He seems like a good paramedic."

"I was glad you got partnered with him. He has the respect of many people in the field. Learn everything from him you can."

"I plan on it. Listen, I gotta go, but don't be such a stranger." Jacob hung up the phone. He wasn't in the mood to listen to Stitch's endless banter. How was he ever going to face Bridgette again? It wasn't like he could avoid her forever. She worked in the ER they frequented.

Making so many mistakes was foreign to Jacob. He'd been a standout high school athlete and anything he set his mind to, he was able to accomplish. The harder he tried, the more mistakes he made - both personally and professionally. It was strange to him. One way or another, he was going to succeed and not give up. He had his father to thank for his resiliency.

Jacob's cell phone vibrated across his oak nightstand. He sat down on his bed and picked it up. "Hello?"

"Hey, Jacob. It's Matt. You up for some overtime and a little bit of experience with patient care?"

"I could always use the extra cash."

"Good to hear. Someone called out sick today for one of the Tempe trucks. It's a basic unit. You're partner, Bradley, isn't allowed to be in the back of the ambulance. He can only drive."

"Why is that?"

Matthew sighed. "He's had issues with some of the fire department paramedics. They've requested he only drives. So, you'll be the attendant. It'll be great experience for you, getting patient contacts."

Jacob glanced at his clock; it was ten in the morning. Crew change was normally at six. "I'll need to take a shower and get ready. I can be there in forty-five minutes."

"Great! I'll let the crew member know that's holding over until you get there. I appreciate it. Remember, no matter what Bradley says, he's not allowed in the back of the ambulance when you are transporting. That's very important!"

Jacob chuckled. "You got it, boss."

"Thanks again for helping out. Have a great shift!"

Jacob closed his phone and set it down on the nightstand. He was curious what Bradley had done in the past to anger the fire department. Oh well, not for him to worry about. Excitement filled him. His first chance at being the attendant in the back of the unit. He stripped off his clothes and jumped into the shower.

The one thing he learned so far was that being an EMT meant a whole lot of driving. In order for him to be able to be in the back of the ambulance full time, he would have to become a paramedic.

Jacob joined Bradley in the day room. He was leaning up against the tough textured wall and flipping through a magazine.

"Want to go get some ice cream?" Bradley asked.

Jacob never turned down the chance to devour ice cream; it was his weakness. "That sounds great. Tell ya what, my treat."

Bradley shot up from his recliner. "I'll never turn down free food. Let's go!"

They left the station and headed out to the ice cream shop. The setting sun bathed the horizon in an orange glow. Mill Avenue buzzed with students on bikes. They appeared to be in their own little world, oblivious to what was happening in real life. *To be a college student and not have any worries in the world, wouldn't that be nice?*

"So, how long have you been an EMT?" Jacob asked.

"Six years now. I've tried to get into paramedic school, but I haven't been able to pass the entrance exams. I have major test anxiety. I know the stuff, but I freeze up when it comes to taking the exams. How about you?" Bradley asked.

"For a few months now. I really like it. I keep messing up, though." *Feels like it'll never stop, either!*

"We all did when we first started, so don't worry about that. I've known guys in the field for years and you couldn't tell. Just keep learning."

Knowing he wasn't the only clueless one set Jacob at ease. He felt like he had come a long way, but there was still much more to learn. The tones sounding on the radio interrupted the silence that loomed in the ambulance.

"Ambulance 79, we have a head on collision on the corner of College Place and Fourth Street. Three victims; two victims not breathing. Fire department has been dispatched and two additional ambulances," the dispatcher said.

"Right on! I love trauma! It's only a mile from here. Let's go get some!" Bradley shouted. He flipped on the lights, kicked on the sirens, and sped toward the scene.

A surge of adrenalin shot through Jacob's body. This is why he left his office job, to have the chance to help people. He tried desperately to slow his breathing and think of all the things he would need to do. No freezing up on the call this time. They were taught in EMT class that trauma was easy. Find the hole and plug it. With trauma, you could see what was wrong with someone rather than with medical, where you had to dig to find out.

As they approached the scene, Jacob's mind went numb. His heart felt as if it was frozen in his chest. Two newer model cars were entangled. With all of the twisted and intertwined metal, it was difficult to tell where one car began and the other ended. Jacob looked over next to one of the cars, and there was a young woman sitting on the ground sobbing. At least she's crying; that means she isn't hurt as bad. Two men were lying face down and hanging out of the passenger door of one of the vehicles. They weren't moving.

Bradley pulled their unit up to the scene. "Ambulance 79 is on scene. We have a head on collision, no entrapment, with three patients thus far. Stand by for additional report," Bradley said. "You go check on that girl sitting there and I will go see what's going on with the other two guys."

The scene resembled a war sight in a movie. His hands trembled and he felt his heartbeat thumping in his ears.

Jacob put on his reflective vest, and ran across the steamy asphalt toward the girl sitting down on the ground. He tripped on debris from the wreck and landed face down in the middle of the road. Jacob raised up to his knees and looked around. *Thank God, no one was looking.* He lurched up from the road and approached the girl. She was moving all of her extremities and breathing without any trouble, which was a good sign.

"Are you hurting anywhere?" Jacob asked kneeling down in front of her.

She cried. "Yes, my neck and back are killing me. Are they okay?" she asked trying to look around Jacob at the accident scene.

"What's your name?"

"Tisha. Please, dear God, tell me they're okay," she said.

Sirens echoed in the distance. *Please God, let them get here quick. We need help!*

"We can't worry about them right now. I need to concentrate on you. Are you having any trouble breathing?"

"No, you jerk! I already told you where I'm hurting. Go check on them. Please," she screamed.

She doesn't have to be so hateful. I'm just trying to help her. "Ma'am, I have to stay with you. Did you have any loss of consciousness?"

"No. I remember everything."

"Are you having any trouble breathing? Were you wearing a seat belt?"

"I already told you I was breathing okay. Yes, I was wearing a seat belt. Why do you keep asking me the same questions?"

She had a point. He was so nervous he kept forgetting what he had asked her thus far. "Were you thrown out of your car?"

"No, I got myself out and walked over here."

"We have more help on the way. I need you to sit really still, and don't move your head. Do you understand?"

She complied while fighting back the tears. Jacob jumped up, and ran back to the ambulance. He grabbed a c-collar, straps, and a long spine board. Once he got back over to her, he placed the c-collar on her, and held her neck. It was very important that he hold the manual c-spine until she was secured to the backboard, as he was taught. Sweat poured down his forehead into his eyes. The stinging sensation blurred his vision.

"What are you doing? I need help over here. These two guys aren't breathing!" Bradley shouted from next to the other vehicle.

"I have manual c-spine. I can't let go," Jacob quickly replied.

"I don't care about that. I need your help. Get over here!"

Everything in his body told him to go help Bradley, but Jacob didn't want to go over to him. The girl he was with was still breathing and in stable condition. With this girl, he knew she was going to be okay. He wasn't about to let go. The cracking noises of Amber's neck from the boating accident echoed through his mind. He wasn't going to allow this woman to be further injured. A moment later, a fire truck and two more ambulances arrived at the scene with lights flashing, sirens blaring, and chaos all around. *Thank God more help has arrived.*

A firefighter and two crewmembers from another ambulance ran toward Jacob.

"What do you got?" a firefighter asked kneeling down next to him.

"A female patient with neck and back pain. She had no loss of consciousness," Jacob answered.

"Okay. I'll take over c-spine. You need to go and help your partner. Looks like those two are in bad shape." He leaned in and took over holding her neck.

Jacob ran over to Bradley. There were two men laying secured to backboards side by side on the ground. Bradley was tending to one of them; a man in his early twenties who had several facial lacerations. Jacob noticed that he also had a small area on his forehead that was slightly caved in. Through narrow eyes, Bradley glanced at Jacob.

"Grab the end of the backboard. We need to move him to our cot," Bradley ordered.

Jacob scurried over to the head and did as ordered. Once secured with the belts, they raised the cot and raced towards their unit.

"We have two paramedics riding with us - Ted and Ben. You'll be in back. Do whatever they say," Bradley said.

Jacob caught Bradley's gaze. His lips were thin and his face tense.

The two paramedics joined Jacob and Bradley with their equipment bags in tow as several law enforcement officers secured the area to keep the curious onlookers away. The news media arrived on scene. They were setting up their camera perimeter, trying to get a shot of the horrific scene. Here they were trying to save people's lives, and there were the media vultures feeding off the gruesome scene.

As they approached the back of the ambulance with the cot, a firefighter flung the back doors of the unit open with such force Jacob was almost struck in the face. How embarrassing that would be, to be knocked to the ground while some camera guy filmed it for the world to see?

"We need to get him in the truck now. I need to intubate him!" said Ted.

"It's my turn to intubate. You're not stealing my tube. You just worry about getting the IV," Ben yelled.

The two paramedics glared at one another like a couple of spoiled three-year-olds. Tension loomed in the air above the chaotic scene. Jacob wanted to throttle both of them. What was it about this job that always brought out the inner toddler in everyone? He pushed past them and locked the cot in place. Ted threw a bag at his partner. "Here, get my intubation stuff so I can get this guy tubed," he ordered.

"Do I look like your slave? Get your own crap ready. I have enough to do," Ben said. No one was performing CPR. Jacob went into auto-pilot, jumped into the CPR seat and pumped on the man's chest, silently counting in his head. Bradley was still standing outside of the truck looking somewhat dazed. As Jacob was busily compressing the man's chest, a cameraman positioned himself at the back of the ambulance pointing his camera toward them. Bradley's look of confusion quickly turned to anger.

"Get out of here," he barked. He reached up and shoved the cameraman. The man toppled to the ground and his camera skidded across the asphalt. The lens shattered and glass sprayed across the ground.

"What is your problem?" the man screamed at Bradley from the ground.

"You're my problem. We're trying to save this man's life and all you're interested in is getting your big story. Do us all a favor and get out of here!" Bradley yelled.

Jacob stifled his laughter. *Did he just really push that guy down?* It was that occurrence that snapped the two paramedics out of their feud. They looked at one another, laughed, and then got busy working on the man.

"How about you get back to pumping on this guy's chest? The show's over," Ted said.

Without hesitation, Jacob restarted CPR. Jacob's job was easy. He had one task, keep this man's heart circulating blood. The paramedics were responsible for bringing the man back to life.

"Bradley, let's get going. Code three to County Hospital," Ben ordered.

"You got it, boss." Bradley shut the door and jumped into the driver's seat. He flipped the sirens on and headed towards the hospital.

The two paramedics opened IV supplies, prepared the intubation equipment, and threw trash all over the back of the ambulance. Seeing these men at work fascinated Jacob. A shiver shot down his spine.

"You need to compress deeper and faster," the paramedic said to Jacob.

Fatigue was setting in, but Jacob wasn't going to let them know that. Giving into fatigue wasn't an option. CPR was a basic skill, but a very important one. Without this man's heart pushing blood to the rest of his body, everything else they were doing was rendered useless.

Ben plunged an IV needle into the man's arm, blood flashed in the chamber. He secured it and hooked tubing into the hub. Fluid dripped in rapid succession. "I've got IV access. What does his rhythm show on the cardiac monitor?" Ben asked.

Ted turned the monitor towards him and a flat line scrolled across the screen. "It's a systole."

Trent had told Jacob there was no such thing as a stupid question. "What's a systole?" he asked.

"It means there aren't any electrical impulses in the heart," Ted answered.

Ben grabbed the medication kit out of his jump bag. "I'm going to push one milligram of epinephrine." He pulled out a syringe, inserted it into the IV line, and pushed the drug into it. "Next dose will be in three minutes," he said as he glanced at his watch.

Ted prepared the equipment needed to intubate the patient. Once he had assembled everything, he slid the blade of the laryngoscope into the man's mouth. Jacob continued compressions on his chest as he watched

Ted, intently. This was a procedure Jacob had never seen before. *Dear God, I know you haven't been listening to me much as of late, but can you please help this paramedic save this man's life?*

"I can't see the vocal cords," Ted said. Sweat spotted on his forehead as he gritted his teeth. "Ben, I can't see anything."

Ben grabbed the handrail on the ceiling and walked next to his partner. "Want me to take a look?"

Airway was important in a cardiac arrest. Jacob knew that if Ted wasn't successful intubating the patient, the chance of getting him back decreased dramatically. With each tug of the laryngoscope, Ted's facial muscles tensed and the veins on his forehead pulsated.

"Let me take a look. You've been digging around in his mouth long enough," Ben said.

The men switched places. After several failed attempts, neither man could get him intubated. Jacob looked over at the cardiac monitor. It was still a flat line. It felt as if they had been driving to the hospital for hours. But in reality it had only been a few minutes.

"How far out from the hospital are we?" Ted asked Bradley.

"Twenty minutes."

Ted and Ben looked at one another for a few moments. There was an unspoken language going on between them. With Jacob's fatigue at a peak, he didn't know how much longer he could continue doing CPR. The compression depth and rate slowed dramatically.

"We have to do it, Ben. Without an airway this man is dead," Ted said.

Ben shook his head and sighed. "I'm not comfortable with this. Are you sure we're out of options?"

"I've seen it done a few times. I can do this," he said boldly.

Ben moved out of the way and Ted took position at the head of the cot. "Take it nice and easy, Bradley. I'm going to do a surgical-crych on this guy," Ted said.

"What do you mean surgical-crych? You're going to cut his throat?" Jacob asked.

"Yes, unless you have a better idea."

This was Jacob's first trauma, and now he was about to witness a very risky procedure. And they said trauma was easier! Ted was right, though. If they didn't do something now, there would be no hope of bringing him back. As Ted took out the scalpel, his hands trembled. A bead of perspiration streamed down his forehead, down his nose, and fell onto the patient's face. The blaring sirens suddenly became quiet, and time stood still.

"You can do this, Ted. I have faith in you," Ben said. He placed a hand on Ted's shoulder.

Ted looked at Ben and then back down to the patient. The ambulance swayed side to side as they sped towards the hospital. Ted rested his hand on the right side of the patient's neck, trying to steady it. Ted sucked in a deep breath, and then cautiously approached the man's neck with the scalpel. Just as he began to cut the skin, the ambulance jerked to the side. The scalpel slid off the patient's Adams apple, and sliced down the side of his neck. A fountain of blood gushed from the man's neck covering the floor. Ted's face turned pale. He grabbed a handful of gauze and shoved them against the wound he'd just created. Ben and Jacob looked at one another in complete horror.

"Well, he's dead," Ted said grimly.

Jacob had never seen so much blood in all of his life. He used an entire bag of rags to clean up the mess. The blood was thick and clumpy. Now coagulated, it resembled dark red jello. Ted and Ben were inside talking to the trauma team and doctors. Jacob and Bradley hadn't said two words to one another since they arrived at the hospital; Jacob knew he was angry. The site of the blood didn't bother him, which was surprising since he hadn't been exposed to it until this point.

A few minutes later Ted and Ben walked outside. Their fire truck idled outside of the emergency department entrance, waiting to pick them up. They walked over to the ambulance to retrieve their equipment bags.

"Gentlemen, I just wanted to thank you both for your help. I really appreciate it," Ben said.

Bradley peeled off his gloves and walked towards them. "I wish there was more we could've done."

"Nothing was going to change the outcome. He was pretty much dead anyway," said Ben.

Jacob looked over and noticed Ted sitting on the bumper of the fire truck, arms on his knees, head hanging low. Jacob overheard the captain yelling at one of his fire fighters.

"Are you stupid or what?" the captain asked.

"No, captain. It was a mistake," the firefighter answered.

"A mistake? People die when we make mistakes. It's really simple. When we're on a vehicle accident you have a charged fire hose out and ready. What if one of the cars had caught on fire? What would've you done then? I'll tell you what you would've done: watched them burn to death!"

"You're right, captain. It was a mistake. It won't happen again."

"You're damn right you won't do it again. If you do, I'll kick your butt all the way to Canada."

This call created so much misery. Out of three patients from the wreck, only one survived. Ben sat down next to Ted on the bumper, and placed a hand on his shoulder. At the beginning of the call, these two men were trying to kill each other. Jacob felt as if he was a passenger on an emotional roller coaster. This was a part of the job he had never thought about. *Am I going to be able to handle all of this? Every time I think things will even out they fly out of control again.*

"You doing okay, Ted?" Ben asked.

Ted sat up and leaned against the back of the truck. A sigh slipped through his lips. "Yeah, I'll be fine. I feel horrible about screwing up on that poor guy."

"You have no reason to. You know that don't you? He was already dead."

"Well, I certainly didn't improve his chances by cutting his throat."

"You didn't hurt him either. You did what you had to. Without an airway, he didn't have a chance anyway. Short memory brother; we'll get the next one."

They grabbed the equipment bags and placed them back in their fire truck. During the decontamination the call volume subsided, which was a welcome change. The smell of Pine Sol and Sanishield filled the air. Jacob glanced around, making sure he didn't miss anything.

Bradley sat down on the bench seat next to Jacob. "Boy that was a call gone bad."

"You could say that," Jacob answered shaking his head.

"I was trying so hard to drive smooth. I didn't even see that pothole in the middle of the road. Is that when Ted cut that guys throat?"

"Yeah. I could tell he was nervous doing it. His hands were shaking just before he tried to make the incision."

"Wouldn't yours be if that had been you? I've never seen a surgical-crych performed in the field. You have one up on me already."

"Honestly, I could not care less to have that honor. It was horrible. I've never seen so much blood." Jacob glanced over at Ted. "It doesn't look like he's taking it very well."

"I don't blame him. He basically killed that guy."

Jacob's brow furrowed. "You think he killed that guy?"

"He did cut the man's throat and bled him out," Bradley said.

"I know I'm new out here, but Ben said he did nothing wrong."

"Of course he did. The firefighters stick together no matter what. Even if Ben had thought Ted killed him, he wouldn't say it."

Jacob wanted to punch him. It took everything in him to keep his mouth shut. *What is your problem? Ted did what he had to do to try and save that man's life. Just because you swerved the damn truck wasn't Ted's fault.* Even with so many emotions swirling around and a boatload to learn, Jacob still felt he belonged in the field. Something inside him kept urging him forward, telling him he could somehow make a difference.

"Who's that?" Bradley asked, nodding toward the ambulance entrance of the hospital.

Jacob looked up to see a beautiful red head smiling at him. Her teal eyes held his gaze.

"I have no clue."

She gave him a little wave and then turned and walked into the hospital.

"She acted like she knew you. Are you sure you don't know her? If it was me, I would definitely be accepting her invitation."

"What are you talking about?"

"Are you blind or something? That woman wants you."

Jacob shook his head and headed for the passenger side door. He couldn't put his finger on it, but something about that woman was familiar.

Chapter Ten

Jacob had three days off from work. For the short time he'd been in the field, he gained a fair amount of experience. It was nice having a job that he looked forward to. The one thing that was so captivating to him was that he never knew what experiences the next call was going to bring.

As he was sitting in his lazy boy, thinking about the recent calls he'd been on and surfing through the channels on his TV, his cell phone vibrated across the oak end table. "Hello?"

"What's up, my brother from another mother?"

"Hey, Stitch. How's it going?"

"Doing great. How about we go grab a drink?"

His offer was enticing. "Sure. Where do you want to go?"

"How about our favorite place, The Rusty Nail?" he asked.

"Sounds like a plan. What time do you want to meet?" A knock sounded at his front door. "Hold on, man. Someone's knocking." Jacob strolled across the thick carpet in his living room and opened the door. Stitch stood in the doorway, grinning.

"Are you going to invite me in or make me stand out here looking like a fool?" Stitch asked clicking his cell phone shut and slipping it into the front pocket of his jeans.

"Dude, really? You could've told me you were coming over."

"That ruins the fun, rookie," he said with a grin on his face.

Jacob couldn't resist; he shut the door in Stitch's face, walked across the living room, and flopped down in his cushy recliner. The front door flung open and Stitch causally walked in.

"Nice manners. Why don't you just come in?"

"I thought you'd never ask." Stitch walked over, took the remote control out of Jacob's hand, sat down on the couch, and flipped through the channels.

"Were you raised in a barn?"

"Nope." He continued watching TV, ignoring the fact that he had left the door open. He could be so irritating at times. Jacob got up and slammed the door shut.

"Easy there, Hercules. You don't want to take it off the hinges."

Jacob walked into his bedroom and threw on a pair of blue jeans and a white t-shirt. Even though Stitch could be a pain, Jacob enjoyed hanging out with him. Once he was dressed, they headed to the Rusty Nail. Stitch was unusually quiet on the way to the bar. Jacob wasn't sure what was going on with him, but he decided to enjoy the rare silence.

It always took a few minutes for Jacob's eyes to adjust when walking into the Rusty Nail. He couldn't help but wonder if the reason they kept it so dark was so people couldn't see the ugliness that surrounded them. As they strolled through door, a man grabbed Stitch from behind and put him in a chokehold.

"What the....?" Stitch said gasping for air. Standing behind him, with his arms wrapped around his neck, was Trent.

Jacob laughed. "Man, Trent. I was about to scissor kick you in the head."

Trent released the hold and patted Stitch on the back. "You can't kick that high, young buck," he said to Jacob.

"Freaking eh, Trent, that wasn't cool. I almost passed out," Stitch said holding onto his neck.

"Oh, quit being a big baby. I barely had a hold of you."

The three of them walked over and sat down at the bar. Jacob glanced around and noticed the usual crowd that frequented the bar. The combination of cigarette smoke and musty alcohol hung in the air.

"Hey, guys. What'll it be?" the bartender asked.

"Whatever they're having. I'm not picky," Jacob said as he shot a glance over at his friends.

Stitch reached for his wallet, looked inside of it, and disappointment washed over his face. "Guess I forgot to get some cash. Do you take cards?" he asked looking at the bartender.

"Sure do."

"So, I have some good news for you," Stitch said to Jacob.

"What's that?"

"I'm transferring to your station. The lack of call volume has me bored. It's time to get back in the action."

"Jealous of all the fun stuff that I've been getting to do?"

"Jealous? Of you? Never," said Stitch laughing.

"It's okay to have call envy. I would if I were you."

"Look at you now, rookie. Getting a big head are we?" Stitch said as he tossed back his beer. "You need to calm this guy down, Trent."

"I've been trying to. You can see how far I've gotten," Trent answered, shaking his head.

"I don't have a big head, but my chin is quite large, haven't you heard?"

Stitch spit beer over the bar. The bartender didn't look pleased as he walked over with his cleaning rag.

Reaching over, Trent hit Jacob on the shoulder. "Look who's sitting over in the corner?"

Jacob turned around and smiled.

"What are you still doing over here? Go talk to her," Trent stated.

"Who are you guys talking about?" Stitch asked.

"I can't, Trent. I already sounded like a complete idiot the last time I saw her, remember?" Jacob's stomach tensed. There she was, even more beautiful out of her work uniform. It didn't appear that she had noticed them. She was too busy looking down at the table and playing with the straw in her drink.

Stitch stared at her for a few moments. "Don't be a sissy. Go talk to her, and if you don't, I will."

Jacob wished he had a few drinks in him so he would be powered by liquid bravery. The way she sat, held her glass, wrapped her lips around the straw…

"Jacob, it's time to man up. It's obvious you're attracted to her. Wouldn't you agree, Stitch?"

Stitch nodded his head and laughed. "I think he's in love with her already,"

"So, do yourself a favor and just go talk to her. This time, might I suggest, you don't do a face plant in front of her," said Trent.

"I'm glad I'm entertainment for you two."

"Seriously, Jacob. Just go talk to her. What's the worst thing that can happen?" asked Stitch.

Jacob's shoulders slumped. "That's what I'm afraid of."

Stitch and Trent turned around and focused their attention on the TV that was showing highlights from a basketball game. Everything in his body told him to get up and go to her table, yet he was glued to the seat with fear of rejection. In the past, he was too shy to try talking to women. Jacob sat trying to muster up his courage until finally he stood up and walked toward her. His heart thumped in his chest. Walking toward her table, his mind raced. *What am I going to say? This is crazy!* As he arrived at her table, she looked up and smiled. *This was a good sign, right?*

"Hi, aren't you Jacob?" Bridgette asked.

He couldn't form any words. His tongue stuck to the roof of his mouth. She looked at him quizzically, and her smile disappeared.

"I...um...I...I need to go pee," Jacob said, then turned and headed toward the bathroom. *Oh my God! I didn't just say that to her! I am a complete idiot.* He blew it again. What was it about this woman that rendered him completely helpless? Anytime he was around her, his brain shut down and some mindless twit took over. The funny thing was he didn't even have to pee. He couldn't think of what to say and found his nearest escape route. After spending several minutes standing at the mirror in the bathroom looking at himself, he decided he couldn't stand in there forever. As Jacob walked out of the bathroom, he looked over at her table and she was gone. Sitting across the bar were Stitch and Trent, laughing hysterically. Not only did he look like a fool in front of her, but also his friends. Jacob stood there for a moment trying to decide if he should leave or face the ridicule he was about to receive from them. With a new career, his clumsy mistakes, and now being a failure at talking to Bridgette, it felt like his life was spinning carelessly out of control.

"Nice one, rookie," Trent said laughing.

"Jacob, am I going to have to show you how to talk to the ladies? That girl is hot. You looked like a hopeless idiot!" Stitch said shaking his head.

Whatever in the world is it about this woman that caused him to turn to jello? Jacob took a seat next to the guys. As he tipped back his beer, taking large gulps he thought, *that is strike two.*

The three men had a few more beers and shared stories of their recent calls. Jacob was amazed at the types of calls his friends had been on over the years. Some of them he had a hard time believing, but just talking about the experiences they had, helped him learn more about the job. After settling their tab, they walked outside. They each said their goodbyes, and Trent left. Jacob and Stitch walked over to his truck. Out of the corner of his eye, Jacob noticed a yellow Mustang pulling up behind them.

"You've got to be kidding me!" Stitch bellowed. "Give me a minute," he said to Jacob and walked over to the car.

A slender blonde hopped out of the car and walked around to the front, meeting Stitch.

Jacob tried not to stare, but couldn't help himself. *Who is this gorgeous woman?* He looked over and noticed a small boy, maybe five or six, with sandy blonde hair and large blue eyes watching them from the front seat of the car.

"What are you doing here?" he could hear Stitch ask.

"I need some money," the woman said crossing her arms on her chest.

Stitch stuck his hand in the front pockets of his jeans. "I don't have any cash on me right now. You should've already gotten the check anyway."

She glanced at the bar and then back to Stitch. "Hmm…you don't have any money, yet you're out drinking at the bar with your friend," she said looking at Jacob and crinkling her nose.

Stitch shook his head. "I didn't say I don't have any money. I just don't have any cash. Besides, what does it matter what I'm doing. You lost the right to be concerned when you divorced me."

The small boy bounced up and down on the front seat. "Daddy, Daddy…come give me a hug."

Daddy? Stitch has a kid? He never told me that.

The woman looked over at the boy. "Daddy can't see you right now. Sit down and buckle up your seatbelt."

Stitch turned to walk toward the passenger door, the woman grabbed his arm. "Don't go near my son. If you can't give me money to take care of him, then you can't see him!"

Stitch ripped his arm from her grip. "Don't touch me! If I want to see my son, I can!" His body tensed; his brow furrowed. "Why don't you ask your boyfriend for some money? You know, the man that used to be my best friend!"

"It's not his responsibility. It's yours!" The woman ran around to the driver's side of her car. "You want to see Bentley then pony up some cash!" She jumped into her car and slammed the door shut.

Stitch knelt down and reached through the window to hug the boy. "I love you, son."

Tears streamed down Bentley's cheeks. "I love you too, Daddy."

The woman slammed down the gas pedal and peeled out of the parking lot spitting rocks and dust into the air.

Stitch stared as she drove away. He stood up and hung his head. Jacob was speechless. He wanted to console his friend, but he didn't know what to say. After a few moments, Stitch turned and walked toward Jacob's truck. He glanced at Jacob with tears welled in his eyes.

"Who was that?" Jacob asked.

Stitch wiped the tears from his eyes. "My ex-wife, Angela."

"I didn't know you had a kid. You never talk about him."

Stitch shook his head. "That's because she doesn't allow me to see him. His name is Bentley and he's six years old. She gets child support; I pay religiously, which is my responsibility. But if I want to get visitation, I have to take her to court. The system's messed up. I will tell you that. When we got divorced, she had someone in her back pocket and got full custody, even though she was the one who cheated on me. To take her back to court would cost money I don't have, and she would probably find someone new to manipulate and I would lose again. Besides, I don't have the kind of money it would take to fight it." He leaned against the truck, looking at the ground with his shoulders slumped.

Jacob walked over and stood next to him, placing a hand on his shoulder. "I'm sorry, man. That's horrible. I can't imagine."

Stitch rubbed his eyes and then ran his hand through his hair. He stared into the night sky. His bottom lip quivered. Jacob's heart sank at the sight of the pain in Stitch's eyes. It angered him that the woman used their son as a pawn to hurt his friend. He never understood why people used their children as a weapon. In the end, the child was the one that suffered the most.

"You know what you need?" Jacob asked.

Stitch caught Jacob's gaze. "What?"

"Let's go to the lake tomorrow and maybe camp out overnight. I know I could use some fresh air."

Stitch's lips tugged up lightly, forming a half smile. "Yeah. That sounds fun."

Chapter Eleven

Jacob and Stitch loaded the last of the camping gear into his truck. He weaved a rope over the load and secured it.

"Looks like we're good to go. You ready?" Jacob asked Stitch.

"Yeah."

The two jumped into Jacob's truck and headed toward Apache Lake. It was forty-five miles east of Phoenix and sat in the middle of the Tonto National Forest. The lake held the horrible memory of what happened to Amber. This was going to be the first time either of them went back since the boating accident. However, it was important in their job to force their way through things like that and move forward with life. If a person in their line of work was unable to do that, it would evidentially devour them and leave a bitter and nasty shell of a human.

Stitch spent most of the time staring out the window, not talking. Jacob didn't blame him; in fact he found his own blood boiling over the fact that Angela was using that sweet boy as a pawn for pain. Every child deserves two parents! In this day and age it wasn't often that a father wanted to be a part of their child's life. How could she rob Bentley of that right? Jacob glanced over at his friend and he remained quiet. It tugged on his heart, seeing Stitch hurting. *Why didn't he tell me he had a child?*

An hour later, they arrived at Apache Lake. He drove down the road looking for a spot for them to pitch a tent off the beaten path. Just ahead, Jacob spotted a dirt road that trailed off to the left. He slowed down and navigated the turn. A thick cloud of dust trailed behind them. The truck lurched over the rough road, tossing them like rag dolls from one side of the cab to the other. The cooler full of ice and beer slid back and forth in the bed of the truck.

Stitch laughed as he grabbed hold of the door handle, bracing himself. "Hold up there, buckaroo. This bronco is taking off for the rodeo."

Jacob grinned as he maneuvered the sharp turns and twists in the road. He was unsure if it led them closer to the lake. He wasn't going to ask Stitch. He didn't want to appear like a fool aimlessly driving around the lake. He'd made enough mistakes and couldn't handle further ridicule from his friend. For once, he wanted be the knowledgeable one.

Twenty minutes later, the road opened up to a large clearing and with it, the mood in the cab lightened. Beyond the meadow, which led to a cliff overlooking the lake, the sunlight sparkled off the water. A sigh of relief slipped through Jacob's lips. He pulled the truck to a stop and shifted it into park, suppressing the jubilant feeling that bounced in his gut.

Jacob peered at Stitch. "Look like a good place to set up camp?"

Stitch scanned the area. "Sure."

The two men hopped out of the truck and Jacob loosened the rope that secured the stowed gear. They pulled out the equipment and sat it in an organized pile. Once the truck was emptied, Stitch grabbed the tent and pulled it out of the bag.

"I'm going to find some wood for a fire," Jacob said.

"Sounds good," Stitch replied. He grabbed the poles and begun to thread them through the tent.

Deadwood was scattered all over the ground. Jacob walked around picking it up and dropping it in a pile where he wanted to set up their campfire. He found several pieces of small wood to use as kindling. Once he retrieved enough firewood, Jacob found several rocks and lined them up in a circle, forming the fire pit. He knelt down on the ground and placed a pile of kindling in the middle. Glancing over his shoulder, he noticed Stitch stood watching him. The tent was erected.

Jacob pulled out his flint, a knife, and started running the blade across it. Sparks flew.

Stitch had a puzzled look on his face. "What are doing?"

"What does it look like? I'm trying to start our campfire."

Stitch grinned. "This is the Boy Scouts?"

Jacob sighed. "I used to be good at starting fires this way. I didn't tell you how to set up the tent, did I?"

Stitch laughed. "Whatever you say, ranger. Have at it. When you're done, let me know and I'll light a match."

Jacob's brow furrowed. Aggravation brewed within his stomach. He could take the easy way out, but his stubbornness wouldn't allow that. He was determined to start the fire the way his father showed him as a child. He ran the blade across the flint and sparks flew, but it wasn't catching the kindling on fire. A bead of sweat traced down his cheek. He wasn't going to give up, no matter how much ridicule Stitch threw at him. He ignored Stitch, who was lounging in a folding camp chair with his feet propped up on the ice chest, hands crossed behind his head, grinning like the damn Cheshire Cat. Jacob made several more passes across the flint, yet still no fire. *Can't I do anything right?*

Out of the corner of his eye, he saw Stitch walking toward him. He turned his back on him and furiously struck at the flint. Suddenly a stream liquid hit the kindling. A match dropped into the fire pit and flames shot up. Jacob jumped up, staggered a few feet back, and fell onto his backside barely avoiding the flames.

"What the hell, Stitch! You almost caught me on fire!"

Stitch leaned over resting his hands on his knees, laughing. "That was hilarious!"

Jacob scurried up from the ground and wiped the dust off his clothes. "I'm glad you're amused."

"Ah come on, rookie. Don't get all butt hurt. You weren't close enough to get burned."

Jacob's anger vanished and he grinned broadly. It was a relief to hear Stitch laugh. Stitch walked over and placed the deadwood over the kindling. A short time later, the fire danced.

Once the rest of the campsite was set up, Jacob plopped down in a chair next to Stitch. He reached into the cooler, pulled out two beers, and tossed one to Stitch. They sat watching the flames sizzle. The crackling sounds of the fire echoed through the air. Jacob enjoyed the smell of the burning wood. It brought back many memories of the camping trips he took with his dad as a kid.

Stitch chugged down the remnants of his beer, stood up, and walked over to the edge of the cliff that bordered their campsite. Jacob joined him.

Stitch stared at the calm green water. "I bet it would be fun to jump into the lake, don't you?"

Jacob glanced down. "Man, that's crazy! It must be fifty feet down. You don't know if there are any rocks down there." Flashes of the first day on the river came back to Jacob. "Stitch, remember that girl that took the top of her foot off?"

Stitch grinned. "That's what makes it exciting." He reached into his pockets pulling out his wallet and cell phone. He trotted a few feet back, turned, and faced the lake. "No time like the present!" Running toward the cliff, dust kicked up from under his feet.

Jacob held up his hands, waving for his friend to stop. "Stitch!

Don't!"

Before Jacob could grab him, Stitch leapt off the cliff edge. "Banzai!" he screamed, his arms flapping and legs kicking as he fell toward the water. Pulling his arms to his side and his feet close together, an enormous splash of water sprayed into the air as he entered the lake.

Jacob peered over the edge of the cliff. The water radiated out into a large circle of waves. "Stitch!" He didn't see his friend as the water settled. A lump formed in his throat. His stomach tightened. What if he was hurt? How was he going to help him? He was about ready to jump himself when he saw Stitch swim up to the surface with an enormous smile on his face. "Woo hoo! Man that was fun!" he said treading water.

Jacob's shoulders relaxed. "You're crazy." He shook his head. "I can't believe you did that."

Stitch continued to tread water. "Jump in!"

"Are you crazy? I'm not jumping in there!"

"Come on, rookie. You only live once! Don't be a baby."

Jacob stifled the nausea that rolled through his stomach.

"Seriously, come on! I did it," Stitch yelled from the lake.

Jacob's shoulders slumped. He'd never jumped that far before. Stitch got lucky and wasn't injured. What if he hit a rock that wasn't visible? He pushed down his fear, emptied his pockets, and stepped out of Stitch's view. Forcing his feet forward, he stood where Stitch started his run. He sucked in a deep breath and slowly exhaled. *This is crazy!* Nevertheless, he was tired of Stitch thinking he didn't have a backbone His heartbeat thumped in his ears and his chest tightened. He ran toward the cliff; his feet kicking up dirt. He ran faster, and faster until the edge of the cliff came into view. He pushed off and leaped into the air. He looked down and saw the lake quickly approaching. *Dear God, I have lost my mind!* He dropped his hands to his sides as his legs hit the water. The cool water enveloped his body. Jacob spread his legs and arms to slow his decent and then pushed against the rushing water. He paddled vigorously, swimming toward the surface. He sprung out of the water and sucked in a deep breath. A surge of endorphins rushed through his body. He did it!

Jacob glanced over and saw Stitch smiling at him. A sense of accomplishment coursed through his body. He'd never been much of a risk taker so he felt very euphoric. The two men swam to shore and climbed out of the lake. They stood on the bank, water streaming from them onto the rock, and smiled like a couple of giddy teenagers.

"Good job, brother," Stitch said slapping Jacob on the shoulder.

Jacob smiled. He reached up and ran his fingers through his wet hair. Glancing back to the lake, he noticed a rock protruding through the water - a mere few feet from where he landed.

"Did you know that was there?" Jacob sputtered.

Stitch Grinned. "Yeah, after I was already in the lake."

Jacob couldn't believe his ears. Stitch knew it was there, yet he still coaxed him to jump. "I could've...we could've been hurt - killed!"

"Sometimes you have to take a leap of faith. I don't know what you're mad about. Nothing happened. Let's get back up to camp," Stitch said. He stomped up the path with Jacob following behind.

Water sloshed out of their shoes as they walked up the dirt path. Mud formed on the top of their shoes. Stitch walked over to the truck and grabbed two fishing poles.

"You up for some fishing?"

"Sure." He grabbed the fishing pole from his friend and followed him back down to the lake. Jacob wasn't a good fisherman, but he was enjoying the peace and quiet that wasn't interrupted by station tones and sirens. More importantly, Stitch was acting like his normal self. That alone was worth its weight in gold.

Jacob stood on the shore of the lake. He glanced over at Stitch pulling out yet another fish. He removed the bass from his hook and strung it with the other fish he'd already caught. Jacob had a couple of bites, but hadn't caught one yet. Stitch grinned at him after he placed the stringer back into the water. Jacob was frustrated. *This guy is unbelievable!*

After several hours of fishing, the two men trekked their way back to their campsite. Stitch took the fish and cleaned them while Jacob restarted the fire. Once the flames blazed in the dusk, he sat down in a chair and cracked open a beer. The cool liquid quenched his thirst. Stitch approached the campfire and prepared to cook their dinner. This was the life. No outside distractions and nothing to worry about except enjoying what Mother Nature had to offer.

A pale orange glow stretched across the sky as the sun nestled on the horizon. The lake water had the appearance of smooth glass and a light breeze blew in off the water, sending chills down the back of Jacob's neck.

He was glad he brought Stitch out to go camping. His friend needed the distraction. He was curious why Stitch hadn't ever mentioned his son. If Jacob had a child, he wouldn't be able to hide that from anyone, but then again, he hadn't gone through the circumstances Stitch had.

Stitch pulled the aluminum foil wraps out of the coals of the fire and handed one to Jacob. The smell of garlic, butter, and fish wafted out of the foil as he opened it. He'd never seen anyone prepare a meal like this; not even his father who was an avid camper.

Jacob's taste buds exploded in satisfaction with each bite. After consuming two foil wraps, he leaned back in the chair full and satisfied. The sun had set and the bright orange glow of the fire surrounded the campsite. The yipping howls of coyotes bounced off the cliffs.

"Man, that was a great meal. Thank you."

"Anytime, amigo."

Jacob leaned in his chair, facing Stitch. "I'm glad you came. I've had a great time today."

"I'm the one who should be thanking you." Stitch reached over and patted Jacob on the shoulder. "You're a great friend. I'm sorry I never told you about my son. It's a difficult subject for me and hurts that I don't get to see him very much, you know?"

Jacob shook his head. "I feel for ya, and for your son. I wish there was something I could do. It isn't right."

"You're doing everything you can by helping me forget about that hateful woman." Stitch stood up and stretched. "Can you do me a favor?"

Jacob sat up straight in his chair. "Sure."

"Quit trying so hard. It's causing you to make mistakes. Settle down, think about what needs to be done on calls and do it. Trust me. There isn't a mistake you've made that I haven't made in the past."

Jacob weakly smiled. "I highly doubt that."

Chapter Twelve

As he was lying in bed, the urge to ignore his alarm was more enticing than facing the ridicule he was sure to receive. Up until now, he couldn't wait to get to the station, but he feared Trent was going to have a field day with him once he arrived at work. Having to do the walk of shame didn't sit well in the pit of his stomach.

He pulled into the parking lot and saw them. Standing outside of the door were Trent and Stitch. He looked in the rear view mirror and watched them laughing. He couldn't delay the inevitable at the risk of clocking in late. Grabbing his gear, Jacob walked across the parking lot. The closer he got to Trent and Stitch, the harder it was for him to breathe.

"Before you guys start in on me, I know. I'm a loser," Jacob uttered.

"I didn't say you were a loser: just starting to think you may be gay since you can't seem to get your foot out of your mouth when you're around Bridgette," Trent chuckled.

He still couldn't put his finger on it; there was something about the woman that terrified him. Was it her beauty or his fear of rejection? "I'm not freaking gay. I love women."

"Well, you'd better get it figured out. I'm sure we'll see her at the emergency room at some point today," Stitch said.

The thought of seeing her again terrified Jacob. Regardless, he needed to get his head together and prepare for the shift. Jacob walked by the guys and put his belongings in his room. As Jacob stretched the sheets onto his bed, there was a knock at the door.

"Hey Jacob, you're not mad at us are you?" Trent asked peeking around the door.

He couldn't be angry with them. It wasn't their fault that he acted like a moron around Bridgette. "No, it's all good." Jacob sat down on his bed; his shoulders slumped. "I am an idiot, though. I don't know what it is about her that makes me feel so foolish."

Trent walked into the room and leaned against the wall. "Women will have that effect on you. I don't know what to tell you. Don't worry about it. Let's go out and have some fun today. What do you say?"

"Sounds good to me." Once his bed was assembled, he went out to the bay to check off the ambulance. This was how they started every shift to make sure all of the equipment was accounted for. It took twenty minutes to complete the check off when the radio beeped alerting them they had a call.

"Medic 61, you have a call at 1257 Parkview Terrace for an unknown medical. Fire department has been dispatched."

Pulling the radio off his belt, Jacob answered, "Medic 61 copies." Excitement crept throughout his body as he trotted toward the ambulance. Trent shook his head and grinned. The two men climbed into the ambulance.

"Trust me when I tell you this Jacob, the newness will wear off."

"What makes you say that?"

"Every time we get a call, you can't stop smiling. Some would say that's not normal behavior."

"Is it wrong to love your job? Not too long ago, I had a mindless office job. Now I have a job that has meaning." Jacob glanced in the side mirror. "What's up with that red Charger? It's been following us since we pulled out of the station."

"Have you ever thought they might be going the same direction?"

Jacob laughed at that as he turned into the cul-de-sac. He noticed a fire truck sitting in the driveway of a brown stucco house, so he navigated the turn and pulled in next to them. Two firefighters sat on the tailboard of their truck talking. It must not been too serious if they were outside while their partners were in the house.

"You boys won't need anything. I think they're trying to get a refusal," one of the firefighters said.

"What's going on?" Trent asked.

The two men couldn't stop laughing. "Go inside and find out."

Jacob looked at Trent, puzzled. From the sidewalk, they could hear a woman yelling at the top of her lungs. Jacob closely followed Trent down the walkway toward the front of the house. The wind whisked through Jacob's hair. He reached up and brushed a few strands from his eyes.

Pulling the screen door open, they walked through the doorway. The spring of the door creaked and then slapped shut behind them.

"I want to go to the hospital," the woman said.

"Meghan, there's nothing wrong with you. Why do you want to go?" one of the paramedics asked.

"Are you blind? I've been shot!"

"Where? I don't see any bullet wounds on you."

Meghan stood up, lifted up her shirt, and pointed in the middle of her chest. "Right here. Can't you see it?" she asked.

Standing in front of the firefighters, with her shirt up and no bra, was a woman in her mid-fifty's. Her hair unruly, shirt covered with coffee stains, and wearing a pair of faded shorts that were two sizes too big. Jacob felt uncomfortable seeing the half-naked woman in front of him. He turned his attention away, glancing around the room.

"Meghan, there aren't any bullet wounds. Have you taken your medication today?" the paramedic asked.

"I was shot. Why won't you help me? I'm calling 911 and getting another ambulance that will help me," she said. She walked across the room and grabbed her phone. Two officers from the Police Department knocked on the door and then walked in.

"What's going on?" one of the officers asked.

"I've been shot and these guys won't do anything to help me. I need to go to the hospital before I bleed to death!"

The officer shook his head and grinned. "Meghan, there's nothing wrong with you. We talked about this last week. How about these men get back into service so they can help someone who really needs it?" The officer looked over at the guys. "You can go. We'll take care of it from here."

The men all turned, and headed for the door. Jacob couldn't believe this woman called 911. Were there people like this that called EMS for ridiculous reasons?

"Does she really think she was shot?" Jacob asked.

"That was Meghan. She is bipolar and has schizophrenia. I've been out to this house at least six times in the past two weeks. Each time she calls it's for something stupid. It gets old coming out here. If you call 911 you get us regardless," the paramedic from the fire department said.

"This is my first time here, but we have several people just like her. I get so aggravated because there's bound to be that one time when you're dealing with them, someone around the corner will be having a heart attack and you're stuck," Trent said as he climbed into the truck.

Jacob's eyes narrowed. "Stuck? You can't leave and go to someone with a life threatening injury?" Jacob asked.

"No. Once you're on scene, you have to either get a refusal or take them to the hospital. If you leave without a signature you can be charged with patient abandonment," the paramedic explained.

"We just left her without her signing anything. Isn't that construed as abandonment?" Jacob asked.

The firefighter laughed. "You're full of questions. We left her in the custody of the police. We don't need one."

Jacob was stunned. He never really thought about a situation like this. It would be horrible, sitting at this lady's house while a kid wasn't breathing somewhere, a multi patient car accident happening, or someone having a heart attack. It made no sense. *Talk about feeling handcuffed.*

The firefighters got into their truck and roared away. Diesel exhaust spewed from the tail pipe and floated in the air. After Trent and Jacob climbed into their ambulance, he looked over to see Trent grinning from ear to ear.

"What?" Jacob asked.

"You want the good news or the bad news?"

Jacob was afraid to answer. It appeared that he wasn't going to like it either way. "I guess the good news."

"Well, you're about to have a chance to redeem yourself, or fall flat on your face again."

He didn't like the sound of that. Jacob was afraid to find out what Trent meant. "What are you talking about?"

Trent shifted in his seat. "We need to go to Mount Prospect Hospital. I need to get a narcotics order filled."

Jacob's worst fear was coming true, having to face Bridgette. He knew this would happen eventually, but he wasn't prepared for it. Not yet. Trent sat back in his seat, and with a satisfied look on his face, snapped his seatbelt into place. He reached down and picked up the microphone to the radio. "Medic 61 dispatch."

"Go ahead Medic 61," the dispatcher answered.

"We're going to be clear of this scene, and en-route to Mount Prospect."

"Dispatch copies."

Jacob leaned back in the seat.

"What are you waiting for? Let's get going, rookie." Against his better judgment, Jacob shifted the ambulance into drive, and headed towards the hospital. A hundred scenarios ran through his mind. It wouldn't be difficult to take the easy way out and sit in the ambulance while Trent filled his order, but how many times was he going to be able to avoid her? Eventually their paths would have to cross, especially if they brought a patient into the emergency room. A knot formed in his throat, and sweat spotted his upper lip. *Get a grip on yourself. This is just a woman like the hundreds of other women you have had roaming around your life for the past twenty-three years now.* The last words he spoke to her echoed through his mind, *"I have to pee, I have to pee, I have to pee."* *I am such an idiot!*

"Medic 61, what is your location?" the dispatcher asked.

Trent reached for the microphone. "We're a few miles from our station."

"We have a call for you at 567 East Greenfield Road. You have a forty five year old male patient with back pain."

"Copy that. We'll be en-route," answered Trent.

That was music to his ears. For now at least, he wouldn't have to worry about facing Bridgette. Jacob could tell by the look on Trent's face that he was annoyed. He didn't care. Anything that kept him from having to see her was a saving grace until he could get control of whatever it was that turned him into a blubbering idiot in front of her.

"What a way to start our day, having a bull crap call," Trent said.

Jacob reached down, switched on the lights, and turned on the siren. Trent reached across and shut everything down. "We're not going code three to this. There's no sense in risking our lives and the lives of the people on the road for someone who probably doesn't need an ambulance."

At times, Trent could be overbearing. He was the paramedic, so whatever he said, goes. The motorists behind them were confused. One minute, an ambulance pulls into traffic with all of their emergency lights on, and the next, everything is shut down. A couple early morning commuters shot dirty looks at them as they passed by. Then the red Charger with the sunroof open pulled up alongside the ambulance. *It's that same car*, Jacob thought. Confusion filled him as he gazed down at the red headed driver. She glanced up and smiled briefly before pulling out in front of the ambulance. That was the same woman who had waved at him from the ambulance door just a few days ago. He knew it was! What were the changes of her being on the same road? An eerie chill crept up his spine.

Ten minutes later, they arrived on scene. As they were pulling in front of the address, a man walked out carrying a suitcase. Trent shook his head and threw his clipboard onto the floor. Jacob had never seen him this angry before. He was shocked.

"Medic 61 dispatch," Trent said in an angry tone. "We're on scene." Before the ambulance was placed in park, Trent was out the door walking toward the man. He was angry and Jacob didn't understand why.

He pulled up next to the curb, put on the emergency lights, and climbed out. As Jacob got closer to Trent and the patient, it appeared they were arguing.

"So what's the problem? Why did you call an ambulance?" Trent asked him.

"My back hurts really bad. I need to go to the hospital," the man answered.

"It must not be hurting you too bad. You walked out here," Trent said through pursed lips.

The man bent over, grabbed his lower back, and cried, "Yes it does. I can't take it anymore. I couldn't wait for you to get here so I came out to you."

"I don't think you need to, but if you want to go to the hospital, get in the back of the ambulance," Trent said.

"I can't climb up in there. You're going to have to get your bed out."

"Well, if you want to go to the hospital with me, you're going to get in the back of my ambulance," Trent said sternly.

Bewildered by Trent's behavior, Jacob walked toward the back of the ambulance to get the cot, but Trent stopped him. It was obvious this man wasn't in as much pain as he was leading them to believe, but still, he was a human being. Jacob felt sorry for him. What *if* he was in pain, but they just couldn't tell yet?

The guy walked over, climbed into the side door of the ambulance with his suitcase in tow. Trent looked at Jacob, shaking his head, and climbed in behind him. The patient sat down on the cot and slowly leaned back.

"Can you give me something for pain? Fifty milligrams of Demerol and twenty-five milligrams of Phenergan usually do the trick," he said.

"I'm sorry, sir. We can't give you anything. We have specific criteria that you have to meet in order to receive pain medications, and you don't meet them," Trent said.

Jacob climbed into the back of the ambulance and placed a blood pressure cuff around the man's arm. He caught the man glaring at Trent. The man closed his eyes and cried out.

"I'm in some serious pain!"

Trent shook his head. "What are his vital signs?"

"Blood pressure is 126/82, heart rate of 72, and a pulse ox of 99% on room air," Jacob said.

Trent turned towards the patient. "You see sir, your vital signs show that you're not in that much pain. If you were, your blood pressure and heart rate would be elevated."

"That doesn't mean anything. Give me something. I can't stand it anymore," he pleaded with Trent.

"Like I said, I can't. You want to go to the hospital, fine. We can do that, but you won't get any pain medication from me. You'll have to wait until you get to the emergency room," Trent said.

"What hospital do you want to go to?" Jacob asked.

"Mount Prospect," he answered.

Mount Prospect? You've got to be kidding me! No! Trent looked at him and smiled. Jacob removed the blood pressure cuff from the man's arm and climbed out of the back of the ambulance. As he drove down the road, Jacob listened to the patient whine about not receiving any pain medications. It was irritating, but at least it kept his mind off Bridgette. What was this, the wolf criers' convention? Two fakes in one shift? What if someone was having a life-threatening emergency? They weren't able to break away and render the aid that could save someone's life because of this bozo. He was quickly learning that not everyone needed an ambulance.

A short time later, Jacob pulled into the ambulance parking at the hospital, got out, and opened the doors. The patient continued to beg Trent for pain medications. Trent climbed out of the back of the unit with a disgusted look on his face.

"I can't stand drug seekers," Trent said under his breath.

"I heard what you said. I'm not a drug addict," the man shouted at Trent.

The patient sat with his arms across his chest and a scowl on his face. Jacob pulled the cot out and pushed him toward the emergency room doors. His amusement was quickly replaced with the realization that he was about to see Bridgette. His only saving grace would be if she wasn't working today. As they entered the emergency room, he glanced around the department and didn't see her. He choked down a wave of nausea.

"What do you got, Trent?" Alice asked.

"This fine young man is complaining of excruciating back pain. He met us out on his driveway carrying his suitcase," Trent said snidely.

She stared at the patient shaking her head. "Well, administration is complaining that we put too many people in triage. I guess room twenty-six will work. I'll send a nurse in as soon as I can."

"Can I get some pain medicine?" the man asked.

Alice's brow furrowed. She leaned on the counter toward the patient. "Sir, you're going to have to wait until the doctor can assess you first."

"Can't you see how much pain I'm in? I came in by ambulance; I need to be treated, now!"

Her eyes narrowed. "Sir, you're not in any immediate danger. You can wait your turn. Just because you came in by ambulance, doesn't put you ahead of the critical patients we have. Now, if you don't mind, I would like to get back to tending to the patients that have life threatening conditions."

"Fine, whatever. I'm telling you now, if I don't get treated soon you'll be hearing from my attorney," he crossed his arms over his chest.

"That would be fine. Send him our way. Of course, he'll have to take a number. There's a line of attorney's chomping at the bit to sue us. Be my guest," Alice said as she turned and stomped away.

It took everything within Jacob not to burst out laughing. The nerve of this guy! Thirty minutes ago, he was walking out to the ambulance carrying a suitcase.

As they headed over to room twenty-six, there were several people gathered in the hallway outside of the rooms. Jacob could only imagine what they were dealing with. Some of them were quietly talking, while others were holding each other crying. Sadness lingered in the air like a thick storm cloud. Before Jacob could navigate the stretcher close to the bed, Trent stopped him. He pushed the button that lowered the cot, a few feet away from the bed.

"All right, sir. You can get off and get onto the bed," Trent said.

"Are you kidding me? I'm in too much pain. You guys can lift me over to it," the patient said.

Trent stiffened up and let out a sigh. "No, you walked to the ambulance; therefore, you can get off our cot and into the bed."

The patient unbuckled the seat belts and angrily flung them off him. "This is crap. Do you treat all of your patients like this?"

"Only the ones that deserve it," Trent said.

For a man that was in so much pain, he was able to get up, stomp over to the bed, and then throw himself onto it easily. Jacob pulled the dirty sheets off the cot. A familiar voice spoke behind him; his body stiffened.

"Hey guys, what did you bring me?" Bridgette asked.

Trent had an enormous smile on his face. Jacob tried to gulp down the knot in his throat. He turned around, face flushed, and weakly smiled. *I can do this. Don't act like a fool, this time.*

"He has back pain and is requesting pain medication, immediately," Trent said.

"Is he now? Well sir, I'm going to assess you, and then the doctor will be in when he has a chance. Until then, you're going to have to wait," Bridgette said.

Jacob finally got the nerve and set his fear aside. This was his chance to redeem himself and not look like an idiot in the process. He mustered up the courage and decided to speak. "Hi," was all that came out of his mouth.

Bridgette had an amused look on her face. "So, do you have to pee?"

Trent tried to cover his laugh with a cough.

"No, I'm good." *Breathe.* "How's your shift going?"

Bridgette smiled. "It's going good. I've been really busy, but nothing to complain about."

They stood there, staring at one another for what seemed like an eternity. Jacob had successfully navigated his first obstacle; not sounding like an idiot while talking to her. A sense of accomplishment washed over him. He was holding a real conversation with this gorgeous woman. All right, it might be kind of a lame conversation, but at least it was a conversation.

"I hate to break up this reunion Jacob, but we need to get ourselves back in service. I'm going to scribble out this report real quick while you get the cot made," Trent said.

Jacob flung the seat belts back onto the top of the cot and walked out of the room. He didn't really say much, but the fact that he said anything was a step in the right direction. He pushed the cot over by the ambulance entrance and readied if for their next call.

"I'll be back in a moment to assess you," Bridgette told the disgruntled patient. She followed Jacob over to the ambulance entrance. "I'm glad you know how to talk."

Jacob turned around to face her, nodded, and continued to dress the cot. It felt like he had made a monumental accomplishment. Nothing was going to ruin this moment. Feeling quite euphoric with his recent victory, he decided to talk to Bridgette a little bit more. She looked so heavenly, like an angel that had been sent from above. He cautiously approached her trying to think of something witty to say.

"So, you come here often?" Jacob asked. As the words slid through his lips, his confidence slipped away.

Bridgette smiled and shook her head. "Yes, actually. Twelve hours a day, three times a week."

"I would kill to only work twelve hours at a time. I could do that standing on my head."

The corners of Bridgette's lips tugged upward. "I would like to see you try that, standing on your head for twelve hours. It wouldn't end well for you."

"True, it may not. If I passed out, would you give me mouth to mouth?" With each passing moment, Jacob's confidence soared. *Where is all of this coming from? I've gone from speechless to Casanova!*

"We don't do that anymore. I would just use a bag valve mask on you," she grinned.

"Well, you can't blame a guy for trying. Look, I apologize for the other night at the Rusty Nail. I can only imagine what you were thinking."

"I was thinking that you're socially retarded."

Man she's good. "Touché! I deserve that. If you wouldn't have run off, I would've bought you a drink."

"I highly doubt that. I think you're too scared to talk to me."

She had a point. Jacob wanted to tell her why, but the fear of what she may think stopped him cold.

"Bridgette...."

"My friends call me Bridge."

"Am I your friend?"

She continued to flip through a chart she was holding. "You could be, if you weren't so afraid of me," Bridge said without looking up.

"Bridgette...I mean Bridge, I have a confession to make." She had curious look on her face. "You intimidate the hell out of me."

She looked at him, slightly tilting her head sideways. "I intimidate you?"

"Yes, very much so. You see, you're so incredibly beautiful that I find myself stumbling on my words. I can't help it. It's all your fault."

Her face turned a rosy red. She looked down at the ground, avoiding eye contact with Jacob. For the first time, the tables were turned. Now *she* was speechless. This was a welcome change from his previous encounters.

She looked up at Jacob with a captivating smile. "I don't know about that. I'm not that beautiful. Moderately attractive at best."

"I beg to differ. I'm not usually this forward, but it's time that I come out of my shell."

Trent ran up to Jacob, grabbed his arm, and pulled him toward the ambulance entrance. "Hate to interrupt your conversation, but we've just been dispatched to a rollover accident with multiple ejections."

Jacob glanced over his shoulder and noticed Bridge smiling at him. His insecurity and intimidation toppled down like the Berlin Wall.

Trying hard not to fall on his face, he turned and ran alongside Trent. His heart pounded in his chest. Trauma had that effect on him.

"Is it far from here?" Jacob asked.

"It's on Superstition Highway. We're the eighth ambulance dispatched to the scene. Multiple people lying in the road. Get your head straight. I need you on this one,"

The sound of their leather boots pounding into the asphalt echoed through the parking lot. Jacob jumped into the driver's seat, flipped on the lights, and sped out of the lot.

Trent held onto the handle in the door and grabbed the radio microphone. 'Dispatch Medic 61, we are en-route to the rollover accident."

"Dispatch copies. All radio traffic for this call is on tactical channel two. Please switch to that channel and acknowledge you're on your way," the dispatcher ordered.

Trent flipped through the radio channels, but couldn't find it. "Where is this damn channel?" he said with frustration. Jacob couldn't offer him any guidance; he wasn't sure. Finally locating the proper channel, Trent keyed up the microphone. "Medic 61 is en-route to the traffic accident on Superstition Highway."

"Dispatch copies. Once you're approaching the scene, check in with Superstition Command to receive your assignment."

Jacob's hands trembled; his palms were sticky with sweat. Memories of his last trauma flashed through his mind. He had frozen. That wouldn't be the case this time. He was going to stay calm and do everything he could to help Trent. Restoring Trent's faith in him was his first priority.

Traffic was light. The cars that were out graciously yielded the right of way. Thankfully, this increased their response time. Sweat traced down the back of his neck. He glanced at Trent who had his game face on. Jacob felt lucky to have him as a partner. The one quality Jacob was hoping would rub off on him was his calm, cool, and collected demeanor. Calls never rattled Trent.

After a few miles, Jacob took the highway on-ramp and headed east. A few miles down the road, emergency lights illuminated the skyline. Jacob sucked in a deep breath through his gritted teeth. Trent was still cool as ice as he put on a pair of gloves. He slid a few extra pairs in his pocket.

"What's with the extra gloves?" Jacob asked.

"There are multiple patients, and its poor form to use the same pair on different people."

These were pearls of wisdom that Jacob wouldn't have thought about. As they approached the scene, Trent grabbed the radio microphone. "Medic 61 to Superstition Command."

"This is Superstition Command. Go ahead Medic 61," the man answered.

"We are approaching from the east. Do you have an assignment for us?"

"Come to the staging area and await further instructions."

"Medic 61 copies."

They had to sit and watch the firefighters do all of the important work? That didn't seem right to Jacob. He didn't go through all of his training to sit on the sidelines. His adrenalin surge halted. He pulled off the highway and next to the line of ambulances parked on the desert roadside. Trent and Jacob stepped out of their ambulance and joined Stitch and the other crewmembers gathered in front of their units, talking. Approximately two hundred yards from where they were positioned, there were three fire trucks and a suburban strategically placed on the highway. Off the side of the road, was a pickup truck that was barely recognizable. The roof of it was level with the bed, a twisted piece of metal. By gauging the damage of the truck, there was no way anyone survived.

"So what's going on?" Trent asked.

"There are eight patients. Mom and Dad were in the cab with all of their kids in the bed of the truck," Stitch said.

"Are you kidding me? They had their kids in the bed?" Trent asked.

"Yes. We haven't been called over yet to transport anyone. I overheard command on the radio requesting five helicopters. They've shut down the highway."

Jacob was disgusted. He couldn't believe a parent could put their kids in harm's way. If he ever had children, this was something that he wouldn't allow. When he was a kid, riding in the bed of a truck was common practice, but times had changed. It took everything in him to stand still and not go running into the scene and try to assist the firefighters.

"Command to Medic 61, Engine 46 needs your assistance with a pediatric patient. They have him in the treatment area next to their apparatus."

Trent grabbed his portable radio. "Medic 61 copies." Still keeping his cool demeanor, he looked over at Jacob. "Time to get to work. Let's go, rookie."

Jacob was relieved they didn't have to sit back and watch any longer. "Do we need to grab anything?"

"No, let's just go over and see what they need."

Jacob and Trent bolted across the highway towards their assignment. As they approached the engine company, the firefighters were hovered around a small child secured to a backboard and IV's were in place. The boy had several lacerations and was covered in blood. Jacob's heart sank. Children weren't supposed to be hurt like this. Parents were supposed to protect their children. Trent walked over next to one of the firefighters tending to the child's injuries.

"What do you need, Captain Ballard?"

Feverishly working on the child, he snapped at Trent. "Go get your cot! We need to wheel this little boy over to the landing zone. We're landing five helicopters."

"Where's my mommy? I want my mommy!" the boy cried.

"It's okay, buddy. She's with the other firefighters getting her owies fixed. You'll see her at the hospital, kiddo," the captain said.

"Jacob, go get the cot. Have one of the other guys in the staging area help you."

"Got it." Jacob ran toward their ambulance. All of the other ambulance crews were standing around talking. Stitch was in mid-sentence laughing, when he saw Jacob running towards them.

"You need something?" Stitch asked.

"I have to get the cot and get back to the patient. We're going to wheel him to the landing zone," Jacob said out of breath. He leaned over for a moment trying to slow down his breathing.

Stitch followed Jacob to the back of the ambulance. Jacob reached up, wiped the sweat off of his brow, and pulled the door handle. He stood there, speechless.

"Jacob, where's your cot?" Stitch asked.

Horror filled him. "I forgot to put it back in the ambulance."

Stitch laughed. Jacob didn't know what to do, or how he was going to explain this to Trent and the captain.

Stitch reached up patted Jacob on his shoulder as he was laughing. "Sucks to be you, brother. It was nice working with you."

His heart sank. Stitch walked over to the other crews in the staging are—their laughter rang through the air. Jacob could see Trent, and the firefighters, looking over at him curiously. He had no other choice but to go and explain what he had done. As he was walking back to where the patient was, the first helicopter landed on the freeway approximately a hundred yards from the accident scene. Dust floated into the air and tumbleweed rolled across the road.

"What are you doing? Where's the cot?" Trent asked angrily. Captain Ballard and the other firefighters looked at him quizzically.

"I forgot it at the hospital," Jacob softly answered.

"You did what?" the captain shouted, competing with the roaring engines of the helicopters.

"Sir, I'm sorry. I have no excuse. It's at the hospital." The men stood looking at him in disbelief. It felt as if he had shrunk to three inches tall.

"Are you stupid?" Trent asked angrily.

"Look, getting angry won't do us any good right now. Let's just carry this little boy over to the helicopter. Everyone grab a corner of the backboard. Except for you," the captain said looking at Jacob. "You've done enough. Go stand by your ambulance and make sure you don't forget it, too," he barked.

They grabbed the backboard and walked toward the waiting helicopter. As ordered, Jacob went back to his ambulance. No matter how hard he tried, he was always making mistakes. The other crews were helping with the other patients. Jacob sat down on the bumper and watched the other helicopters land on the highway. He felt like he was a child in time-out. The more he tried not making mistakes, the more it happened. He felt like he was in a pit of quicksand. The harder he fought, the faster he sank. Jacob wasn't accustomed to being a screw-up. He prided himself on being efficient and productive, but things had changed since his accident. He had less control of his emotions, tired more easily; things he never gave a thought to before bothered him. Was he ever going to recover and be productive member of the team? Jacob questioned if he made the correct choice in becoming an EMT.

God, if I get fired then I deserve it. Please help me to stop screwing up. After the firefighters and Trent loaded the little boy into the helicopter, they walked back towards the fire truck. The captain was yelling at Trent. A few minutes later, Trent signaled Jacob to join them. It felt like he was going to the principal's office. Jacob stood in front of Captain Ballard and Trent. It was obvious they were attempting to control their anger before they spoke.

"So, have you ever done anything like this before?" Captain Ballard asked.

Jacob looked down at the ground, unable to look him in the eye. "No, sir. This is a first. I can't apologize enough."

"In the field we have a rule. Anytime you do something for the first time, you have to buy everyone ice cream. My crew and I, we like chocolate. I'm betting there will be plenty of it at my station by our next shift."

A wave of relief rolled over him. Was he serious? This was his punishment for his monumental mistake? "Yes, sir. I'm sure there will be."

Chapter Thirteen

For the next two days, Jacob tried to digest his recent mistakes. Sure he was new, but these were things that he shouldn't be doing. He felt horrible about forgetting the cot. He had tunnel vision while talking to Bridge. Because of that, he looked like a complete fool in front of his coworkers and the fire department. His career resembled quick sand. The harder he tried not to make mistakes, the quicker he sunk into a sea of errors.

Seeing Stitch laughing really angered him. They were supposed to be friends, but if the tables were turned, Jacob might've done the same thing. Who was he kidding? He *would* have! It was a new shift, a chance to redeem himself - something that was becoming a habit lately. He was tired of trying to make things better only to make them worse.

Jacob trotted through his house, making sure he had everything to get through the next twenty-four hours. After grabbing his duffle bag, the chocolate ice cream he owed Captain Ballard, and his bedding, he headed out to his truck. The orange glow of the morning sun peered through the blinds into his house.

Driving toward the station, he felt his stomach in knots. He reminisced about his childhood when he wished his father would take the long way home when he knew he was in trouble. His father; he really missed him. With the trying times he was experiencing, he wished his father was there to reassure him that he made the right career choice. He couldn't shake the nagging feeling that he'd make a mistake working on the ambulance. Maybe he just wasn't cut out for this kind of stress.

The drive, unfortunately, seemed faster than normal to work. As was the case every morning, everyone was standing outside talking.

Trent and Stitch saw Jacob, and walked inside of the station. This wasn't a good sign to start off his day.

Jacob gathered his duffle bag and made the dreadful walk towards the station. The more he thought about what happened at that car accident, the more foolish he felt. What little confidence he had in his skills, had quickly dwindled away.

Trent and Stitch stood in the kitchen area, glaring at Jacob. "We need to talk," Trent said.

"Can I put my stuff in my room first?" Jacob asked. Trent didn't respond. What made him feel even worse was that Stitch wouldn't make eye contact with him. Talk about feeling unwanted. He walked past them and put his belongings in his room. Shrugging off the fear, Jacob went back to the kitchen and put the ice cream in the freezer.

Trent leaned against the wall, arms across his chest. His jaw was tense, eyes narrowed. "So, here we go again, another screw up."

Jacob's face turned pale. "Look, I know what you're going to say...."

"You have no clue what I'm going to say. Jacob, you made a major mistake our last shift. Not only did you make yourself look bad, but me too. How could you forget the cot at the hospital?" Trent growled.

Jacob's eyes dropped to the floor. He felt like a scolded six-year-old. He couldn't force his lips open to respond.

"Don't you have anything to say?" asked Trent.

Jacob's shoulders slumped. "Trent, I know I screwed up. I was too busy trying to impress Bridge, and didn't do my job. I have no other excuse."

Trent and Stitch stared at each other for a moment and then looked back at Jacob.

Stitch shook his head. "I know I was laughing at you at that scene, but man, this is huge. If administration finds out, you'll be fired."

"Captain Ballard said...."

"Who cares what he said, Jacob? That's not the point. The fact is you screwed up so bad that I don't know if anyone will ever trust you again. In this job, the only person you have is your partner. You must have each other's back. Personally, if you were my partner, I would never trust you again!" Stitch fumed.

"Good thing you're not my partner then." Jacob had enough of his patronizing, "You're not so perfect. What, you've never made a mistake before? How soon you forget that you and Charles nearly came to blows on that boating accident. That wasn't very professional, now was it?"

Stitch uncrossed his arms, and stomped toward Jacob. The hollow sound of his boots echoed through the station. "So that's your defense? Bring up the past, and try to make yourself feel better?"

"That's not what I'm doing. I know I screwed up, but you two are tag teaming me here. You're not my partner, Stitch. So get your nose out of it. What do you care, anyway?" Jacob's heartbeat pulsed in his temples. It wasn't any of Stitch's business. The only person that should be angry was Trent.

Stitch stood inches away from Jacob's face. Trent tried to separate them, but Stitch pushed his hands away. "Why do I care? I got you this job! I vouched for you. Matthew didn't want to hire you, but I told him we worked together at the river and that you'd be a great EMT. Now, all I hear about every day is your screw ups, and that makes me look bad."

"You two need to calm down. Stitch, go take a walk and cool off," Trent ordered.

Stitch pushed Trent's hands away again. "Yeah, maybe I should go cool off. As for you, Jacob, go find yourself another friend." He turned, pushed the front door with his boot bouncing it off the wall, and walked outside.

"Why is he so angry? It's none of his business," Jacob asked looking at Trent. He caught his gaze and a shiver shot up his spine.

"He has a point. You're making him look foolish with all of your mistakes. Look, every one of us were new at one time, but leaving the cot was an unforgiveable mistake. We got lucky on that call. Had they not flown the little boy, what would you have done then?"

That caught Jacob off guard. He had no clue what they would've done. It would be impossible to transport a patient without a cot. The realization of that, made him feel that much worse. He had to find a way to halt the myriad of mistakes he'd been making.

Trent put his hand on Jacob's shoulder, and looked him square in the eyes. "Jacob, you ever pull this again, I will personally beat you. Are we clear?"

"Crystal."

The tension, which was stretched like a tight elastic band, snapped as the station tones went off. "Medic 61 and Medic 62, we have a traffic accident with entrapment at the corner of Greenfield and Main. Fire department has been notified," the dispatcher rambled.

Stitch ran back into the station with his partner, Jeff. "That's only a few blocks from here."

"Yes, it is. Let's saddle up, boys," Trent said.

"Make sure you have your cot," Stitch bellowed.

This was no time for Jacob to let Stitch's words bother him. There was work to be done; lives to save. The four men ran to their ambulances. The sound of their boots pounding on the pavement reminded Jacob of the Soviet Army marching in formation. Once again, his adrenalin coursed through his body. This was the feeling he enjoyed the most about this job, the fear and excitement of going into the unknown. They jumped into their ambulances, flipped on the lights, and pulled out into the busy morning traffic.

"Medic 61 and Medic 62 are en-route to this accident. Do you have anything further?" Trent asked over the radio.

"You have two vehicles with major damage. It is unknown on how many patients. Fire department is en-route from station 14. Station 12 is on a structure fire. They should be on scene within ten minutes," the dispatcher answered.

"That station is on the other side of town. It's going to take them some time to get there," Trent said to Jacob. He reached over and grasped the door handle, steadying himself as the ambulance swayed on a sharp turn.

Stitch followed close behind. Traffic was heavy, and in the distance, Jacob could see several cars stopped. As they drew closer, Trent noticed there was thick black smoke billowing from under the hood of one of the vehicles.

"Stop just before the accident scene. Looks like we have a car that could possibly be on fire," Trent said. "Medic 61 to dispatch."

"Go ahead Medic 61," the dispatcher answered.

"We have two vehicles with major damage. One of them is possibly on fire. Advise the engine company to expedite. Also, law enforcement hasn't arrived on scene. Get an ETA. We're going to need traffic and crowd control," said Trent.

One of the vehicles was a small, compact four-door car that had been t-boned by a full size truck on the front passenger door. Black smoke billowed from the engine compartment of the car. There was a man slumped over the steering wheel of the truck. Several vehicles stopped in the middle of the road, looking on.

Jacob pulled a short distance before the two vehicles. Jeff and Stitch parked directly behind them. Trent ripped off his seat belt, and flung open the door. The four gathered to assess the scene.

"Stitch, you and Jeff go to the car and see what you have. Jacob and I will go check on the patient in the truck," Trent ordered. Being the senior paramedic on the scene, everyone looked at him for direction.

Jacob sprinted to the back of their unit, retrieved the cot, and the necessary equipment to spinal immobilize the patient. As he hurried towards the wreckage, a gold sports car slammed on their brakes and laid on the horn a few feet away from him. The driver shot Jacob a dirty look and then sped off around him. *Where is the police to control this traffic?*

Trent wedged open the door of the truck. A petite man with short grey hair and aging lines etched into his face leaned against the bent steering wheel. A large trail of blood traced down the side of his face dripping onto his white shirt. Trent glanced up and noticed the starred windshield. The seatbelt dangled next to the man's left arm.

"Sir, can you hear me?" Trent asked touching the man's shoulder. "He's not breathing. We need to get him out of this truck now!" Trent placed a c-collar around the man's neck. Jacob moved the cot over next to the open door, slid a backboard under the man's butt with the assistance of Trent, and pulled him out of the truck. Once he was on the board, they moved him in front of their ambulance.

Trent pressed his fingers against the man's neck through an opening of the c-collar. "He has no pulse. Begin CPR."

Jacob interlaced his fingers, found the appropriate spot on his sternum, and compressed his chest rhythmically. Trent moved at a feverish pace, getting the cardiac monitor onto him and his IV set up. Jacob glanced up and saw Jeff pulling a woman from the front seat of the car while Stitch was ripping at belts in the back seat.

"Jeff, I can't get these belts undone!" Jacob heard Stitch scream.

"My daughter is back there. You have to get her out!" the woman pleaded with Stitch.

The black smoke from under the hood of the car grew thicker. Jeff was trying to restrain the woman from running back to the car.

"I need to go and help Stitch!" Jacob yelled. He stopped compressing the man's chest and stood up.

"No, are you kidding me? This person needs us. Keep doing CPR," Trent shouted.

Everything inside of Jacob wanted to stop and go help Stitch. A child was trapped in a car seat. To him, she was more important. The flames shot out from under the hood and blazed over the top of the car, quickly approaching the back seat. *Where is the fire department? They should've been here by now!*

"She's freaking stuck, Jeff. I can't get the belts undone!" Stitch said again.

"Use your trauma shears to cut the damn things," Jeff ordered. The mother of the child ripped at his hands, trying to free herself from Jeff's firm grip. Her pleas for help echoed across the roadway, silencing the sounds of the raging flames.

"I don't have mine. I left them in my car."

Jeff pulled out his and flung them across the top of the car to Stitch. He reached up, retrieved them, and frantically cut the belts. With every passing second, the flames grew closer and closer. Jacob's anxiety was building and it showed in his CPR. He was pushing so hard and fast on the man's chest, that he was certain every rib was broken by now. Jacob's attention was solely on Stitch; he no longer noticed what Trent was doing.

As the flames reached the back seat, Stitch ripped the small child from her car seat. He turned and sprinted away from the fire-engulfed car. Tires screeched, Stitch stopped and turned around. A black four-door sedan slammed into him thrusting him and the little girl underneath it.

"Nooo!" the child's mother screamed. She pulled herself free, ran to the front of the car, and frantically tried pulling her limp daughter from underneath it.

Time stood still. All of the commotion and the chaos went silent in an instant. Trent stopped what he was doing, and Jacob sat frozen. There were screams from all around and people started running to the car. The sight of several police cars and a fire truck pulling up to the scene broke Jacob's catatonic state.

"Jacob....Jacob!" Trent yelled. "Get back to CPR. We can't help them right now. This man needs us."

As if from far away, Jacob heard what Trent was saying, but his body moved as if someone else was controlling him. He got up and walked, staring at Stitch pinned under the car. Just a few minutes ago, he was arguing with his friend. Now, his body was crumpled up underneath the vehicle.

A moment later, a young man in his early twenties stumbled out of the car and staggered across the asphalt. "What...what happened?" the man asked. He slurred his words as he spoke. His eyes were bloodshot; the heavy aroma of alcohol filled the air. Two police officers grabbed him and took him back to one of their cruisers.

Two firefighters ran up to the burning car with a charged fire hose, and saturated the flames with water. A short time later, the fire was extinguished.

"My baby! Save my baby!" the woman screamed. Three more officers grabbed her from the ground, and pulled her away from the car.

"Let's get the airbags under this car," a firefighter ordered. Another fire truck arrived. Their crew reported to Captain Ballard of the first arriving engine company, received their assignments, and went back to their truck to retrieve equipment. Jacob felt a hand on his shoulder. Glancing back he saw it was Trent. They both stood, observing the emergency crews at work.

Jacob watched as the firefighters lifted the front of the car, exposing Stitch and the small child. Jeff and Trent knelt down and shook their heads. They stood as one and approached Jacob.

"Stitch is dead," Trent said solemnly.

"What do you mean? You haven't even done anything!" Jacob yelled.

"Both Stitch and the girl have open fractures of their skulls with brain matter showing. There isn't anything we can do."

"Yes we can. We have to! We can't give up like this." Jacob tried to push past him, but Trent grabbed him by both arms. The more Jacob tried to fight him off, the tighter he squeezed.

"Jacob, stop! I'm sorry. He's gone. They're both gone."

Jacob's legs buckled and Trent caught him under the arm to keep him from collapsing. Tears sprang to his eyes. "No! No. He was fine a minute ago."

A police officer walked over. "The guy we have in custody is complaining of neck and back pain. My sergeant said he needs to be taken to the hospital."

"He can die for all I care," Jacob spat. This drunk just killed Stitch and an innocent child. Now, they were expected to help him? Are you kidding? Jacob would love nothing more than to get him in the back of the truck and beat him senseless. How could they be expected to render aid to a murderer?

"We'll get our stuff and be over there in a minute," Trent said.

A heavyset officer approached. "I know it's not a good time right now, but I'm going to need statements from each of you."

"Has someone talked to the mother of the baby yet?" Trent asked.

"Yes. We put her into one of our cars and let her know about her daughter. The guy that hit them didn't even know what he had done. Once we told him, he shook his head and laughed."

Anger boiled to rage inside of Jacob. He pulled away from Trent, wiped his eyes on his forearm, and tried to regain his composure. Looking over at the bodies covered with sheets, was a reminder of what could happen to any of them at any given moment. *Our lives are on the line every time we put on the uniform.* Thoughts of doubt shrouded his mind. Was it worth it dying for someone he didn't know? It wasn't the right time for him to speculate. He had a job to do.

"Go get the cot, and the spinal immobilization stuff. Let's get this over with," Trent said.

Jeff grabbed Jacob's arm. "I'm sorry. I know the two of you were friends. The brass are on their way here so I have to stay. Call me later if you want to talk."

Jacob tried to force a smile, but couldn't. He turned and walked to the ambulance to retrieve the equipment. He wanted nothing to do with taking care of the drunken man. Why did he deserve treatment? He killed two people.

The media arrived on scene and set up their cameras around the perimeter set by the police. *Of course, the vultures coming to get their five minutes of fame.* The sound of whipping helicopter blades hung high above the scene. Jacob fought off the urge to look up. They were taught in orientation that you never looked to the sky when the news media were filming the scene. He'd asked Matt what the reasoning was, but couldn't get a clear cut answer other than not to do it.

After Trent and Jacob retrieved their equipment, they walked over to the police car where the drunk was sitting. As they passed the blood-covered sheets that hid the bodies, Jacob's eyes welled up with tears. He had so much pain and didn't know how to control it. Even Trent, who was known for the ice in his veins, became misty eyed.

There were several officers standing around a patrol car, where the drunken man stood with his hands in cuffs, behind his back. He leaned against the car oblivious to the carnage he created with a smug look on his face.

Trent's voice quivered as he spoke. "What's going on?"

"He's complaining of neck and back pain. Policy states he has to be taken to the hospital for medical clearance. Not that he deserves it," the officer said.

He could barely stand without someone holding him up. He reeked of alcohol. Jacob suppressed the nausea that rolled through his stomach. He felt evil not caring about the man's well-being. His job was to care for the injured; regardless how it happened.

"What's your name?" Trent asked.

"Forget you. I don't have to tell you a damn thing," the man replied. He stared squarely into Trent's eyes and spit in his face. Two officers grabbed the man. "Hey, easy. Don't make me sue for police brutality," the man sneered.

Trent wiped the mucous off his face.

"His name is Buck Childers." An officer handed over a piece of paper to Trent, "Here is his information. He's under arrest, so his handcuffs will have to remain on. One of my officers will follow you over to the hospital." He stepped close to Trent. "If he shows up with some bruises, I'll back you saying he resisted arrest and got them from the scuffle."

Trent's eyes narrowed and a small grin tugged at the corners of his lips. "So, where are you hurting?"

"Are you deaf? I said forget you. I don't have to tell you anything," Buck answered swaying from side to side.

Trent stepped inches from his face. "Listen, I couldn't care less what you have to say. You're a murderer and you don't deserve to live. You want to play hardball, that's fine with me. Your hands are shackled, and I have very sharp needles that can inflict large amounts of pain."

Buck laughed. "You can't hurt me. If you do, I'll press charges."

"Whatever happens in that ambulance, no one will ever know. I'm going to take you to the hospital so you can get cleared, and then you're going to rot in a jail cell for the rest of your pathetic life," Trent said.

Jacob stood next to Trent, forcing back the urge to punch the man in the gut. "What do you need me to do?"

"Lower the cot, put the backboard on it, and let's get him secured to it," Trent said.

"What do you want to do about his hands? Want us to take the cuffs off and lock them to your bed?" an officer asked.

Trent's eyes narrowed. "No. Leave them behind him."

The officer's mouth hung open. "Are you sure? That won't be very comfortable."

"I don't care."

"I have rights. I want to talk to my lawyer," Buck said slurring his words.

"After you've been medically cleared, you can call him," an officer responded.

Trent and Jacob got on each side of Buck, sat him down on the cot, put a collar around his neck, and then laid him flat on his back.

"Ouch, that hurts!" Buck blurted out.

They ignored his complaints. Comfort wasn't something he deserved. He tried to sit up. Trent put a hand in the middle of his chest and pushed him back down, holding him there while Jacob secured the spider straps over his body. Trent never looked away from his eyes.

"You hit me! All you cops saw it!" Buck screamed.

"Nope. We didn't see a thing," an officer said.

Once he was secured to the backboard and loaded into the ambulance, Jacob closed the doors. He turned and looked at the innocent bodies lying under the sheets. Jacob climbed into the ambulance.

"Medic 61 to dispatch," Jacob said on the radio.

"Go ahead Medic 61."

"We'll be en-route to Mount Prospect."

"Dispatch copies. Medic 61. Our hearts here are with you all."

"Medic 61 copies."

Jacob drove in a daze, oblivious of what was going on around him. He couldn't get the picture of Stitch and that little girl out of his head. He turned the radio to his favorite station and increased the volume to drown out the obscenities streaming from Buck's mouth. As thoughts of never seeing his friend filled his mind, he forced the tears back. He had to be tough; Stitch would've wanted it any other way.

The parking lot near the ambulance entrance overflowed with media. They noticed the ambulance pulling up and rushed towards them. Jacob held up his hand shielding his eyes from the flashes of their cameras. A few reporters ran alongside of the ambulance, banging on the window with the butt of their microphones, asking questions.

"Trent, we have a problem," Jacob yelled.

"What's going on?" he asked. He peeked his head through the opening from the back of the ambulance and noticed the circus outside. "Let's go around to the surgery entrance and take him in there."

Jacob rushed past the horde of media vultures, and found his way to the surgery entrance. There was no one there; this was a relief. Once the ambulance was parked, Jacob and Trent pulled the drunken man out. He was still screaming profanities at Trent.

"I'm going to sue you guys!" Buck screamed.

"Go ahead. I'm sure you'll have plenty of time to find an attorney while you're in prison," Trent replied.

The police officer that was following pulled up and jumped out of his car. "I was wondering where you guys were going until I saw all the cameras. Good call."

They pushed the cot inside and navigated their way toward the emergency room. Jacob was thankful Trent knew where he was going. After several turns, they finally arrived at the emergency room. The nurses looked puzzled.

"What do you have?" Alice asked Trent.

"Drunk driver that struck and killed two people. I called in the report already."

Her brow furrowed. "Take him to trauma two."

"Get me off of this hard board!" Buck screamed.

Trent stopped the cot and stood over him. "Listen, you're in a hospital. There are sick people here that don't need to hear anything coming out of your pie hole. Now do us all a favor and shut up!"

Jacob and Trent entered the room and prepared Buck to be moved. Jacob looked up and there she was: Bridge. She had a concerned look on her face. As they lifted the board, and moved it over to the bed, a doctor stormed into the room. "Why are this patient's hands behind his back?"

Trent and Jacob looked at one another, but didn't speak.

"I asked you a question. Why are his hands behind his back? Is this how you treat all of your patients?" he yelled.

Bridge walked over, leaned up close to his ear, and whispered. His facial expression turned cold and hard. "Never mind. I'll be back later to assess him." He turned and left the room.

Bridge walked over and placed her hand on Jacob's arm. "We just heard. Are you okay?"

Tears threatened to fill his eyes. "I'm fine. I have to get the cot back." Jacob turned abruptly and pushed the cot into the hallway.

Bridge ran behind Jacob, grabbed his arm again, and gazed into his saddened eyes. It took everything he had not to burst into tears. After a few moments, Jacob pulled away and headed down the hall. Thankfully, he remembered how they got to the emergency room. He loaded the cot back in the ambulance, put clean linens on it, and then stepped out. He sat down on the bumper and stared into space. Unable to control his emotions any longer, he broke down and sobbed. *How could you, God? How could you allow this to happen? What did Stitch ever do to you? He even told me he believed in you. And that innocent little girl... why?*

Chapter Fourteen

"No—No—Stitch. Watch out!" Jacob bolted up out of his bed, soaking wet with sweat. It was a dream, he had to convince himself. Looking around the room, realizing where he was, Jacob flopped back against his pillow trying to slow his breathing. He couldn't get the images of the accident out of his head. It replayed in his mind repeatedly, whether asleep or awake. The sheets were soaked with sweat. He reached up and wiped the beads off his forehead. Looking over at the clock, it was three-fifteen in the morning. After a few minutes, his breathing slowed to normal, but he couldn't fall back to sleep. A sigh slipped through his lips.

After several hours of tossing and turning, Jacob slid his sleep-deprived body out of bed. Each night the accident replayed in his mind, and he woke up screaming Stitch's name. Critical incident debriefing was available to him, but he wasn't a big fan of sharing his feelings with complete strangers. Reluctantly, Jacob donned his uniform and headed to work. Uncertainty coursed through his body. He had a passion for this job, but now his drive was quickly dissolving. Everywhere he looked, he saw Stitch. It had been several days since he died, and it wasn't getting any easier.

The morning traffic was hectic as usual. Someone could sit in the vehicle next to the morning commuters with a gun pointed at their head, and they would be oblivious. Ignorance is bliss—Jacob thought. He pulled into the parking lot of the station. None of the employees were outside socializing. It resembled a ghost town. There was an eerie feeling in the air, like something wasn't right or missing. After parking his truck, he grabbed his bag and walked across the parking lot to the station door. Despite the warm morning sun bathing his face, birds chirping, and a slight warm breeze, he couldn't let go of the pain. This was his first shift since Stitch's death. It was going to be very difficult with him gone.

Jacob walked through the door. The previous shift's crew were sitting around, not saying anything to one another. Standing in the corner was a new face that he hadn't seen before.

He eagerly approached Jacob. His uniform neatly pressed and the shine on his boots nearly blinded Jacob. "Hi. It's my first day here. What's your name?"

Jacob looked at him, shook his head, and walked by and into his room. He wasn't in the mood to socialize. While unpacking his bag, there was a light knock on the door.

"Hey, how are you doing?" Trent asked standing in the doorway.

Jacob looked back down to his bag. "Not too good. I can't stop seeing that car hit Stitch and that little girl. I'm not sleeping, and when I do, I wake up screaming." Jacob swallowed the knot that formed in his throat.

Trent had a concerned look on his face. "That was a horrible day. I didn't see what you did. I can only imagine."

"I feel horrible, Trent. I wish I could take that fight back. I've run that call over and over in my head. Could we have done something differently?" Jacob looked at Trent, studying his face for answers. Anything that could suppress the anguish he suffered was welcomed.

Trent crossed his arms on his chest. "I've asked myself that very question over a hundred times. I still don't know the answer. The only thing I know is that life goes on. We have a job to do. As tragic as losing Stitch was, we have to move on."

His words cut through Jacob's chest like a sharp knife. "Are you serious? How can you be so uncaring and callous? We just lost our friend, and you're going to act like it's no big deal? You can be so cold hearted at times." Jacob ripped his spare uniform from his bag and slammed it down on the bed.

Trent uncrossed his arms and stood stiffly. "I do care. Sulking around about it isn't going to bring him back. We still have a job to do, patients to take care of. I miss him, trust me, but I'm not going to allow myself to die with him. Think about that," Trent said as he turned and walked away.

Jacob wanted his friend back. He knew that wasn't going to happen. The thought of having to be here, at this station, made him sick to his stomach. He searched for answers, but couldn't find any. For a fleeting moment, he thought about praying. When you need answers, give it to God, is what his father told him numerous times throughout his life. *God doesn't listen. Why even bother?*

The station tones blared over the speakers. "Medic 61, we have an unknown medical call at 710 North Waley."

Trent walked around the corner. "You ready? We have a call."

"Yeah, I'll be right there."

Trent went out to the ambulance. Jacob stood, staring at the ground, not sure what to do. In reality, he didn't have a choice. He was bound by the "Duty to Act" law. If he refused to go on any 911 calls while on duty, not only would he lose his job, but also his license. In some aspects, Jacob admired Trent's ability to put his feelings aside and do his job; he wasn't Trent.

As Jacob walked out to the awaiting ambulance, Trent had an inpatient look on his face. The crews had one minute to be en-route to a call. Jacob didn't care if it took any longer than that. The motivation that had driven him before was gone. The urge to leave tugged at his heart.

"We need to get going," Trent said.

Jacob climbed into the ambulance, switched on the emergency lights, and pulled out into traffic.

"Where's your head at?" Trent asked.

"It's here. What else do you want?" Jacob asked glaring at his partner.

Trent shook his head. "Get your head into the game. I need your help."

Everything inside of him wanted to pull the ambulance over, get out, and say forget it. "I'm glad it's so easy for you. He was my friend. You didn't watch that car barrel over him like I did. Right now, I couldn't care less about anything. I'm one step away from calling it quits."

Trent leaned back in his seat and stared out of the window. "Are you going to his funeral tomorrow?"

Jacob hadn't thought about it. He'd never attended one and he wasn't sure he could handle seeing Stitch's body cold and stiff inside of a coffin. It would give him closure and maybe the healing process would begin. "I don't know."

"Seriously Jacob, you're starting to make me angry. You're sitting over there and drowning in a sea of self-pity. I lost him too. If Stitch were here...."

Jacob flew into a rage. "But he's not; he's dead! A drunk killed him, and I don't know how to deal with it. Every night, when I go to sleep, I see him under that car. Every morning, when I wake up, I hope and pray it is all just a dream, but it isn't. I don't know what to do!" Jacob screamed.

Silence filled the truck.

A few moments later, they arrived at the address. "Dispatch Medic 61 is on scene," said Trent through the microphone.

"Dispatch copies."

Engine 14 was already on scene. Jacob got out of the ambulance, slammed the door shut, and stomped to the back of the ambulance. Trent walked around the corner to help him retrieve the cot. As they pulled the cot out, Captain Ballard walked out of the house.

"You guys can cancel. She doesn't want to go to the hospital," he said.

"Why did she call?" Trent asked.

"She's on home oxygen, it got kinked, and she freaked out and called 911. We got it fixed for her. She's all better now."

"Gotta love the easy calls," said Trent.

"Look, we're really sorry about your friend, Stitch. Everyone in our house is busted up over it. If there's anything we can do, don't hesitate to ask," he said placing a hand on Trent's shoulder.

"We appreciate that. You guys have a safe shift."

"Dispatch Medic 61, are you going to be transporting?" the dispatcher asked.

Trent grabbed his radio. "Negative. The patient has decided not to go. We're available if you need us."

"We have a traffic accident on the corner of Power and Main. We have two vehicles involved, unknown on extent of injuries. Fire department has been dispatched."

"Medic 61 copies. Show us en-route," Trent said. "No rest for the weary. We'll see you on the next one, captain."

"You guys be careful," he said.

Jacob nodded, and then went to get in the front of the ambulance. This was going to be one busy shift, but he didn't mind. The busier they were the less chances he had to think about Stitch. Silence rolled through the cab on the way to the next call. Jacob wasn't in a social mood. He approached the accident scene from the south. Two compact cars sat in the right lane; one struck the other from behind just before the stop light. The trunk of the front car was flattened up against the back window. It was obvious the impact was from a high rate of speed.

Trent surveyed the accident. "Medic 61 dispatch, we're on scene. We have two vehicles, moderate damage."

One of the firefighters approached the ambulance. "Hey guys, you're only going to have one patient. He's complaining of neck and back pain. I'll help you get your stuff."

"Why don't you two grab everything while I go and see what we got?" Trent asked.

Jacob couldn't get mad at him. He was just doing his job. The paramedic always went to assess what the patient's needs were. He grabbed the spinal immobilization equipment and placed it all on the cot. With the assistance of the firefighter, they pushed it toward the accident scene. Police were talking to a woman in the front car. She didn't appear injured, just crying uncontrollably. Trent was checking on the man that struck the lady's car. He was standing up, outside of his car, slightly swaying. Trent and another firefighter were asking him questions, but he wouldn't answer.

Jacob joined Trent assessing the patient. A distinct odor caught his attention. "Are you kidding me? You're driving drunk? What's wrong with you?" he shouted at the man, inches from his face.

Trent spun around towards Jacob. "Shut up! You're out of line."

"I'm out of line? How about the jerk that is driving around drunk? I think he's the one out of line!" Jacob yelled.

Everyone on scene stopped what they were doing and stared. Jacob couldn't care less about this man's feelings. He was drunk driving. More innocent people could be killed because of it. Trent looked over at the other firefighter. "You got him for a second? I need to talk to my partner."

"Sure thing," he said.

Trent grabbed Jacob's arm and pulled him around to the back of the car. "What is wrong with you? We have a job to do. Regardless if we agree or not, we still have to treat him like a human being. Now, get your head out of your butt and do your job!"

Trent let go of his arm and went back around to where the patient was standing. "Sir, you're not answering my questions appropriately. We're going to have to put you on this backboard, and take you to the hospital." Looking over at Jacob, he suggested, "Let's get that collar on his neck."

Jacob hesitated for a moment, shook his head, and then stomped over to the cot. He grabbed a c-collar and ripped it out of the plastic packaging. Once the collar was secured around the man's neck, they moved him over to the cot and secured him to the backboard. The firefighters raised the cot, pushed it to the ambulance, and loaded him inside. The click from the locking mechanism holding the cot in place echoed through the back of the truck.

Trent jumped up in the back and gathered the supplies he needed to start an IV. "Jacob, get some vital signs for me," he commanded without looking at him.

Jacob shook off his anger, climbed into the ambulance, and placed the blood pressure cuff around the man's arm. As he inflated the cuff, the patient finally spoke.

"Ouch man, that freaking hurts!" he yelled.

Trent glanced at Jacob. "Sorry, sir. You're blood pressure must be pretty high. Just relax your arm and it will be over in a minute," Jacob said. The man relaxed his arm and sighed. "His blood pressure is 136/74, Trent."

"Put him on 4 liters of oxygen with a nasal cannula," Trent instructed Jacob. "Sir, I'm going to start an IV on you. You're going to feel a slight pinch in your arm. Try not to move. If you do, I could lose the IV and I'll have to stick you again. Do you understand?" he asked the man.

"Yeah, I guess so," the man mumbled.

Trent placed the tourniquet on his arm, located a vein, wiped it with an alcohol pad, and then grabbed the IV catheter. With a concentrated look on his face, he slid the needle into the man's arm.

"Ouch! Why did you use such a big needle?" the man shouted. He tried pulling his arm away, but Trent tightened his grip.

Jacob felt gratified seeing the man in pain. It was wrong, but he couldn't help it. He was a drunk driver, and deserved every bit of pain and discomfort coming his way. His patience and tolerance for drunk drivers had died with Stitch.

Trent taped down the man's IV, and then handed the catheter to Jacob. "Get a blood sugar off this," he said.

Jacob took the catheter from Trent and performed the test with the glucometer. After it counted down from five, the word "HIGH" scrolled across the screen. Trent looked down, scowled at Jacob, and shook his head.

"You see, Jacob? He isn't drunk. He's in Diabetic Ketone Acidosis."

Jacob felt like a fool. He remembered learning in school about DKA. It was a build-up of ketones that gave the patient a fruity odor on their breath, which could easily be confused for alcohol. This man wasn't drunk; he was a diabetic. He treated the man poorly because of his assumptions. Jacob hung his head, his shoulders slumped. *Yet again, I screw up. Is it ever going to stop?*

"Let's get going to Mount Prospect. Get up there and drive," Trent ordered.

There was nothing Jacob could say that was going to make a difference, so he did as instructed, and got out of the back of the ambulance. The two firefighters that were standing at the back of the truck shook their heads at Jacob as he passed by. He broke the cardinal rule. He made an assumption, and was wrong. Jacob climbed into the ambulance and leaned back against the seat. A sigh slipped through his lips. *I can't keep doing this. I'm not cut out for this job.*

"Medic 61 dispatch," Jacob said into the microphone.

"Go ahead Medic 61."

"We'll be en-route to Mount Prospect, code one with one patient."

"Dispatch copies."

On the way to the hospital, Jacob thought of how he was going to apologize to the patient and Trent. Jacob pulled to a stop at a red light and glanced over at the playground of a school. Several children chased one another around, playing. Jacob ached for the simplicity of childhood. Life was so uncomplicated then. The biggest worry kids had was what they were going to have for lunch and who they were going to hang out with at school. *If they only knew what kind of pain and anguish they were going to suffer as adults....*

"Medic 61 to dispatch, we've arrived at Mount Prospect."

"Dispatch copies."

Jacob climbed out and went to the back of the ambulance. As he opened the doors, Trent was still visibly upset. While on the way to the hospital, he had hung a bag of saline, and was running it wide open. This was the preferred pre-hospital treatment for DKA; load them up with fluid. Trent jumped down from the back of the truck and they pulled the patient out. Upon entering the emergency room, there were several doctors and nurses busily working. It never ceased to amaze Jacob how busy this place always was.

"Afternoon, boys. What did you bring me today?" Alice asked in her usual gruff voice.

Trent shot a quick glare at Jacob before answering her. "Patient in DKA that rear ended another vehicle. His chief complaint is of neck and back pain."

"Do you think he meets the criteria for a trauma?" Alice asked.

"No, I think this is more medical than anything. His blood glucose is over 500 from my IV start."

She turned and glanced at the patient board behind the nurse's station. "Put him in room seventeen. I'll get a nurse in there for ya as fast as I can."

As they were wheeling the patient over to the room, Jacob caught a glimpse of Bridge smiling at him. Just the sight of her made his day better. Not that long ago, he couldn't find the courage to talk to her. Now, he reveled at the chance to be around her. One of these days, he was going to muster up the courage to ask her out on a date.

Once the patient was moved over to a bed, the nurse walked in to receive the report. As Trent talked to her, Jacob pushed the cot out into the hallway. One thing was for sure, he wasn't going to let the cot out of his sight until it was safely secured in the ambulance. While putting clean linens on the cot, Bridge approached him.

"Hey, handsome. How are you doing?"

"Okay, I guess. I'm really having a hard time with Stitch's death. I thought I smelled alcohol on this patient's breath, and I went off on him. Turned out he was in DKA."

Bridge placed her hand on Jacob's arm. "It's okay. That's an easy thing to mistake. It's understandable, with everything you've been through lately."

He wanted to believe her, but couldn't. There are life-changing events and this certainly qualified as one. The question was whether he was ever going to be able to bounce back from it? "I appreciate your kind words, but you don't have to. I'll be okay."

Bridge put her arms across her chest. "You know, that's what friends are for. So rather than push me away when I'm trying to be there for you, how about you embrace the fact that I care, and show a little gratitude?"

Jacob was shocked to silence. Finally he said, "All right, all right. I'm sorry. Can you ever find it in your heart to forgive me?"

The corners of her lips tugged into a smile. "Tell you what. I'll forgive you if you take me out the Rusty Nail for a drink tomorrow night."

The Rusty Nail? Anywhere but that place. "Bridge, I can't go there. That's where Stitch and I used to go hang out."

She stepped closer to him and put her hand on his arm. "I know, but it's also the place you brushed me off for your bladder."

Jacob laughed. That was one embarrassing moment in his life he would've loved to take back. "I don't know. It'll be too hard."

"You need to start healing. I know it's only been a few days, but you need to start somewhere. That's one place that will hold good memories for you. I'll even pick you up, say around eight?"

How could he say no to her? "All right. It's a date."

"Cool. I'll see you then. I'm sure I'll see you plenty today, the way the ambulances have been bringing in patients left and right."

Jacob smiled. He pushed the cot through the ambulance entrance doors and wheeled it across the parking lot toward their ambulance. Once he locked it in place, a sigh of relief slipped through his lips. Trent stomped across the parking lot toward him. His jaw clenched and eyes narrowed.

"Are you stupid or what? You're out of control, Jacob. You accused a man of being drunk, and then proceeded to treat him like garbage. You're an idiot!" Trent screamed.

Jacob looked at the ground, unable to look up. It was difficult controlling his emotions. "Trent, I'm sorry. I...."

"You're always sorry, Jacob. Every time I turn around you're screwing something else up. Look, I'm hurting too. He was also my friend, but you're going to have to put this behind you and do your job. We encounter all kinds of pain and heartache, but we have to move on. Fortunately for you, he won't remember how you treated him. He's pretty much out of it."

Trent had a point. While at work, Jacob had to find a way to control his emotions. He couldn't keep taking his pain out on the patients that need him. This was a hard life lesson to have to learn. The question was could Trent keep tolerating Jacob's mistakes?

Trent didn't say much more to Jacob for the rest of the shift. Twenty-four hours could be an eternity if you aren't getting along with your partner. On his way home, Jacob was having an internal battle over whether to attend Stitch's funeral or not. He had never been to one, but it felt like he owed that to Stitch.

After arriving home, Jacob peeled of the uniform and boots. It was a welcome comfort being barefooted. His feet were throbbing. It was nine o'clock and Stitch's funeral was in a few hours. He was still undecided as to whether or not he was going to attend. A knock interrupted him. He walked over and opened the door.

"Can I come in?" Trent asked.

Jacob really didn't want to talk to him, but he couldn't be rude. "Sure."

Trent stepped just inside of the door. After Jacob closed the door, he sat down in his recliner. "Have a seat."

Trent sat down on the couch directly across from him. He sat bent over, with his elbows on his knees. He let out a sigh before he spoke. "Look, I'm sorry I was so hard on you yesterday."

His apology was welcome, but unwarranted. "It's okay. No need to apologize. I was wrong for the way I acted."

"Jacob, believe it or not, I'm hurting too. I just hide it better than you do. In our field, we have to be able to set our emotions aside and do our job. I'll be honest; it took me several years to be able to do that."

Jacob rocked in his recliner, looking up at the ceiling. He avoided eye contact with Trent. "I don't know if I'll ever be able to. I'm trying, but everywhere I look, I see Stitch."

"There's nothing else I can say that's going to make anything better. The fact that you're this busted up over Stitch's death, shows that you're human. I would worry more if you weren't upset. You're going to be fine, Jacob. I know that. Now all you need to do is believe it too. I need you on the truck. That's why I'm so hard on you because you have potential to do great things."

"You have a funny way of showing it."

Trent shook his head and let out a little laugh. "You're not the first person to tell me that and probably won't be the last. Stitch's funeral is in a few hours. I hope you'll be there." Trent got up, opened the door, and then turned around. "I'm telling you this, Jacob. If you don't go, you'll regret it for the rest of your life. Trust me. I know." He smiled and then walked out the door.

Jacob was battling so many mixed emotions. Part of him wanted to go, but the other part of him wanted to avoid it. Whatever decision he made would be the one that would haunt him for the rest of his life if it wasn't the right one.

Chapter Fifteen

The road in the cemetery was lined with vehicles from every emergency agency in the area. Several firefighters, police, EMT's, dispatchers, and paramedics donned their Class A uniforms. A low grumble of the attendants quietly talking to one another surrounded the graveside.

Stitch's coffin was perched on a green pedestal with the lid open. He was dressed in a dark blue pin stripe suit. Jacob stood at the coffin, gazing at his friend. He choked down a wave of nausea that purged up from his stomach. The funeral home was able to mask the injuries to Stitch's head and face. At that moment, Trent walked up to Jacob and placed a hand on his shoulder. The two men stared at their fallen friend, a hero. His eyes welled up with tears. The last words they had were forever burned into his mind. Jacob reached down and touched Stitch's shoulder.

"I'm so sorry, my friend. I didn't mean the things I said to you. I would give anything to have those few moments back. I'm going to miss you, amigo." Tears streamed down his cheeks. He walked away, trying to hide his weakness. He stopped next to a headstone a few feet away from the tent that covered Stitch's casket. The shadow of leaves sprinkled across the grass as the wind tossed them like playthings. It wasn't common to see such lush landscape in the desert terrain. Jacob reached up and dried his eyes. He peered back to the tent and noticed Stitch's family gathered at his casket. It was heart wrenching seeing his family in so much pain.

Jacob walked over and stood behind Stitch's family, with Trent by his side as the service was called to order. It was heartwarming seeing the EMS community come together to grieve the death of a fallen brother. Stitch would've been proud to see the support his family received. As if from a different dimension the sound of a lone bagpipe floated through the air, playing the mournful strain of "Amazing Grace." He glanced around and noticed people mouthing the words, Jacob refused to. He didn't understand why God would let his friend die. He was young and full of life. Then his thoughts shifted to the little girl. Why did she have to suffer such a tragic death? She was so young and innocent. His heart sank at the thought of what her mother must be going through. There was no grace in that; no grace that could cover this pain.

And as it began, so did the cry of the bagpipe fade and disappear into the clouds as they drifted overheard. The pastor began the eulogy. Out of the corner of Jacob's eye, he noticed Angela, Stitch's ex-wife walking up to the tent with Bentley. Tears streamed down her cheeks. Following closely behind her was a man; Jacob assumed it must've been the man she left Stitch for. A quiet mumble rolled through the crowd. She approached his coffin, put a hand over her face, and cried. Angela placed a hand on his coffin and cried aloud.

Jacob took a step toward her, but Trent grabbed his arm.

"Don't. This isn't the time or place," Trent said barely in a whisper.

Angela lifted Bentley so he could say his final goodbyes to his father.

"Daddy, get up. Why are you sleeping? Talk to me, Daddy," Bentley said reaching for his father.

Stitch's parents burst into tears. Angela pulled Bentley close to her and briskly walked away from the graveside service. Jacob's anger brewed. *How could she possibly do this? Just A few days ago, she dangled Bentley in front of Stitch like a carrot trying to coax more money out of him. Now here she is exposing the boy to Stitch's death and acting like she cares.*

The service ended and the crowd dispersed. Jacob felt someone brush up behind him. He turned as a petite woman, her head covered with a black shawl, pressed a small envelop into his hand.

"My heart goes out to you," she gazed up at him briefly. A single tear slipped from the corner of her eye as she turned and walked away. The wind caught her shawl and ripped it from her golden red hair cascading down her back. *The woman from the Rusty Nail again.*

Jacob sat in his car staring at the note. "I will always remember Stitch and what he meant to me. Just know my thoughts will be with you always. Becca." *I wonder if he was dating her? She must have been with him at the Rusty Nail before I arrived.* Jacob tossed the note on the passenger seat in disgust. It was just like Stitch to keep him in the dark.

He went home to get ready to meet with Bridge. He wasn't in the sociable mood, but he promised Bridge they would go out for drinks; he wasn't going to pass up the chance to be with her. Besides, it would be nice to take his mind off everything. The downside was that she wanted to go to Stitch's favorite bar. She insisted that they go to The Rusty Nail to honor Stitch, but he still didn't think it was a good idea.

After a long hot shower, he stood at the mirror looking at himself. What could she possibly find attractive about him? This woman was insanely gorgeous. She could have any man that she wanted. What did he have to offer? A miniscule salary as an EMT? Jacob shook the doubt out of his mind and finished preparing for his date.

Once he was dressed and ready to go, there was a knock on the door. His heart jumped into his throat. He stood at the front door and grabbed the cold metal doorknob. He sucked in a deep breath. It would be embarrassing to appear overly excited. Once Jacob opened the door, his breath was taken away. It was difficult not to stare.

"Take a picture, it will last longer," Bridge said.

"Sorry. I...."

"You're too cute, Jacob." Bridge smiled as she strolled past him into the house.

Not too long ago, he felt like a blubbering idiot around her. He had a newfound confidence. Being afraid of talking to her was no longer a problem. After shutting the door, Jacob turned around and noticed her pillaging in his cabinets. She went through cabinet after cabinet, examining their contents.

"Please, make yourself at home."

"Sorry. It's a bad habit I have, going through cabinets to see what kind of eating habits people have. From what I'm seeing here, you eat out a lot."

A smile tugged at the corners of his lips. "I hate to cook for myself." Jacob shut the door and walked into the kitchen. He leaned against the granite countertop and crossed his arms over his chest.

"So you know how to cook? That surprises me. Not many single men know how."

"I never said that. I can get along okay. Occasionally I've been known to burn a pot of boiling water."

Bridge snorted. A shocked look washed over her face. She reached up with her hand and covered her mouth.

"Did you just...."

"No, I didn't," she replied and playfully slapped in on the arm. "Where was this sense of humor the first time I talked to you?"

"It was in my back pocket. I was saving it for a rainy day."

After going through each of the cabinets, refrigerator included, she took a seat in Jacob's Lazy Boy recliner.

"Well, just make yourself comfortable."

With a devilish grin she replied, "Don't mind if I do."

"You do know that a man's recliner is his throne, don't you?"

Bridge sat in the recliner, legs kicked up, with a satisfied look on her face. "You must be single because there's a saying: if momma isn't happy, then no one is happy."

"As a matter of fact I am single, but it's by my choice. I just haven't found the right woman to catch my attention."

Bridge looked at him inquisitively. "Oh, really? What kind of woman catches your attention?"

Jacob sat down on the couch across from her. "A woman that can be comfortable farting or belching in front of me, and not be embarrassed; a woman who doesn't always have to be dolled up, one who can go out and get muddy. I have yet to find that kind of woman."

Bridge slightly turned her head to the side. "Where I was raised, that's not very proper of a lady."

"Now you know why I'm single. I have yet to find a woman who fits those criteria."

Bridge shot up out of the recliner. "Jacob, I'm hungry. How about you take me out to dinner and then we'll go have some drinks? You're buying of course. After all, I'm still a lady."

Jacob laughed and opened the front door. "Ladies first. I insist."

Bridge smiled and walked toward the door. "You know Jacob, there may be hope for you yet." She walked past him and toward his truck.

Once he locked the front door, Jacob turned around to see her standing by the passenger door, waiting. He humored her, walked over, and opened the door. Once she was inside, he shut the door and walked around to the driver's side.

"Very good, Jacob. You do have manners."

"My mother raised me to be a gentleman. After a few drinks, that may be a different story." Jacob fired up the engine, threw it in drive, and squealed out of the driveway.

"Easy there. This isn't a race," she said while holding onto the door handle.

"If the community trusts me to drive fast, so should you."

"Where are we going to eat?"

"I was thinking of grabbing a burger and fries. Do you object?"

"Well Casanova, don't spare any expense on my behalf."

"It's the first date. If you go out with me again, I'll upgrade you to some seafood."

Bridge sat there with a bewildered look on her face. To know what she was thinking would be priceless. As they drove down the road, there was an uncomfortable silence in the truck. Jacob didn't want to sound foolish again, so he chose not to speak. After a few minutes, she reached over and turned on the radio. As she was flipping through the stations, the only thing Jacob could think was please don't pick country music. He hated that music. Of course, she stopped on the first country station she came across.

"Why the long face? Don't you like this music?"

"To be honest, no. I hate it."

"You obviously don't appreciate good music."

"On the contrary, I love good music. I just don't see the need to be punished by listening to some cowboy sing about how his Ford truck broke down, his dog died, and his woman left him. It's really depressing if you think about it."

Bridge smirked at his statement. "Let me guess. You listen to that metal crap that has some guy screaming into a microphone?"

"No, I actually like music from the eighties."

Bridge laughed aloud. "That's not real music. It's funny how a man can have long hair and wear makeup, don't you think?"

"That was the style back then. It was sociably acceptable."

"It's not acceptable in my book. Men aren't meant to wear make-up."

Not only was she beautiful, but she had a great sense of humor and he enjoyed being around her. Jacob felt like he was one lucky man to be on a date with such a gorgeous woman. If this was an audition, he hoped he would make the first cut.

After getting something to eat, they sat in the parking lot of the Rusty Nail. Jacob fiddled with the mirror in his truck. Bridge reached up and took his hand. Her touch was magical. It had a soothing affect.

"It's okay, Jacob. I'm here if you need me. Trust me; you're going to be all right."

Everything within him was hoping she was right. She let go of his hand, sat back in her seat, as if waiting for something. Realizing what it was she wanted, Jacob sprung out of the truck, ran over to her door, and opened it.

"Such a gentleman. You're a dying breed, you know that?"

Feeling quite enamored with himself he added, "And don't you forget that."

For a moment, she was able to help him forget what he was about to walk into. That feeling quickly subsided as they were approaching the front door. A wave of depression rolled over him. There were too many memories, and this place certainly didn't help. Once inside, Bridge led him to the table where he first saw her. The memory of standing in front of her professing he needed to pee flashed through his mind.

"Your favorite spot?" Jacob asked.

"You can say that. I like sitting here so I can people watch. It's a bad habit of mine. I find it humorous watching all of the intoxicated heroes flexing their muscles and telling their lies. I don't drink to get drunk, just to feel good, and find humor in others."

As they took a seat at the table, Jacob looked around to survey the surroundings. There were several people sporadically placed around the bar. Once his eyes adjusted to the darkness, he could see the wear and tear the bar had blessed upon its patrons. There were several older men, looking upon the female bar flies with eager anticipation of what they could possibly take home with them for the night. With the right amount of alcohol, any of these women could be easy prey.

"Are you doing okay?" Bridge asked.

Not to appear weak, he lied. "Yeah, I'm doing okay." Her caring eyes sent a warmth over his body. Everything within him wanted to get up and run out of the door.

Bridge pushed a few strands of hair out of her eyes. "You don't look like it."

"I'm fine. It feels weird being here. I half expect to see Stitch clowning around. Of course, that isn't going to happen."

There were several emotions flowing through him; guilt, uneasiness, but most strongly, hatred. He was amidst a room of people drinking, who probably would make the same bad choices as the man who killed Stitch and the innocent little girl. He will never fully understand why it had to happen. They were just doing their job, trying to save people's lives, and then in an instant, it went completely wrong. Jacob couldn't help but wonder if they were there a few minutes earlier or even later, would the outcome have been different?

Bridge reached over and gave his arm a reassuring touch. Once again, it soothed him. "So, tell me more about yourself, Jacob. What makes you tick?"

"Nothing much to tell, I guess. I had a boring job, but that quickly changed one night."

"What happened?"

"I suffered a spinal cord injury that nearly landed me in a wheel chair."

Bridge's eyes widened and her mouth dropped open. "You did? Looks like you recovered nicely, or you wouldn't be able to walk through that door."

"I was lucky. The neurologist said I suffered a spinal cord contusion. After several months, I completely healed."

"How did it happen?"

"I wish it could've been more glamorous, but I did it doing a head first dive into home plate in a city league softball game."

"You're kidding me," she said, "city league softball? Really?"

He felt like a complete idiot. Why couldn't he lie and make the injury more spectacular? "Yeah, city league softball."

"I don't mean to make your injury sound...."

"Funny?"

Bridge sulked in her chair and her shoulders slumped. "I didn't mean to down play your injury. I'm sorry"

Jacob's heart sank. The last thing he wanted to do was make Bridge feel bad. He was embarrassed by the way he was injured, but was surprised to realize he was thankful for it happening. Had it not, he wouldn't have taken a job in EMS. On the other hand, he wouldn't be sitting in his dead friend's favorite bar either. "It's okay. It's embarrassing admitting how I was injured, but it happened."

"What did they do?"

"I was flown from the ball field to the neuro trauma center where I spent the next two months learning how to walk again."

"That had to be difficult."

"It was. Let me tell you though, it gave me a new appreciation for the simple tasks in life. There's nothing worse than not being able to wipe your own backside."

Bridge chuckled. "Sorry. I shouldn't laugh at your expense. I can't imagine. You've come a long way though."

A waitress approached their table. "What can I pleasure you with?"

Jacob looked over at Bridge and then back at the server. "Allow me. We'll take two beers and a shot of tequila each."

"Very good. Be right back with your drinks."

When he looked back over at Bridge, she had a pleased look on her face. "I like a man that can take control."

Another point scored. Jacob felt proud. His confidence continued to build. "It was a humbling experience. My dad flew in from Missouri and spent a week with me. It broke my heart, and his, when he had to leave."

"I bet. So, what got you into EMS?"

"That injury did. I'm a firm believer that we go through things in life that lead us in a specific direction. I truly believe that injury happened to get me where I am today." Jacob leaned back in his chair. Flashes of that fateful night rolled through his mind. The fear that struck him when he couldn't move, the grueling healing process, wondering if he'd ever be the same again and in a lot of ways he wasn't the same person. He was afraid of making mistakes and that caused him to keep making them. Was he trying too hard? He knew what to do. He just needed to settle down and let his actions flow naturally.

The server returned with their drinks. "Will that be all for you?" she asked.

"For now." He handed her his debit card. "Can we start a tab?"

"Sure thing, sweetie," she said as she winked at Jacob. Bridge didn't notice.

He slid one of the shot glasses over to Bridge and picked his up. "Shall we toast?"

She grabbed her shot glass and raised it in the air. "Sure, what to?"

"Friendship... and maybe more."

That elicited a smile from Bridge. "Cheers," she said as they clinked the shot glasses together.

The tequila burned all the way down. Trying to appear tough, Jacob didn't use the lime. Bad choice! Once the shots were gone, they each took a swig of their beers.

"Want to hear the most embarrassing moment of my life?" Jacob asked.

"Dare I ask?" Bridge tipped back her beer and took a mouthful.

"It's a doozy. While I was on the step down floor, I had a gorgeous nurse that was taking care of me. During a sponge bath, I got an erection."

Bridge spit beer all over the table. While choking on her drink, she reached up to wipe the beer off her chin. "Are you serious?"

"Unfortunately, yes. I am. I was so humiliated. Not being able to move, I had no way of running out of the room."

Bridge couldn't stop laughing. "I'm sorry. I shouldn't laugh, but that's funny."

"I'm glad my misery brings you joy," Jacob said feeling a little irritated.

Bridge sat back in her seat with a disappointed look. "I'm sorry, Jacob. I shouldn't laugh. You have to admit, it's a little funny."

He couldn't be mad at her for long. "Maybe a little. Who am I kidding? It was horrible."

She smiled. "Well, I can imagine. I'm sure she kept a professional attitude about it. On the inside, she must've been really freaked out. I know I would be."

Jacob shook his head. "Not as freaked out as I was. That was a turning point during the healing process. Shortly after that, feeling returned and my body started to heal. Tell me more about you. I've been spending all of this time talking about myself. Your turn."

"There's nothing really to tell. I'm on a travel assignment for the next ten weeks, and then I'll head back home."

Jacob's eyebrows raised. "Where's home?"

"Boise, Idaho. I miss it. I've spent my whole life there. Decided to travel a little, but there's no place like home," she said as she clicked her heels together.

Jacob scooted his seat back and looked around on the floor and underneath their table. "Where's Toto?"

Bridge laughed.

"I'm guessing you're single?" Jacob asked with eager anticipation. *Please say you are!*

Bridge smiled. "Yes, I am. I've had a few relationships, but nothing serious."

YES! "I find that hard to believe."

"Seriously, just haven't found the right guy."

Jacob was hoping he could change that. "Are you about ready to head out of here?"

Bridge tipped back her beer bottle, swigged the remaining contents, and then slammed down the empty bottle. "I'm ready." A woman after his own heart.

After he paid the tab, the two slipped out of the front door of the bar. Just as before, he walked over and opened the truck door for her. She gave him an approving smile, sat down, and put on her seat belt. This evening had gone better than he ever could've imagined, so far. As they were driving back towards Jacob's house, he reached up and put the radio on a country music station. Out of the corner of his eye, he saw Bridge smile. It was yet another small victory in his battle to win over her heart. Once back at Jacob's house, he went over to open her door. She slid out of the truck, and stood in front of him, smiling. This was his chance, an opening; he leaned in to kiss her. Just as he reached her lips, she turned her head.

"Jacob, I...I can't." She took a few steps away from him. "Look, I'm not here for very long. I can't get into a serious relationship. I'm going back to Idaho after this contract is up. I can't very well ask you to come with me."

Jacob felt rejected and hurt. Bridge wouldn't look him in the eye. They each stood there, looking at the ground. This whole night, Jacob felt like they were making a connection. Now, it felt as if he had taken six steps backwards.

"I have to go. I've got the early shift in the ER tomorrow. Thank you for tonight." She walked over to her car and left.

Jacob stood there for a moment in complete disbelief. Where did he go wrong? Did he misread the evening? With more questions than answers, he decided to go inside of his house. He kicked off his shoes and walked towards the recliner. A few hours ago, Bridge sat in his throne. How he wished she was still here.

Jacob threw the cardiac monitor on top of the freshly dressed cot. He glanced over and noticed Trent staring at him, smiling.

"What?" Jacob asked.

Trent shook his head. "How long are you going to keep me wondering? How was the date last night?"

This was the question Jacob was hoping to avoid. The first part of the evening was great. All the way up until he tried to kiss her and she left. "It went all right, I guess."

Trent turned his head to the side and looked at him puzzled. "You guess? What happened?"

The sting of Bridge's rejection still haunted him. "Nothing really. That's the problem."

"You didn't turtle up again, did you?"

It was the exact opposite. "No, the night was going good. When we got back to my house, I leaned in to kiss her, and she shot me down."

Trent laughed hysterically. "I'm sorry, I can't help it. That sucks, man."

Sucks wasn't the word that was coming to mind. "She gave me the whole spiel about not wanting anything serious, that she's only here for a short time, blah...blah...blah."

"I'm sorry to hear that. It's better to find out now, rather than after awhile when feelings begin to develop."

"Yeah, I guess you're right."

"Well, speak of the devil," Trent said and gave him a nod. Jacob turned around and standing behind him was Bridge.

"I've got the cot. At least this way I make sure it goes back in the ambulance," Trent said laughing as he took it away.

She looked at Jacob, and a tear trickled down from her eyes onto her cheek.

"Bridge, what's wrong? Was it because of last night? I'm sorry. I...."

She reached up and wiped the tear away. "No, it's nothing that you did. Jacob, I really do like you, but I was informed today they're ending my contract. I'm heading back to Idaho tonight," she said with a crackle in her voice.

His heart sank to the ground. For the first time, he found a woman that he knew eventually, he could fall in love with. "Can they do that?"

"Yeah, I'm really sorry. This is why I didn't want to get involved." Her eyes welled up with more tears.

There were so many things he wanted to say, but couldn't. The last thing he wanted to do was make her feel worse. If she only knew. He yearned to pull her into his arms.

"Bridgette, your patient in room one is coding. We need you, stat," a nurse yelled from across the emergency room.

She walked over to Jacob, placed a hand on the back of his neck, and pulling him close to her, kissed him lightly on the cheek. "I'll never forget you, Jacob," she said, and then ran towards room one.

Chapter Sixteen

"Are you ready? This is everything you've been working for," Matthew, the district manager, said as he handed Jacob the drug keys.

Jacob's hands trembled, but he clamped his jaw in determination and nodded. He took the keys and walked to the ambulance. His new partner, Collin, was a seasoned EMT. He couldn't think of a better person to be working with. Shortly after Bridge left, he was accepted into paramedic school. There were times he wanted to quit. After the many losses and turmoil of the previous year, his mind was all over the place. He wasn't a disciplined student and it had been a difficult year. Trent was his rock and helped him trudge through school. Now that he had completed and passed all of his licensing tests, he was about to have his first shift on the ambulance as a licensed paramedic.

Jacob climbed into the back of the truck and tried to compose himself. He was the leader now. The last thing he needed was to have his partner worried that he was incompetent and going to soil his pants. It wasn't that long ago he was fumbling around and making stupid mistakes. Granted he had worked through his fear and the mistakes had become few and far between. Now he realized the fear was clutching him by the throat again, but this time if he made a mistake, it could cost someone their life. He had to get control of himself!

His new station assignment was on the far-east side of Mesa, on Medic 67. He did most of his ride along time on this ambulance during paramedic school, so he was already familiar with where all of the equipment was located. This area of town was saturated with an elderly population. If you came across someone fifty years old, it was the equivalent of a pediatric patient. The east side was known for cardiac and breathing problem calls. *You are going to be fine*, he said to himself. He reminded himself that he was good with Advanced Cardiac Life Support. It wasn't uncommon to run three to four cardiac arrest calls on a daily basis.

"You nervous?"

Jacob jumped in his seat. "No, I'm good."

"You're a bad liar. It's okay to be scared. If you weren't, I would be worried. It takes a few years to become comfortable as a paramedic. It's the ones who think they know everything that get people killed," Collin said.

Jacob weakly smiled at Collin and continued to flip the drug keys through his fingers. Collin was an above average sized man. He reminded Jacob of a star football player he once knew in high school. The one thing Jacob hoped was that Collin wasn't a bully like that football player had been. He pulled the drug box out and counted all of the narcotics. Thankfully, they were all there. As he was signing the narcotics log, the tones rang out across the radio.

"Medic 67, we have a seizure call at Leisure World. You have a fifty-six year-old male actively seizing." Leisure World was a fifty-five and over gated community. They had a nurse who would go to the home and do an assessment to determine if they needed an ambulance or not.

Holy crap! I'm not on duty for more than ten minutes. His heart thumped in his chest and a knot formed in his throat. "Right out of the gate. Just like I like it," Collin said with a smile on his face.

Hesitantly, Jacob stepped out of the side door, shut it, and climbed into the passenger seat. It felt strange sitting on this side. He had become accustomed to driving all of the time. Collin flipped on the lights and sirens, surging into traffic.

Oh dang! I need to call dispatch. Jacob grabbed the mic. "Medic 67 dispatch. We're en-route." He remembered how Stitch scolded him for trying to talk on the radio when they were partners at the river. Another reminder of how much he missed his friend.

"Dispatch copies. A nurse on scene stated the patient is still seizing."

Those were words Jacob didn't want to hear. His first call as a paramedic and he was going to have to push drugs. At least it wasn't a pediatric call—wait—he shouldn't think that way. Before he took a job in EMS, he wasn't a superstitious person. Now he watched what he thought and said in fear of it coming true. The one word that no one in EMS spoke was "quiet." It never failed that the moment you said that word, all hades broke loose.

"Okay, IV. Get an IV. Blood sugar, check it from the IV. Valium, five milligrams of Valium. That will stop the seizure. Cardiac monitor -

put that on after the seizure has stopped. What if it doesn't stop? Oh crap, I hope it stops," Jacob mumbled quietly.

Collin glanced over quickly. "Are you okay?"

"Yeah...I'm fine." Who was he kidding? He was terrified. When he was in training, there was another paramedic there to make sure he didn't do something that would harm a patient. The thought of not having that crutch terrified him. He knew the day would come when he had to make decisions on his own. The thought of making a mistake and harming someone haunted him. Jacob sucked in a deep breath, trying to slow his rapid heartbeat. If he wasn't calm, he would be no good for his patient.

Collin shut down the siren as they approached the guard shack at Leisure World. At the front entrance, a metal framed globe of the world perched in the center of a circular pool. The shrubbery was neatly trimmed and an eight-foot concrete wall surrounded the property. A portly elderly guard handed Collin a map and showed him how to navigate to the house. Collin pulled through the gate, glancing at the map, making the appropriate turns. The community reminded Jacob of a maze. *How in the world could anyone find their way around here?*

They pulled into a cul-de-sac and saw the nurse's response vehicle parked in front of a large and lavish house. The lawn was neatly manicured; the bushes were trimmed to look like they came from a mold, and a new BMW was parked in the driveway. Standing at the door was a nurse. She didn't appear overly excited. This was a good sign.

Jacob and Collin grabbed the cot and the equipment bag. The sound of their boots stomping on the concrete walkway and the creaking of the cot's wheels echoed through the air. As they neared the door, the nurse frowned.

"I don't know you," she said to Jacob.

"It's my first day on the job," Jacob replied.

"Great. Just what I need, a rookie."

Jacob inwardly sighed. Would he ever get rid of that name? He chose to ignore her. "So, what's going on?"

The nurse turned around and walked into the living room. "You have a fifty-five year old male patient with a seizure history. He has been in an active seizure for approximately five minutes now. I looked at his medicines. It appears he hasn't been taking his anti-convulsion medications."

The nurse led them through the living room, down a narrow hall, and into a small bathroom. The walls had several pieces of décor, which their bags kept striking. The nurse stepped aside and let Jacob into the bathroom. The patient was flopping on the ground like a fish that had just been pulled out of the water. Assessing the bathroom, there wasn't enough room to get next to him.

"Hey, Collin. You think we should move him into the living room? There isn't enough room in here."

Collin peeked his head around the corner of the door, surveying the layout. "Yeah, we're going to need to lift him out of here."

"Anything I can do?" the nurse asked.

"Yeah, get out of the way," Collin barked at her.

She flashed him a dirty look, shook her head, and walked down the hall.

She was just trying to help. No need to be so rude, Jacob thought.

Collin positioned himself behind the seizing patient. Jacob reached down and grabbed his feet. As they were carrying him to the living room, they realized it was next to impossible to hold onto the man. With each jerking movement, Jacob had to reposition his hands so he didn't drop the man onto the ceramic tile floor. Once in the living room, they slowly lowered him to the floor.

"I'll get him on oxygen while you get your IV ready," Collin said.

Oh yeah, he needs an IV—Jacob remembered. He reached over and pulled out the IV bag. The nurse stood behind him studying his every move. As if the call wasn't stressful enough, now the nurse was perched behind him, like a hawk, waiting for him to make a mistake.

Collin placed a nasal cannula onto the patient, and then stood watching Jacob. Being the center of attention was foreign to him. Jacob grabbed the IV bag of saline and the drip set. "Spike this bag for me, please," he said.

Collin took it, pushed the pointed end of the tubing into the bag, and ran fluid through it. Once Jacob had the tourniquet on the patient's arm, he wiped the area clean with an alcohol prep and grabbed the IV needle. Jacob sucked in a deep breath through his gritted teeth. *I can do this. Calm down, it's just an IV.*

"Collin, I need you to hold this arm still."

Collin sat the bag of fluid down, took position by the patient's shoulders, and straightened the man's right arm trying to hold it still. Jacob pushed down with a finger until he found a vein in the bend of the inside of the man's elbow. Sweat formed on his forehead and traced down his nose. He slid the needle into the man's arm. Right away, there was a flash of blood in the chamber of the IV catheter; he was in the vein. Jacob slowly advanced the catheter the rest of the way in. "I need the IV tubing," he said to Collin.

"You got his arm?" he asked.

"Yeah, I got it." Feeling nervous about losing the IV, Jacob held it firmly and pressed the man's wrist against the cold wood floor.

Collin retrieved the bag, and handed it to him. He reached down, and held the patient's arm while Jacob took the needle out of his arm.

"Sharps on the floor," Jacob said loudly. He grabbed the tubing, plugged it into the catheter, and taped it down.

"Let's run some fluid in so I make sure the IV didn't infiltrate," Jacob said.

Collin stood up, holding the bag in the air, and released the clamp. Fluid dripped in the chamber rapidly. Jacob looked down at his arm; no signs of infiltration. Grabbing the medication bag, he found the Valium. The patient continued to flop on the ground. After grabbing a syringe, Jacob drew up five milligrams of the medication. He placed the syringe into the port of the IV tubing and then slowly dispersed the contents into the tubing. Once that was accomplished, he flushed it with saline.

"Want me to check his blood sugar off of the IV catheter?" Collin asked.

He's almost forgotten. Jacob was grateful that Collin was an experienced EMT. "Yeah."

A minute later, the patient's seizure slowly subsided. Jacob heaved a sigh of relief.

"Blood sugar is 144," Collin said. He bent over and retrieved the IV needle and placed it into a sharps container in their jump bag.

Once the seizure stopped, the patient's breathing regulated. A sense of relief washed over Jacob. He looked over his shoulder and the nurse nodded at him approvingly.

"I guess we're ready for some vital signs," Jacob said to Collin.

Collin placed the blood pressure cuff on the patient, grabbed the stethoscope, and pumped up the bladder. Slowly releasing the pressure, he intently watched the gauge as it deflated. "His pressure is 156/78," he said pulling the stethoscope from his ears.

Jacob looked back to the nurse. "Do you have his medical history, medications, and allergies?"

She reached into a file, pulled out a small stack of papers, and handed them to Jacob. "Right here."

He glanced over them and then shoved them into the bag. "Alright, Collin, we're ready to move him onto the cot."

Collin replaced the equipment back in the bag. They lifted the limp patient onto the awaiting cot. Once he was secured with the seat belts, they grabbed the equipment and headed for the door, pushing the cot. As Collin was getting the front door prepared for departure, Jacob looked back at the nurse. "Thank you for your help."

She smiled. "You did a good job. I'm impressed. You might want to talk to your partner about his bedside manner though. He's not very professional."

Jacob nodded and headed out the door. Collin opened the doors to the ambulance, and once the cot was in place Jacob stepped in and took a seat next to the patient. "Sir, can you hear me?" he asked as he shook the patient attempting to get a response. The man's eyelids fluttered open and then closed.

Collin stood at the back of the ambulance with the doors open.

"Let's go to East Valley Hospital," Jacob instructed him.

"You got it," Collin answered and closed the doors.

The patient remained groggy during the transport. Jacob forced himself to remain calm by reminding himself the combination of the seizure and receiving Valium, it was normal for the patient to be less responsive. He watched the monitor afraid he would miss the tiniest blip.

Once Jacob gave report to an emergency room nurse, they went back to the ambulance where he sat down on the rear bumper of the ambulance. The muscles in his shoulders finally relaxed and he heaved a sigh of relief. Collin sat next to him.

"Good job. You did great. I wouldn't have guessed it was your first call as a paramedic," Collin said.

"Thank you. I'll admit it. I was scared. Does it get any easier?"

"How would I know? I'm an EMT, remember? I've been in the field for a long time. But I don't understand what it's like to be in your shoes. I can only imagine the pressure." He shifted, now facing Jacob. "I promise you this. If there's anything you need, I will get it for you. We're a team."

"I appreciate that. I'm sure I'll need lots of help."

Collin smiled and stood up. "Let's go get something to eat. My treat."

"Who am I to turn down free food?" Jacob said as he got up and walked to the passenger side of the ambulance. He looked out of the window, deep in thought. Would he be able to cut it as a paramedic? Only time would tell, but he felt up for the challenge.

Jacob spent his four days off lounging around the house. He grabbed his cardiology book, reviewing the things he had learned in school. His instructor said that just because you're out of school, doesn't mean you quit learning. He ran his fingers across the glossy page that showed the electrical pathways of the heart. It amazed him how a simple muscle was the centerpiece to life. Glancing over the various heart blocks, he was surprised at how much he'd forgotten since school. His main instructor told the class that they would be lucky to retain fifty percent of what she taught them. It was evident that she was right.

During paramedic school, Trent was an inspiration and a wealth of knowledge. There were many nights Trent would stay up late to explain something in detail until Jacob understood it. Each time Jacob became too frustrated and threatened to quit school, Trent was the voice that kept him going. They'd forged a tight friendship and Jacob often bounced scenarios off him to see what he would do. Though Jacob completed school, he felt his learning had just begun once he started working on the streets by himself.

Not a day went by that Jacob didn't think of Stitch. The sleepless nights grew fewer and fewer as time passed. The man that was responsible for killing Stitch and the little girl was sentenced to twenty-five years in prison. In Jacob's opinion, it wasn't long enough. The mother of the little girl that died in that accident killed herself a few months later. Family and friends told the local media she couldn't bear living without her daughter. In Jacob's opinion, that drunk driver was responsible for her death as well.

Jacob's heart sank even lower when he thought about Bridge. Just when it felt like they were starting to grow closer, like a whisper in the wind she was gone. She had a spirit that drew him in, wanting to know more about her. Several times, he'd thought about leaving Arizona and going to Idaho. Family wasn't tying him down; just the fear of starting over. These days, his loneliness was at a peak. Jacob was longing for the love of a woman. In his field, it was a difficult thing to find. Not many women understood, nor accepted the long hours away from home. Still, he wasn't going to give up on love. One day, he was certain that special someone would walk into his life.

Collin drove Jacob crazy at times. He was eager to run calls and would be in a virtual sprint to the ambulance when they received a call. In a way, he wished he could be more like him. Jacob had a hunger for his job. But being a new paramedic, his fear of making mistakes held his excitement to a dull roar. He knew his confidence would grow, but he couldn't seem to grab hold of the same kind of enthusiasm that Collin had. Remembering how he felt the first day on the ambulance as an EMT helped him believe his fear would subside… so he hoped.

Jacob and Collin walked across the parking lot toward the ambulance to perform their daily check off. It was still early in the morning, yet the temperatures soared well over one-hundred degrees. The soles of Jacob's boots stuck to the melted asphalt as he traipsed across the parking lot. There was only one ambulance at their station. Jacob had become accustomed to having another unit housed with them and other crewmembers to socialize with. In many ways it was lonely because Collin often spent his downtime, when the busy call volume allowed, snoring in a recliner. Jacob had never met anyone who slept as much as Collin did. As far as sleeping goes, Jacob had difficulty falling asleep during the daylight hours. There were a few times he had drifted off to sleep, but for the remainder of his shift, he felt groggy, and in a bitter mood. The downside of not taking a nap when he had a chance was the mind numbing fatigue. Collin inventoried the jump bag while Jacob counted his narcotics and filled out the daily log. The radio squealed their station tones. "Medic 67, we have a call for you at 670 East Reed Avenue," the dispatcher said.

"Whelp, guess we're not going to get our truck checked. I hope everything is here," Collin said tossing the jump bag onto the jump seat.

The two men climbed into the cab of the ambulance and Jacob reached down and retrieved the microphone. "Medic 67 to dispatch. We're en-route."

"Dispatch copies. You have a twenty-two year old female complaining of abdominal pain. You're responding code one. Fire department will not be dispatched to this call."

Collin looked over at Jacob.

"What?" Jacob asked.

"I was just wondering if you're going to crap in your pants like the other day."

Jacob tried to hide his amusement and crinkled his nose at him. "No, I'm fine. I didn't crap my pants: for the record."

Collin shook his head and laughed. "Yeah. Keep telling yourself that."

Although Collin annoyed him, Jacob trusted and enjoyed working with him. He had a laid-back personality and a sense of humor that helped the time pass. Traffic was light at this time of the morning. Fifteen minutes later, they arrived. The home was a modest, Arizona style house. The neatly groomed front yard consisted of rock and cactus. They dismounted the ambulance, pulled out the cot, and the equipment bag. As they walked up the path, Jacob noticed the front door was wide open. He lightly knocked on the doorframe, "Paramedics."

From the living room, a low and sensual voice replied, "Come in."

Leaving the cot outside, Collin grabbed the bag, and they entered the home. Once inside, the Aztec décor caught Jacob's attention. Ivy sprawled across and hung down the main wall. Directly below that, an attractive young woman was sprawled on a couch. Her red hair draped over her shoulders. Like a jolt of electricity, Jacob's internal alarm went off as her brilliant green eyes caught his gaze. The Rusty Nail, the funeral, and now there she is like a spider in a golden web. She smiled up at them.

Collin rushed by Jacob, nearly knocking him down, and kneeled down beside her. "Afternoon, Ma'am. What's going on?"

She never took her eyes off Jacob. "Hello, Jacob. I've been waiting a long time."

Collin looked from her to Jacob, confusion painted across his face. He stood up and walked over behind Jacob. "Do you know each other?" he whispered in his ear.

"No," he mumbled, and as if in a trance, Jacob went into autopilot. He walked over and sat down next to her on her couch. "What seems to be bothering you?"

She reached over, took his hand, and placed it on her stomach. "I hurt here. Can you help me?" she asked gazing into his eyes.

A shiver ran down his spine, the hair on the back of his neck stood at attention. It all felt so wrong. If Stitch had been involved with this woman, why did it feel she was coming on to him? He pushed words past the glue in his mouth. "How long have you been hurting?"

"For as long as I remember, but it's become unbearable since Stitch died." Jacob forced his mind to stay on task. This was a 911 call. Just because she knew Stitch was not a reason for Jacob to crumble into a pile of despair. He had to stay on target.

"Well, it could be any number of things. I have several questions for you. When was your last bowel movement?"

"Yesterday."

"Could you be pregnant?"

"No, but I want to be," she said without blinking.

"Wow!" Collin mumbled.

"Could it be a physical manifestation of grief from the loss of Stitch?"

"Oh, no. It wasn't like that with Stitch and me. He was just my connection with you."

Jacob's thoughts scattered across his skull like crazed ants frantically searching for their tunnel. What did that mean? Perhaps it was the pain causing her to talk nonsense. He grabbed at the next question hoping to bring the conversation back to normal.

"When was your last menstrual cycle?"

"That's a little personal, don't you think?"

The skin on Jacob's face felt flushed. "I don't mean to be personal, Ma'am. I just have to rule out several things."

"It was last week. My goodness you're handsome."

Jacob was speechless. A nervous laugh slipped through his lips. "Well, thank you. How about we just concentrate on you. Do you have any medical history?"

"No, I take a few medications, but nothing significant."

"What do you take?"

"I take Alprazolam, Busperone, and Lithium."

Those are psych medications. How well did Stitch know this woman? "Do you want to go to the hospital?"

"Yes, but only if you're taking me. I want to go to East Valley Hospital," she replied.

"Think you can walk out to our cot? It's right outside of your door, Ma'am." Collin said.

"Yes, I think I can." She stood up and then her legs crumpled. Jacob reached out and caught her in his arms. She looked up at him, laid her head on his shoulder, and exhaled deeply. Collin's mouth dropped open.

"Okay, Ma'am. We need to start walking. Are you okay, or do we need to help you?" Jacob asked.

"I think I'll be okay. My you have such strong arms," she said as she firmly squeezed them.

Jacob felt his mouth go dry and his gut tighten in a sickening knot. She was an attractive woman, but something wasn't right. With determination, he thrust his feet forward and guided her out of the house. He eyed Collin, pleading silently with him to do something. Collin caught the message and jumped into action.

"Here we go Ma'am. Please lie here and let us take you the rest of the way on the cot. Do we need to lock your door?" Collin asked.

She fished the keys out of her purse and handed them to Collin. "It's the silver key." She dropped them into his hand. Once he had the door locked, they wheeled her out to the ambulance and loaded her in. Jacob climbed in the back with her and sat down on the bench seat.

Collin stood at the back doors. "You need anything, boss?"

"No, let's get going." As he was closing the doors, Jacob called, "Collin?"

He stopped and stuck his head slightly inside. "Yeah, boss?"

"Make it a fast code one," Jacob said sternly.

Collin smiled and shut the doors.

This trip can't go fast enough. "I need to take your blood pressure. Is that okay?"

"Sure, that would be fine."

Jacob pulled the blood pressure cuff and stethoscope out of the jump bag. "Ma'am, what's your name?" Jacob felt embarrassed. He'd been with the woman for well over ten minutes and hadn't asked for her name. Normally, that was one of the first questions he asked when making contact with a patient.

"Becca Stevenson."

"How old are you?"

"You sure do have a lot of questions. The next thing you'll be asking me is out on a date."

Jacob's mouth dropped open.

"Twenty-two."

Jacob reached over, took her left arm, and placed it across his leg. She lightly took hold of his hand and held it. Frozen with shock, Jacob looked down at the ground, avoiding eye contact. A moment later, he looked up and noticed Collin watching through the rear view mirror, concern etched across his face. Jacob would give anything to switch places with him right now. Jacob took her arm firmly, put on the blood pressure cuff, inflated it and listened through the stethoscope. Although he was concentrating on obtaining her vital signs, he could still feel her staring at him.

"Your blood pressure is 118/76. That's perfect."

"You're perfect," she murmured.

Okay, that's enough, Jacob thought as he got up and sat in the captain's seat behind her. The last thing he wanted was having her accuse him of sexual harassment. That was a serious charge that could mar his career.

"Where are you going?" she asked. Her bottom lip stuck out.

"I'm sitting behind you, Ma'am. I need to call in a report to the hospital. We'll be there in a few minutes."

A wave of relief rolled through Jacob as they pulled into the emergency driveway. He wanted to get her off their cot and leave as quickly as possible.

This was the first time Jacob brought a patient to this emergency room, and it seemed unusually quiet compared to Mount Prospect. "Whatcha got?" a nurse asked from behind the main desk.

"Abdominal pain," Jacob replied.

"Take her to curtain four."

He gave a report to the receiving nurse, and as he turned to leave, Becca called out, "Will I ever see you again?"

The uncomfortable feeling morphed into agitation. "I don't know, Ma'am. It would be a good thing if you didn't have to," Jacob answered abruptly.

"I beg to differ," she said smiling.

Chapter Seventeen

Jacob and Collin were checking off the equipment in their ambulance, their daily ritual. Collin went through the equipment bag checking off the medications. The station tones rang out over the radio, "Medic 61, we have a call in the parking lot of East Valley Hospital for an unknown medical."

Collin picked up the microphone with a puzzled look on his face. "Medic 61 copies. East Valley Hospital parking lot, is that correct?"

"That's affirmative."

"What's the nature of the call?"

"Unknown at this time. Since the call is on hospital property, protocol states no fire department response," answered the dispatcher.

"Medic 61 copies. Show us en-route," Collin said. With the same puzzled look, he said, "That makes no sense at all. They're in the parking lot of a hospital. Oh well. You call, and we haul."

He threw the equipment bag he was inventorying onto the floor, got out of the side door, and slammed it shut. The ambulance swayed. Jacob exited out of the back, and climbed into the driver's seat.

"You're in the parking lot of a hospital, why in the world would you call 911?" Collin asked.

"You got me. I'm just the rookie, remember?"

"That's right, and don't forget it either."

Battling through rush hour traffic was challenging and aggravating. It was obvious people could care less that an ambulance, with lights flashing and sirens wailing, was charging towards them. As they approached the parking lot of the hospital, a man in his early fifties waved them down. Jacob turned in and pulled up next to where he was standing. The man strolled up angrily to Jacob's side of the truck.

"I need my wife taken to Mount Prospect emergency room right away," he yelled.

"Sir, what's going on?" Jacob asked.

"My wife is having terrible belly pain and needs a doctor. Help me get her into your ambulance," he said as he pulled Collin's door open.

"Sir, you're in the parking lot of a hospital. Why don't you take her inside?"

The man let out a sigh. "Don't you think I've already tried that, Einstein? We've been sitting in that damn waiting room for over nine hours. They refuse to see her and she can't wait anymore."

"What do you mean they refuse to see her?"

The man's face turned red with rage. "Are you stupid or just not listening to me? My wife is in need of medical attention and I want her taken to Mount Prospect. Do I need to call your supervisor, or better yet, another ambulance?"

Jacob sucked in deep breath. "Sir, I will be more than happy to take her there. I was just wondering what was going on. You don't have to be so angry with me. You called 911, and we're here." He stepped out of the ambulance and walked towards the man's vehicle. Collin got out of the ambulance and stood next to Jacob.

The woman stepped out of her car and leisurely strolled toward the ambulance passing by Jacob and Collin. The two of them looked at one another, baffled. Jacob followed behind her, opened the side door, and helped her in.

"Let's get going. I've got this," Jacob said.

The patient's husband ran his fingers through his graying hair. He looked over at Jacob, "Well, what are you waiting for? Get in there and drive!" he yelled.

A security guard noticed the commotion and briskly walked over to the ambulance. "Is there a problem?"

The man put his hands on his hips. "No, there isn't a problem. Your hospital has refused to care for my wife. I'm having her taken to a hospital that cares about their patients." He pushed by the security guard.

Collin shook his head, closed the doors, and climbed into the ambulance. "Medic 61 dispatch, we'll be en-route to Mount Prospect non-emergent with one patient."

"Dispatch copies."

Jacob couldn't believe the nerve of this woman, or her husband. This was absurd; she was already at a hospital. Maybe they were thinking they could get faster attention if they went to Mount Prospect by ambulance? The waiting room was usually full.

All the way to Mount Prospect, her husband followed so closely that, at times, Jacob thought he was going to rear end their ambulance. This drove him crazy. If Collin had to make any type of evasive maneuver, the man would smash into the back of their unit. That would certainly delay his wife getting any type of medical treatment. Once they arrived at the hospital, as Collin was pulling into the ambulance parking, the patient's husband came running up to their unit and flung the back doors open.

"What are you waiting for? She needs a doctor. Let's go!" he screamed at Jacob.

"Sir, you need to calm down. Your wife is doing fine. Why don't you go to the main desk and get her registered. It could speed things up a bit," Jacob offered.

"Medic 61 dispatch, we've arrived at Mount Prospect," Collin announced.

"Dispatch copies."

Collin walked around to the back of the ambulance. The patient's husband glared at Jacob. His upper lip quivered. He nodded his head and sprinted towards the registration area. They pulled the woman out of the ambulance, and walked towards the entrance. Collin was walking with a brisk pace. Jacob had to walk faster to keep up.

The head nurse was standing at the main nurses' desk. "Is this the patient you called in about, Jacob?"

Jacob had a smile on his face. "Yes, it is."

"Okay. Take her to triage."

They wheeled her through the emergency room and out to the waiting area. They lowered the cot and helped her into a wheel chair in the hall. Once she was seated, Jacob wheeled her to the triage desk where her husband was arguing with a receptionist.

He turned around and saw his wife. "What is she doing out here? I had her brought in by ambulance. Why isn't she in the back seeing a doctor?" he asked angrily.

"Sir, she is deemed as non-emergent. She'll be checked in by me and then she'll have to wait her turn, just like everyone else that came in before her," the triage nurse said pointing out to the thirty people sitting in the waiting area.

The veins in his forehead pulsated. "That isn't going to happen!" he shouted, slamming his fists down on the desk. "She is in a lot of pain and needs to see a doctor, now!"

The nurse stood up and leaned across her desk. "You will not come in here demanding anything, sir. She will wait her turn, just like everyone else. Are we clear?"

"No," he answered angrily.

"Security," she yelled out.

A moment later two burly men in security uniforms walked up to the desk. "You can either calm down or I will have you escorted off of the property," the nurse sternly said.

Collin felt a tug on his arm. "Come on, show's over. We need to get back in service," Jacob said.

"It's getting to the good part."

Jacob smiled. "Let's go."

They lifted up the cot and headed back into the emergency room. Collin was helping put fresh linens on the cot. "I'm confused. They called 911. Don't they get to be in a bed first over people in the waiting room?" Collin asked.

"Not necessarily. If they're not in any life threatening condition, we have the option of putting them in the triage area so beds will be available for ambulances that bring in sick people who really need them."

"I guess that makes sense." Collin tucked in the sheets on the cot.

"This was a bogus call. The husband called us thinking since she was brought in by ambulance, that she would get a bed quicker. Oldest trick in the book. I love getting those patients and seeing their faces when I put them out in the waiting room."

Now that Collin thought about it, it was kind of funny.

"Who was that woman yesterday and what was she talking about?" Collin asked as he pulled into the station and hopped out of the cab.

"I don't really know. She knew Stitch, my first partner, from the river somehow."

Collin looked over his shoulder as he entered the station and plopped down in his recliner to face Jacob. "She's pretty hot." Collin rolled back over onto his back, kicked his legs up, and stared at the popcorn-textured ceiling. "If it would've been me, I would've gotten her my number. Of course, the women always fall for the paramedic," he said in a low grumble.

"If we ever see her again, you can be the paramedic," Jacob said chuckling. He joined Collin in the matching recliner and heaved a sigh.

"You've got it."

Silence rolled through the station. The only noise was an infomercial on TV, quietly in the background. Fatigue set in as he watched Collin drifting off to sleep. As he floated in and out of sleep, the station tones blared over the speakers, sending both Collin and Jacob out of their recliners.

"Medic 67, we have a shooting at the corner of Rosewood and Carmichael," the dispatcher frantically rambled.

"Woo hoo! I love trauma!" Collin shouted as he barreled through the door and out of the station.

Jacob raced after him, groggy from his half sleep. Collin was in the ambulance and started pulling out of the parking spot before Jacob could open the door. Collin stopped next to him with the lights and sirens blaring.

"Come on man, let's go. Get the lead out!"

Jacob stepped up on the sideboard as Collin slammed the throttle down, throwing Jacob against the seat and causing the door to slam shut. Luckily, his foot was inside the cab.

"Medic 67, dispatch. We're en-route," Jacob stated.

"Dispatch copies. You have four shooting victims down and possibly not breathing. Three more ambulances have been dispatched," the dispatcher informed.

"Are you in a hurry or something?" Jacob yelled. He grabbed on the door handle.

"It's a shooting! Can't help but get excited about that."

Jacob shook his head. Nausea rolled through his stomach. The thought of multiple gunshot victims scared him. Collin drove frantically nearly hitting vehicles before they had the chance to pull over to the right. Multiple times Jacob was convinced he was about to rear end a car in front of them. Collin followed them closely enough that their license plates weren't visible. At this rate, they weren't going to make it to the scene. Jacob's heart beat fiercely, trying to jump out of his chest.

"Slow down, Collin! You're driving like an idiot!"

"No habla."

As they rounded the corner at Rosewood, it felt as if they were on two wheels. Just ahead, a few blocks away there were a couple of police cars, lights flashing. The officers were running frantically. One officer spotted the approaching ambulance, waved vigorously, and directed Collin to where he wanted the ambulance parked.

Jacob picked up the microphone with a trembling hand. "Medic 67 to dispatch. We're on scene. There are no other units here. Do you have an ETA?"

"The other units will be there within five to ten minutes. Fire department should be on scene," she answered.

Jacob looked around. No fire trucks. *Just my luck.* "Be advised, no other EMS or fire units are on scene." Sweat beaded on his brow and the back of his neck. Every muscle in his body tensed. His greatest fear was unfolding in front of him; multiple patients with life threatening injuries and no other help within sight. He gritted his teeth and exhaled deeply. *I can do this! Prioritize injuries and treat the more critically injured patients. I'm no good to them if I'm out of control!*

Collin pulled up and stopped in front of the officer. Jacob handed Collin a few pairs of gloves, and shoved a few pair in his pocket. He yanked on a pair and they both bolted out of the ambulance to be greeted by an officer.

"We have four young, black men down." He turned and pointed at two men a short distance from where they were standing, "Those two aren't breathing, and the other two are moving around talking to our officers. I don't mean to tell you how to do your job, but you might want to go take care of the ones not breathing. It was a drive by shooting, certainly gang or drug related," the officer said.

Jacob looked around to assess the situation. There were two men, presumed to not be breathing, lying on the sidewalk adjacent to the street. There were two other men, sitting up in the lawn.

"What do you want to do?" Collin asked.

Jacob stood silently, taking a moment to gather his thoughts, make a plan, and more importantly, calm himself down.

"Well?" Collin asked again. He and the officer were looking at Jacob for direction. It was time to make a plan and execute it.

"Okay, let's get our equipment. I'll go to one of the men on the sidewalk. You go to the other. We should have help arriving shortly," Jacob instructed.

After retrieving the gear, they sprinted back to where the men were lying face down on the ground. Collin knelt down next his patient. Jacob sat the monitor down, reached down to his patient and checked for a pulse—nothing.

"Mine is in cardiac arrest!" Jacob shouted to Collin.

"So is mine," Collin replied.

Jacob placed a collar around the man's neck. Blood poured all over the hot pavement from a wound on his neck. The blood coagulated and the smell of iron wafted through the air. "Hey! You, come give me a hand," Jacob shouted to a police officer standing near him. He donned a pair of gloves and knelt down next to the patient.

"What do you want me to do?" he asked.

"I'm going to hold his neck, and we need to roll him onto his back."

Jacob looked on the man's back, no gunshot wounds. "On my count. One, two, three." Together, they rolled him over. He sustained a gunshot wound to the side of his neck. Blood flowed out of the small caliber wound. He reached over to the other side and checked for a pulse again—still nothing.

"Can you do CPR?" Jacob asked the officer.

He hesitated, staring down at the man's lifeless body. "Um, I can try. I went through the training, but I've never done it on a real person before." He stared intently at the patient encompassed with fear.

"It's okay, there's a first time for everything." Jacob moved over, placed his hands on the patient's chest, and compressed his sternum. "You do it just like this, okay?"

He nervously watched as Jacob performed CPR. "Yeah, sure. I'll do my best." He switched places and did as instructed.

"Just go a little faster and harder okay? You're doing great," Jacob said. He compressed the man's chest at a deeper and faster rate. That freed Jacob up to do the other things he needed to accomplish. "You doing okay over there, Collin?"

"Yeah, just doing CPR right now until we get more hands. When are they going to get here?"

"I don't know. My hands are too bloody to get on the radio. Just keep doing what you're doing, and help will arrive… I hope." Jacob pulled out his trauma sheers and cut away the man's shirt exposing his bare chest. As he was getting the cardiac monitor out, and the pads placed on the patient, he heard tires screech right next to them. He jumped back as a black, late model Cadillac abruptly stopped; five men jumped out and fired their handguns at the police officers. The officer that was doing CPR drew his gun, jumped up, and tried taking cover behind a telephone pole a few feet away. He didn't make it as he was hit with bullets in his leg, and then his head. His body fell limp to the ground. Bullets zipped through the air all around Jacob. He didn't know what to do.

A fire truck approached from the east with lights and sirens blaring. One of the gunmen turned and shot several rounds at them. He had placed three shots through the windshield. They lost control, jumped a curb, and slammed into a house fifty yards from where Jacob was sitting. Frozen with fear, he sat there, trembling profusely, not sure where to go or what his next move should be. He looked over to see if Collin was okay. Standing directly behind him was a masked man with a gun pointed to the back of his head. Collin stopped doing CPR, had his hands raised in the air, still sitting on his knees. The gunman fired twice into the back of Collin's head. Blood sprayed all over the pavement as Collin fell face first onto the ground.

"No!" Jacob screamed as he jumped from the ground. The gunmen stared at Jacob and then his attention shifted next to him. Jacob turned around, staring down the barrel of a handgun being held by Hispanic a man, with a bandana covering the lower half of his face. His eyes narrowed.

"Go easy, man. I'm just here to help people. I'm not the police," Jacob pleaded with him.

"La viva La Raza," the man said as he sent two bullets plummeting into Jacob's chest. The flash of the gun temporarily blinded him. A fiery sensation coursed through his body and brought him to his knees. He reached up and put both hands on his chest. As he pulled them away, he looked down. Copious amounts of blood flowed out of his chest, and off his hands. As things grew darker, Jacob could no longer hold himself up, and fell face down on the ground. It became increasingly difficult to breathe. "Bridge," slipped through his lips as he fell into unconsciousness.

The station tones bellowed. "Medic 67, we have a call for you at 670 East Reed Avenue."

A combination of the tones sounding and Collin pushing on him startled Jacob. "Wha...where am I?" He reached up and wiped the sleep from his eyes.

Collin looked at him confused. "You're at work, dummy. We've got a call. Let's go."

"I'm at work?" His head was in a fog. His lips were dry and his tongue was covered in a thick film.

"Yes, you're at work." Collin stood over him for a few moments, "You okay? That must've been one heck of a dream."

"Thank God it was only a dream."

"Yeah, you were dreaming about a bridge."

Jacob sat up in the recliner and stretched. He wasn't sure how long he'd been asleep. "A long story I'll have to tell you about some other time. Where are we going?"

Collin burst into laughter. "670 East Reed Avenue. To see your girlfriend."

"Wait, I don't have a...." and then it hit him. Becca called 911 again. He didn't want to go and deal with her. This was going to make it two shifts in a row. Why is this woman calling again? She can't possibly need another ambulance ride to the hospital.

Once he gained control of his bearings, they headed out to the ambulance. As Jacob walked outside of the station, the bright sun blinded him. He had to squint to be able to follow Collin's feet.

"How long was I asleep?" Jacob asked.

"A few hours. I woke up just before you did. You were squirming all over the recliner, and grabbing at your chest. What were you dreaming about?"

"We were sent to a shooting, multiple patients. While we were taking care of the injured, we were both shot by the guys who came back to finish off the job."

Collin's eyebrows rose. "Well, I certainly hope that dream never comes true."

"You and me both!" He climbed into the ambulance, put on his seat belt, and Collin headed toward the address.

"Medic 67, we're en-route," Jacob announced.

"Dispatch copies. You have a twenty-two year old female with abdominal pain requesting transport to Mount Prospect."

Not only does this woman call again, now she wants to be taken across town? For some reason Collin was quiet. Several times Jacob reached up and placed a hand on his chest. He felt the sting of the bullet wounds, as if it were real. As they pulled up to the front of her house, this time she was sitting in a chair at the end of her walkway. After a quick glance at her, she didn't appear in any type of distress. She immediately made eye contact with Jacob and smiled. Her gaze tore through his body just as those bullets from his dream.

"Medic 67 dispatch. We're on scene"

"Dispatch copies."

Hesitantly, he got out of the ambulance and approached Becca.

"There's my handsome man. I'm so glad you're the one they sent to save my life," Becca said.

"What seems to be the problem this time?"

"Aren't you happy to see me? I'm certainly happy to see you," she said without taking her eyes off him.

Jacob's mood was foul. "Becca, what do you want?"

"You."

With each passing moment, Jacob's frustration grew. He treated all of his patients with the upmost respect, but the games people played got on his nerves. "Becca, we're really busy right now. We don't have time for this."

"Actually, you haven't been busy at all. I've been listening to the scanner. What's the rush? You boys want to come in for a drink or something? I have tea and soda in the fridge."

"Unbelievable," Collin growled.

"Becca, why did you call us?" Jacob angrily asked.

"Stitch told me I could always depend on you."

"Look, I don't know what you had going with Stitch, but it didn't have anything to do with me."

"I didn't have anything going with Stitch. In fact, I only met him that one time at the Rusty Nail. After you had gone out to your truck to change your shirt I asked him who you were. That night changed my life. That was the night Stitch told me I could always depend on you to catch me when I fall."

Panic seized him by the throat and tightened its grip like a vise. He couldn't breathe. He couldn't move.

Collin looked at him in alarm and then turned to Becca. "Listen, you called 911, which means we are legally obligated to take you to the hospital. We don't have time for this. If you want to go to the hospital, then let's go. Otherwise, sign the refusal so we can be available for people who really need an ambulance."

Becca's shoulders slumped; she stood up and walked over to the ambulance and stood by the door. "Is someone going to open the door for me?"

Collin turned around grabbed Jacob by the arm and gave him a slight push, then he opened the door, and Becca climbed into the back of the ambulance.

Every bone in Jacob's body told him to get in the front and drive. Unfortunately, company policy dictated that the paramedic always had to be in the back with the patient. Jacob climbed into the back and sat behind her.

"Let's go, quickly," he croaked to Collin.

Collin slammed the door shut, got back into the ambulance, and whisked them away towards Mount Prospect. Jacob refused to do any vital signs on this woman. That would give her an opening for more unwanted contact.

Becca patted the bench seat next to the cot. "Why don't you sit up here next to me, handsome?"

"I'm fine where I'm at. Thank you, though."

"Honestly, Jacob, I don't know why I even try. Don't you think I'm pretty?"

Pretty crazy maybe. "How do you know my name?"

"It's on your shirt, silly."

This woman was unbelievable. It was frustrating traipsing her across town when she didn't need an ambulance.

"I like listening to your voice on the scanner. It feels like you're talking to me."

"Sorry to burst your bubble, but I'm talking to the dispatcher." *Couldn't Collin drive any faster?*

"One day Jacob, you're going to lose me if you don't stop playing so hard to get. I'm pretty hot you know, and I can have any man I want."

Then go find them. Thankfully, traffic was lighter than normal and Collin was able to drive to the hospital quickly.

Jacob exited the side door and stood next to it peering into the ambulance. "We're not wheeling you in. You can walk, Becca."

She looked up at Jacob frowning. "I guess the honeymoon is over."

"There has never been, nor will there ever be, a honeymoon. Just get out of the ambulance!"

She got up from the cot, walked out the side door, and then towards the emergency room. The fact that she could walk without buckling over in pain affirmed Jacob's suspicions that she was faking. As they entered through the doors of the ambulance entrance, Jacob stopped Becca. "Wait here with Collin. I need to talk with the charge nurse."

"Sure thing, sweet cheeks," she replied.

That elicited an eye roll from Jacob. He walked over to the nurse's station and found Alice, the charge nurse.

"Hey, stranger. I haven't seen you in quite a while," she said.

"Yeah, they moved me to the east side of town. I go to East Valley Hospital mainly now."

Alice rifled through a stack of papers. "I heard you became a paramedic. Congratulations. You're going to be great."

Her kind words yanked him out of his foul mood. "I appreciate that."

Alice stopped flipping through the paperwork and gave Jacob her undivided attention. "So, what did you bring me?"

"A crazy woman, I'm afraid. She's called 911 two shifts in a row wanting to go to the hospital."

"What's her complaint?"

"Abdominal pain. I think she's a great candidate for triage. This time she was sitting at the end of her walkway in a chair, and walked into the ambulance."

Alice sighed. "Yet another drain on society. As if we don't have enough truly sick patients to care for. I'll have a tech go take her out there so you guys can clear."

"Thank you, Alice. I owe you one."

"Jade, take that girl to the triage area," Alice said. The tech walked over and told Becca to follow her.

Becca glanced at Jacob as she walked by. "Thank you," she said softly.

Chapter Eighteen

Jacob sat in his recliner flipping through the channels on his television when he heard a light knock on his door. He glanced at the clock on the wall; it was eight thirty in the evening. He wasn't expecting any company. He dropped the remote on the arm of his recliner and strolled across the carpeted floor to the front door. He grabbed the handle. A jolt of electricity forced his hand to jerk back. He shook his hand and looked down at the carpet; he was wearing socks. Jacob laughed at himself and opened the door. His jaw dropped.

"Dad! What are you doing here?"

Blake grinned. "Are you going to stand there and stare at me or give your old man a hug?"

Jacob chuckled and pulled his dad into his arms. *Oh how I've missed you!*

After a long embrace, Blake eyed Jacob up and down. "Put on a few pounds haven't you, son," he said grinning.

Jacob felt his skin flush. His pants had been feeling a little tighter lately, but he didn't realize that he'd gained that much weight. His dad loved to pick on him, so he wasn't sure if it was a joke or that he'd actually gained weight.

"That's calling the tea kettle black, Dad," Jacob fired back.

Blake patted his stomach. "I can't help it. My wife is a great cook. Plus, I'm not getting any younger. The weight packs on me if I even look at a package of hot dogs."

The two men shared a hearty laugh.

"Come in," Jacob said holding the door open.

Blake winked at he walked past Jacob. He plopped down in Jacob's recliner, grabbed the remote control, and flipped through the channels.

Jacob couldn't help but laugh. He shut the door and sat down on the couch.

"What brings you here? I didn't know you were coming," Jacob said.

"I wanted to surprise you. I'm on my way to California for a diesel mechanic convention. My boss asked me to go this year. They were going to fly me, but I asked if they would rent me a car instead so I could come by and see you. When I go back to Missouri I'm going to fly."

Jacob's heart jumped into his throat. The chance to spend a few days with his dad was exactly what he needed. Since his injury, he hadn't seen him. They kept in close contact, but the last time they saw each other Jacob was pinned to a bed unable to move.

"How long you staying?"

"Only tonight, I'm afraid. I have to get back on the road early in the morning."

Jacob's heart sank. He tried to hide his disappointment behind a half smile. He wanted to have more time with his dad, but he would take whatever time he could get. "That's okay. Tonight is better than nothing." He leaned back against the couch. "You okay? You look a little worn down."

Blake shook his head. "Son, I just drove twenty hours straight. Of course I'm tired!"

"I don't know what you're complaining about. I've had worse scratches on my eyeball," Jacob snorted. Any time Jacob injured himself as a child, his dad would always tell him that. Growing up, he hated hearing it. Now as an adult, he found it humorous to throw it back in his dad's face any chance he had.

Blake laughed. He stood up and stretched his back. Jacob jumped up and darted for his recliner. Before he could get into it, Blake sat down, grinning broadly. "You're going to have to get up early if you're going to pull one over on me, son."

Jacob's shoulders slumped. As miniscule as it seemed, he would've loved the small victory he could pull from his father's grasp. They were ultra-competitive with one another while he was growing up. He was no different than any other kid wanting to best his father every chance he had. Blake always won. The sting of the defeats wore off quickly as another chance to beat him usually presented itself.

"You hungry?" Jacob asked.

Blake slapped his stomach. "Starving. I only stopped once to eat because I wanted to get here to see you."

Jacob trotted into his kitchen. He pilfered through all of his cabinets and the refrigerator. Outside of a few boxes of macaroni and cheese, he didn't have much to offer. "How does pizza sound?"

"Sounds good to me, son."

Jacob pulled his cell phone from the pocket in his shorts and called in an order. He sat down on the couch and watched the various channels his dad flipped through. Growing up, it drove him crazy the way his father couldn't stay on one channel. Just when he became interested in a program, his dad would change the channels. He didn't mind now. At least he was able to spend a little time with him.

After they ate their meal, Jacob pulled a sheet over the couch. He grabbed a few pillows and a blanket, tossing them onto the couch. Blake sat down and pulled off his boots. Jacob watched him from the recliner he reclaimed, only because his father was tired and wanted to lie down.

Blake leaned back against the couch and rubbed his eyes. "I'm so tired. Not as young as I used to be. So, how are you doing with the loss of your friend, Stitch?" he asked watching Jacob with his caring eyes.

Jacob sighed. "Sometimes good, sometimes bad. I miss him." He turned toward his father. "The thing that bothers me the most is that we fought right before he died. I wish, more than anything, I could take that back. I can't and that's something I have to live with."

"It will get easier, son. As time wears on, it will hurt less and less."

Jacob nodded his head. His dad was a wise man. Talking to him helped him bring things into perspective. Like most teenagers, Jacob thought his dad was the dumbest man alive, always boasting that he knew everything. More often than not, Jacob didn't listen and did whatever he wanted to, regardless of the consequences. It wasn't until he moved out on his own that he soon realized his father wasn't a know it all; just a man that tried to pass on his pearls of wisdom to his son so he didn't have to learn things the hard way.

"Dad, there's something that's been bothering me. There's this woman named Becca, and she's been following me lately."

Blake sat up straight. "What do you mean by following you?"

Jacob leaned forward, resting his elbows on his knees. "I bumped into her at the Rusty Nail one night. She's shown up at the hospital and then at Stitch's funeral. At first she claimed she was friends with Stitch. Turns out she didn't really know him; just talked with him once and it was about me. She's called 911 twice in order to get me to her house."

Blake rubbed his temple with his hand. "I've always told you to listen to your gut feeling. It will never steer you wrong. She'll probably lose interest and fade away."

"I know. It's probably nothing." Jacob stood up and kissed his dad on the forehead. "I know you're tired. I'm going to bed. I love you, Dad. I'm glad you came to see me."

Blake smiled. "I love you too, son."

The next morning, Jacob snuck out of the house early and grabbed some groceries. He wanted to go all out and make his dad a full breakfast. Over pancakes and eggs, they talked about how far Jacob had come since his injury, and Blake told him how proud he was of his son. It was heartwarming getting his father's approval. He had missed the father/son time they used to spend with one another.

After a long embrace, Jacob watched as his father pulled away from his house. He wasn't certain when the next time they'd get to see one another, but he was grateful for the time they spent together. He turned and walked toward his house.

Chapter Nineteen

Jacob was settling into his new routine. Most of the calls ranged from chest pain to simple back pain and with each one, his confidence continued to grow. His time off was spent vegging out, lying on his couch and watching TV. He knew he should probably make himself go out more, but it just didn't seem worth the effort.

A loud knock came on the front door. Peeling up from the couch, he lazily strolled over and opened the door. "Hey, Trent."

"Can I come in? We need to talk," he said.

Jacob closed the door and then flopped down in his recliner. Trent sat down on the couch, resting his elbows on his knees. A grim looked crossed his face.

"So what's up?" Jacob asked.

"You've got a big problem."

Jacob's body tensed. "What do you mean?"

"I hear you've been running on Becca Stevenson."

Hearing that name forced him straight up in his recliner. "I've hauled her in a couple of times."

Trent leaned forward. "She's bad news, Jacob."

"You know something I don't?"

"A few years ago she latched on to one of our paramedics. It got so bad that he quit his job, and moved out of state."

"What do you mean?"

"I don't know the specifics. As far as I know, she didn't do anything illegal. She just wouldn't leave him alone. If I were you, I would start praying."

"Are you sure it's the same woman? She and Stitch had something going. She was at his funeral. I'm surprised you didn't see her."

"What? No way, man. Stitch would have said something. He liked to parade his women around."

Jacob stared at the wall. He was more confused than ever. Perhaps he had read more into Becca's relationship with Stitch, but there was no mistaking that she knew him.

"I've got some errands to run. I just wanted to let you know." Trent stood up and walked over to the door. Before he left, he turned around. "Be careful, man. I'm worried about you." He disappeared through the door.

What had she done that was bad enough to drive the paramedic to move out of state? It would be a cold day in hades before he allowed a woman to run him out of town. He thought for a moment about what Trent had said, about praying. Why bother? If there was a God, he sure wasn't in the habit of listening to Jacob anyway. Besides, it was probably a different woman. Stitch wouldn't be involved with a psycho.

Collin finished putting away the dishes and then threw the towel in the dirty clothes hamper in the corner of the kitchen. He leaned against the wall in the dining room.

The unit tones sounded over the station speakers. There was a brief pause before the dispatcher spoke. Jacob's heart stopped.

"Medic 67, we have a vehicle accident on the corner of Greenfield and Main."

"Here we go again, rubber necking morning commuters," Collin said.

Jacob followed Collin out to the ambulance. As they approached the accident scene, they saw a compact car smashed into the back of a truck. The fire department had their engine blocking off the scene, Collin pulled around to the front of the wrecked vehicles. One firefighter was out talking to a couple of people; victims of the accident, Jacob assumed. The other three firefighters were pouring absorbent on the ground where the car was leaking fluid. As usual, commuters drove by slowly, trying to catch a glimpse of the wreck directly in front of a row of small stores. A large group of people curiously looked on.

Jacob and Collin exited the ambulance, donned their reflective vests, and walked toward the firefighters. It didn't appear that anyone was injured, but looks could be deceiving.

"Hey, guys. How's it going?" a firefighter asked.

"Doing great. What do you have?" Jacob asked. Collin stood next to him, looking around.

"I don't think anyone was hurt. The driver of the car is standing at the back of her car. Why don't you go over and make sure she doesn't want to go to the hospital? I checked her out and she said she was just a little shaken up."

"Sure thing," Jacob said. He walked around to the back of the car and found a young woman, smoking a cigarette and talking on her cell phone. "Are you okay, Ma'am?"

She rolled her eyes, continued to talk on her phone, and held up a finger toward him.

"Ma'am, I need you to get off of your phone so I can check you over."

She let out a sigh. "Can't you see I'm on the phone? Give me a minute," she barked.

Jacob turned around and Collin was laughing. "You just got served."

"Ma'am, I really need to make sure you're not hurt. Can you please get off of the phone?" Jacob asked sternly.

She lowered the phone from her ear. "What part of give me a minute do you not understand?" she yelled.

Jacob exhaled deeply through his clenched teeth. He didn't just show up because he had nothing better to do. It angered him how ungrateful people could be. He reached up, took her phone, and raised it to his ear. "Hello? Yes, I'm a paramedic trying to take care of your friend. She'll call you back later." He pressed the end button and handed it back to her.

"You jerk. That was an important call. I'm going to call your supervisor," she screamed.

"That's fine, Ma'am. I just need a…" Someone tapped lightly on his shoulder. He turned around.

"Hi, Jacob. Can I talk to you?"

He felt the blood drain from his face. He opened his mouth and shut it without a sound. "What…how?" There were a hundred things Jacob wanted to say, but couldn't seem to form a complete sentence. He looked over his shoulder to Collin. "Can you take over here for a minute, Collin? I'll be right back."

Collin stared blankly at him. "Sure thing."

Jacob turned around facing Becca. "Follow me." He grabbed her arm and pulled her over to the ambulance.

"*What* are you doing here?" he hissed.

She jerked her arm away from his firm grip. "Ouch, you hurt me."

"What are you doing here? I'm working. How did you find me?"

A smile spread on her face as she stepped closer to him, and took his hand. Jacob quickly jerked it away from her. "What's wrong? I thought you would be happy to see me?"

"You...." It was difficult to keep his voice down. "Becca, you have no right being here. This is the scene of an accident. You can't just walk through here and interrupt our work."

Becca looked back at the woman and furrowed her brow. "You're not leaving me for her are you?"

"What? What are you *talking* about? She's a victim of this accident."

"Well, good! You are too good for her. I don't like her. She was mean to you. No one talks to my man like that."

Fear ricocheted through his body. "I am NOT your man. You need to leave, now!" he yelled. Collin, the patient, and the firefighters all looked over to see what was going on. Jacob wanted to crawl in a hole. He was always professional when dealing with patients, even the uncooperative ones, but he had no idea how to handle this.

"If you keep talking to me like that I'm going to break up with you, Jacob," Becca said crossing her arms over her chest.

The world began twirling out of control. Fear clamped down on him pressing him into the blacktop. A roaring hiss filled his ears as panic engulfed him.

Out of the corner of his eye he caught sight of a police cruiser's flashing lights. It brought him back to reality. Jacob glanced back at Becca. "Wait here."

"Sure thing, baby," she said smiling.

With his heart pounding against his ribcage, he approached the officer getting out of his car. Jacob took note of the officer's name.

"Officer, can I speak to you please?"

"Sure, what's up?"

"Do you see that woman standing next to my ambulance?"

He peered over Jacob's shoulder. "You mean that gorgeous little thing?" He waved at her; she reciprocated.

"Yes. Can you remove her from the scene please? I'm trying to take care of a patient and she won't leave me alone."

He looked confused. "Is she with you?"

"I don't have time to go into details, but she has been stalking me for months... won't leave me alone. Please get her out of here. I have work to do."

The officer shook his head. "I wouldn't be running from her if it were me. She's pretty hot."

"You can have her," Jacob said. Collin and the firefighters were looking at him. Glass crunched under his boots as he stomped toward Collin.

"Anything I should know about?" a firefighter asked.

"Nothing important," Jacob said as he was watching the officer speak with Becca. At first, she was smiling, but then her face contorted in anger. The officer grabbed one of her arms and pulled her away from the scene.

"You're going to be sorry for this, Jacob. You're making a huge mistake!" Becca yelled as the officer disappeared into the crowd with her in tow.

The alarm on Jacob's phone woke him up from a deep sleep. They had gotten back to the station around four in the morning and collapsed on their beds. He crawled out of bed and gathered his belongings. As he was packing them in his bag, Collin walked into the room.

"Dude, someone slashed your tires last night," Collin said.

"Are you serious?" It took Jacob only a moment to realize who had done it. It must've been Becca. He rushed past Collin and went out to his truck. He wasn't kidding. All four of the tires were flat. Once again, anger rushed through his body. "Damn it!" he yelled as he punched the hood of his truck. Pain shot through his hand.

"Who do you think did it?"

Jacob spun around facing Collin. "You and I both know who did it. It's going to be impossible to prove, but I know she's behind this."

Trent was right. He was in trouble. But who is she and why did she pick him to target out of all of the paramedics in the city? How was she involved with Stitch? It didn't make any sense. Stitch didn't seem like the type to fall for someone so obviously off balance. Pulling his cell phone out of his pocket, Jacob called the police. Surely, the officer that removed her from the scene must've heard her threats. His fingers trembled as he dialed the number to the police department.

A short while later a detective met with Jacob. He would've had more luck talking to a brick wall. Without valid proof, there was nothing that could be done. There weren't any surveillance cameras in the parking lot and it was his word against hers. If this was the same Becca that threatened the other paramedic, he understood why the man left the state. "Can you give me a lift?" Jacob asked Collin.

"Sure. No problem."

After loading his bags into Collin's truck, they headed to his house. The mood was somber; they didn't talk. There was so much fear and anger within him that he didn't know what to do. The past year had been difficult enough. He didn't need this stress.

As Collin pulled into Jacob's driveway, a look of disbelief washed over his face. Jacob turned to see what it was he was looking at. Jacob's mouth dropped open. He shot out of Collin's truck before it was stopped, and ran up to the front of his house. Every window in the front had been broken. Glass glistened in the grass and covered the floor inside of his house. He ran around the side to inspect the rest of the house. Every window - shattered. Collin was racing behind him, trying to keep up. As Jacob went through the gate, entering the back yard, he encountered more of the same.

Collin caught up to him. "Jacob, what in the world? What did you do to this woman?"

"What a dumb question, Collin! You know I didn't do a damn thing! You've seen her. She's freaking nuts!"

"Do you want to call the cops again? Maybe someone saw something?"

The urge to punch something raged through him. He knew where she lived; maybe he should pay her a little visit? No, that would be playing her games and wouldn't be wise. How did she find out where he lived?

It cost Jacob a small fortune to replace all of the broken windows in his house, and the tires for his truck. He had the extra money since he was single. It would've been nice to spend it on a vacation or something, but at least he had it. He knew a lot of the guys would have had to borrow the money.

That night at home, his sleep was restless. The smallest of noises sent him sky rocketing out of bed. Most of the time, it was a neighborhood cat howling and digging through trashcans outside. Good thing he had a rare day off, because he was more exhausted than when he had gone to bed. At the same time he wished he was going to work. Anything would be better than doing nothing to keep his mind preoccupied. In an effort to keep his mind busy, he decided to go through old boxes in the attic. Old shirts, textbooks, junk from his childhood, most of it could go. While he was carrying a load of boxes out to the garage for a thrift store run, there was a loud knock on the front door. His heart rate increased as he approached the front door. "Are you Jacob Myers?" a man in a dark blue pin striped suit asked.

"Yes. Who's asking?"

He reached into the breast pocket of his jacket, pulled out a wallet, and showed Jacob a gold badge. "I'm Detective Horowitz with the Police Department. I need you to come with me down to the station."

"I already filed a police report the other day. Do you have new information or something?"

"Sir, I just need you to come down to the station with me. You can ride with us, and after we're done, we'll get someone to bring you home," he said sternly.

This was odd. He wasn't very familiar with police procedure, but certainly this wasn't how a complaint was handled. His nerves were already shot and this didn't help. "Am I in trouble for something?"

"Sir, I need you to come with me. I'll explain everything to you down at the station." His body language stiffened, and Jacob could tell his patience was growing thin. After locking the door, Jacob climbed into the back of his car. He was driving a newer model Cavalier; a rather odd choice of a police car, he thought.

Jacob didn't dare speak to him again. Detective Horowitz was in his mid-forties, had a shaved head, was clean cut, but Jacob could tell the job had wreaked havoc on this officer's body. They arrived at the police station and Detective Horowitz opened the door for Jacob. "Right this way, sir," he said pointing at the front door. As they entered the building, there were several officers in both uniforms and suits, positioned at desks. Jacob had never been in a police department before. He often wondered what it looked like. All of the offices were surrounded with glass, which made it difficult for privacy. While they were walking down the main corridor, Jacob looked over and saw Becca sitting at a desk, talking to a man in a suit, and crying.

"That's her. She's the one that slashed my tires," Jacob said to Detective Horowitz.

He stopped, grabbed Jacob's arm, and pulled him down the hall. "Keep walking. We're going to go into an interrogation room to talk."

She flashed a cold evil smile at Jacob that sent a cold chill up his spine. They approached a room. Horowitz opened the door and led Jacob inside. "Please, have a seat."

The room was small. There was a table with two chairs placed across from one another. Jacob walked around to the opposite side of the table and sat down. The walls were painted a pale grey.

"Will you please tell me what's going on? I've already told you I filed a report the other day. Have you arrested her? I know she's the one that did it," Jacob said.

The detective sat down, pulled out a yellow legal pad and a pen. He stared at Jacob for a moment. "So, how do you know Becca Stevenson?"

Hearing her name sent shivers through his body. "She's a patient that I took to the hospital a couple of times. She's been stalking me. I don't know how she knows Stitch, but she must know me through him."

The officer looked at him questionably and asked, "When is the last time you saw her?"

"On my last shift. She showed up on an accident scene I was working on. I had a police officer remove her. The woman is unbalanced. She kept telling me how she was going to break up with me. We've never even been on a date."

The detective leaned back in his seat, not taking his eyes off Jacob. His lips were thin, his eyes narrowed. "Jacob, she's accusing you of raping her last night. Can you tell me where you were?"

Jacob bolted up from the chair and slammed his fists onto the table. "What? That's a lie. I was at home and didn't go anywhere. In fact, every window of my house was broken when I got home from my shift yesterday morning. I filed a report. Look it up. I spent the entire day getting them all replaced. I hired someone to come and replace them. I had my truck towed to the shop to have new tires put on it. After that, I was at home for the rest of the night."

"You need to calm down. Please take a seat," Detective Horowitz sternly said. "Can anyone collaborate your story?"

Even though he was innocent, this man had a way of making him feel guilty. "No, sir, I can't. I was exhausted and stayed home alone." He sat down and hung his head.

Detective Horowitz leaned forward, put his elbows on the table, and placed his right hand under his chin. "We take these accusations seriously. Would you be willing to submit to a DNA test?"

"Of course. I have nothing to hide." This is unbelievable. Jacob had never been in trouble with the law before.

Horowitz got up from the table, and stepped outside of the room. Jacob was alone for what felt like an hour. He was the victim here, yet he was being treated like a criminal. *Go ahead, do your tests, and then you'll find out I'm innocent.*

A man entered the room with gloves on holding two long, clear tubes. "I need to swab the inside of your mouth," he said coldly.

"That's fine."

The man pulled two long cotton swabs out of the tubes. "Please open your mouth," he said.

Jacob did as asked. Using them one at a time, the man rubbed them on the inside of his cheek, and then placed them back in the tubes. As the officer was leaving the room, Detective Horowitz returned and sat down at the table.

"Okay, this is what's going to happen. We're going to run your DNA and open an official investigation. While we are doing this, you're not to have any contact with Becca Stevenson. Are we clear?" he asked.

It was difficult to control his anger, but he pushed it deep down inside the pit of his stomach. Getting angry wasn't going to help matters. "I understand. One question though. What am I supposed to do if she seeks me out, or calls 911 while I'm on duty?"

Horowitz leaned back in his chair. "If she attempts to make contact with you, I suggest you call the police. As far as if she calls for an ambulance, you know the address, have your dispatch send someone else. We're done here. I'll have a patrolman take you back home. I'll be in touch." He got up from the table and exited the room. A few moments later, a uniformed officer walked into the room.

"Come with me, sir," he said.

Jacob got up and followed him. He looked over at the desk Becca had been sitting at earlier, she was gone. On the way home, he sat in the police car in disbelief. This woman was now messing with his life and his career. What was this going to do to his paramedic license? He worked hard to get where he was. Now it was all in jeopardy. It felt like the longest ride home he had ever taken. When they arrived back at his house, the officer let him out, and then sped down the street. He glanced around; thankfully, no one was out to see him dropped off by a police car.

Jacob went inside and sat down in his recliner, numb to the world.

Chapter Twenty

"He's on the floor of the garage!" the nurse screamed. "Hurry! He's not breathing!"

Collin jumped out of the ambulance, ran to the back, and flung the doors open. "Dispatch Medic 67, we're on scene," Jacob said and then threw down the microphone.

Entering the side door, he flung the equipment bag and the cardiac monitor onto the cot. Jumping out the back of the ambulance, the two rushed towards the garage pushing the cot. The driveway had a steep slope that made it difficult to push the equipment. It was already ninety-five degrees outside. Jacob's brow was saturated with sweat. As they entered the garage, they saw a man flat on his back on the floor. Blood flowed out of his right temple; his right eye was swollen and bruised.

Pacing back and forth was a woman in her fifties. "You have to help him, please. I can't stand the thought of losing him."

A nurse stood behind the woman covering her mouth with a hand.

"What happened?" Jacob asked.

"He shot himself. He has terminal cancer. He said he was tired of being so sick," the nurse explained.

There was a large pool of blood underneath his head. Still in his hand, was a .22 caliber handgun. Jacob knelt down next to him, pressing on the side of his neck, checking for a pulse; it weakly beat underneath his finger. *We don't have much time before he codes.* The nurse walked over, grabbed the gun by its barrel, and placed it on a table against the wall.

"Collin, get the bag valve mask out. I'm going to get an IV going." Jacob looked up at the nurse, "Can you put the cardiac monitor on him?"

189

"Sure thing," the nurse said. She leaped into action, grabbed the monitor, pulled out the leads, and placed them on his chest. Collin pulled out the BVM, attached it to the portable oxygen tank, and pushed oxygen into his lungs.

Jacob pulled out his portable radio. "Dispatch Medic 67, we need a helicopter dispatched to our location. Advise them we have a gunshot victim in respiratory arrest."

"Dispatch copies. Where will the landing zone be?" the dispatcher asked.

Jacob looked out the garage door and surveyed the area. They were in a cul-de-sac, large enough to land a chopper. "Advise them we have an area in front of our location where they can land."

"Dispatch copies."

"Is he going to live?" the woman asked.

He looked up at the terrified lady. "We're doing our best, Ma'am."

Jacob tried to sound optimistic, but it was looking grim. After the patient was prepared, Jacob was able to establish an IV easily. It was difficult trying to keep his composure and appear calm in this chaotic situation. He grabbed the intubation kit so he could get the breathing tube in place. Jacob slid the laryngoscope into his mouth, saw the vocal cords, and slid the tube past them. Collin attached the BVM to the tube, and began ventilation. The man's chest rose and fell each time Collin squeezed the bag. Having an airway set Jacob at ease.

"What's going on? Will someone tell me what's happening?" the woman asked.

"Keep bagging him, Collin," Jacob said. He stood up and walked over to her. "What's your name, Ma'am?"

"I'm Judy," she answered. Tears streamed down her cheeks.

"Right now, his heart is beating, but he isn't breathing on his own. I put a tube in, and now we're breathing for him. Is this your husband?"

"Yes. He's my world. I can't lose him." Her legs crumpled. The nurse rushed over and put an arm around her.

It was so hard having to ask questions when this poor woman was falling apart. "What's his name?"

The nurse looked up. "It's Charles, and he's fifty-two years old."

Jacob's attention shifted to the driveway as two police cars arrived. A portly officer struggled his way toward the garage. Once he was inside, he bent over trying to catch his breath.

"What...what happened?" he asked as he breathed rapidly.

"Self-inflicted gunshot to the head. We have a helicopter on the way. We're landing the chopper here. Can you block off the street?" Jacob asked.

He wobbled back to his car, got in, and did as asked. Jacob and Collin worked methodically getting Charles on a backboard and prepared for the air ambulance. All the while, the nurse continued to console his wife. In the distance, Jacob could hear the whipping of the helicopter blades. Flashes of that fateful night when he was hurt, flooded his mind. He pushed back the memories and concentrated on saving the man's life.

Dust floated through the air as the helicopter slowly descended to the ground. A moment after they touched down, the flight crew briskly walked up to the house with their cot. After giving them a quick report on what had transpired, they loaded him into the helicopter. A few minutes later, they shot straight up into the air disappearing into the blue sky.

Once the ambulance was restocked, it was time to take a quick break while they could. The call volume demanded their ambulance to spend most of the shift on the road. Jacob never would've thought he could get so tired from sitting, but being in the truck a majority of the time grew tiresome.

"You've been pretty quiet today. Something on your mind?" Collin asked.

"Yeah, I've got a lot going on right now," Jacob answered.

Jacob hadn't told anyone about the investigation, but he trusted Collin and needed someone to confide in. Besides, it could have an effect on Collin if Becca was to call 911 again.

"I have something to tell you, but I need you to keep it to yourself, okay?"

Collin sat his sandwich down, and directed his attention toward Jacob. "Talk to me. What's going on?"

He felt uneasy about his impending confession. "The police came to my house a couple days ago and made me come down to the station."

"What for?"

Jacob hung his head. He was afraid of what Collin would think of him once he fully knew what was going on. He shrugged off the doubt. "Becca has accused me of raping her."

Collin's face went blank. "Are you serious?"

"Unfortunately, yes. They took my DNA and told me to steer clear of her while they were investigating it."

Collin exhaled deeply. "That woman is something else. I wouldn't worry about it. She doesn't have any proof."

Hearing Collin say that gave him a little hope. Without any physical proof, surely they couldn't formerly charge him, could they? "I hope you're right. I've worked so hard to get my career. I don't want to lose it over some psycho woman. Trent told me she harassed another paramedic a few years ago. He up and moved to another state to get away from her."

A shocked look washed over Collin's face. "I never knew that, but really Jacob, I wouldn't worry too much. It will all work out, my friend."

Talking to Collin released some of the pressure and Jacob was able to relax a bit. They finished their lunch and were lounging in the recliners watching television when the all too familiar voice rang over the station radio. "Medic 67, we have a call at 314 Daisy Lane for a sick male."

They both got up and trudged towards the ambulance. *No rest for the weary.*

"Dispatch, Medic 67 is en-route," Jacob stated after he settled into the ambulance.

"Copy, Medic 67. Respond code one to 314 Daisy Lane. You have a sixty-seven year old male patient that isn't feeling well," the dispatcher stated.

The nice thing about being at work was it distracted him from everything he was dealing with. *Just keep the calls a comin',* he thought as he gazed out the window at the sunlight sparkling off the desert floor. Collin pulled up in front of the address. As they were getting out of the ambulance, Jacob looked across the street and there she was: Becca, looking at him with that same evil smile he saw at the police station. Jacob closed his eyes for a moment. When he opened them, a woman walking her dog down the sidewalk was there, not Becca. *Come on man, get a grip. It's not her!*

"What are you staring at?" Collin asked.

Jacob shook his head and turned around. "Nothing."

"We need to get inside. We have a job to do," Collin said.

Collin pulled the cot out and they walked to the front of the house. Leaving the cot outside, they went inside to see the patient. Jacob glanced around the living room. There were several pictures on the walls, depicting the many generations of family. Sitting in a chair across the room was an elderly male. He was shifting nervously as Jacob approached him.

To make him feel a little at ease, Jacob knelt down in front of him. "Afternoon, sir. What's your name?"

He didn't answer.

"Sir, can you talk to me? If you don't, I won't know how to help you."

Still, he didn't answer.

Jacob looked back at Collin. "Can you get his vital signs?"

"I'll be right back," Collin said and then walked out of the front door.

Jacob placed a hand on the man's knee. "Sir, I really want to help you. I can't if you don't tell me what's going on."

He glanced around the room. "I'm really embarrassed," he whispered.

Now we're making progress. "There's no need to be. I'm sure whatever is wrong I've seen before."

"My name is Harold. I didn't know what else to do, so I called 911."

"That's what we're here for. So Harold, tell me what's going on?"

He hesitated for a moment, started to speak, but then stopped himself. Jacob leaned in close. "It's okay, Harold. You can tell me."

"I...I can't find it," he answered.

This sparked Jacob's curiosity. "You can't find what?"

"It. I can't find it."

Jacob wasn't very good at riddles. "Harold, can you be a little more specific?"

He glanced around the room once more, and then spoke softly, "I can't find my penis."

Jacob leaned back, biting the sides of his mouth to keep from laughing. He was not sure what to say next. A frown crossed the man's face. Jacob placed a hand on his arm in an attempt to reassure him.

"When was the last time you saw your little fella?"

He cracked a small smile. "Yesterday. I had a double hernia repair surgery a few days ago."

Suddenly the light went on for Jacob. With a hernia surgery there stands a chance to have swelling that could push tissue out and make it difficult for him to find his manhood. "You know, Harold, if that was to happen to me, I would call the National Guard and the local Search & Rescue. It's going to be okay. This happens with hernia surgery at times. Which hospital do you want to go to?"

"Do you think I need to go?"

"Most definitely. We'll get you in so the doctor can figure out what's going on. It won't fix itself, unfortunately."

"East Valley Hospital," Harold answered.

His mood seemed to lighten. Collin walked back inside, holding a blood pressure cuff and stethoscope. After he finished obtaining his vital signs, they walked Harold out to the awaiting cot and then placed him into the ambulance.

"Medic 67, we have a call at 410 East Liberty for an unknown medical," the dispatcher's voice came across the radio.

"We can't seem to get a break today," Jacob said. "Dispatch, Medic 67 is en-route."

"Dispatch copies. Fire department is at low census for available trucks. Advise if you'll need their assistance."

"Medic 67 copies," Jacob replied.

Collin flipped on the lights and sirens. There was a car a short distance in front of them that was pulled over to the right. As they approached, the driver shot over in front of them and came to a complete stop.

"Damn it!" screamed Collin, as he swerved to the left, narrowly missing the car. As they passed the car, Jacob made certain the driver could see the dirty look he shot at him. The driver was oblivious and talking on his cell phone.

It only took them a few minutes to arrive. It was a rundown home, almost looked abandoned. Uneasiness settled in the pit of Jacob's stomach.

"Medic 67 dispatch, we're on scene. We'll advise about the fire department," he said.

"Dispatch copies."

Just like they did several times a day, Jacob and Collin met at the back of the ambulance. The two of them stood staring at the house.

"You getting a bad feeling like I am?" Jacob asked.

Collin replied, "A little. Think we should ask for the police to come out?"

It wasn't a bad idea, but then Jacob's ego took over. He was sick of looking over his shoulder and acting like a scared little girl. "Nah, we can handle it."

They retrieved the cot, the equipment, and trekked towards the front door. The lawn didn't appear to have been mowed in several months. The closer they got to the porch, the worse the house looked. The wood on the front porch was rotting. They left the cot on the walkway, grabbed the equipment, and walked up the steps.

"Watch your step. These boards don't seem too sturdy," Jacob said. The rotting wood creaked underneath each step they took. The two cautiously navigated their way up the steps and stopped at the front door. Jacob knocked on the door.

"Come in," a woman's voice called from inside.

As they walked through the door, Jacob's chest tightened. Collin tried to walk around him, but Jacob pushed him back with his free hand.

Looking down the barrel of a gun pointed in his face was the cold and evil smile.

"What's the matter, Jacob? Aren't you glad to see me, baby?" an icy voice asked from beyond the barrel.

Jacob's muscles tensed. He wanted to turn and run, but the fear of catching a bullet to the back of his head stopped him.

"Becca, what are you doing?" Jacob asked. His tongue stuck to the roof of his dry mouth.

"Getting your attention; do I have it now?"

"Um…yes…yes you do."

"Good. This is what's going to happen. Your partner is going to leave us alone to talk." She looked at Collin. "If you call for help, and I mean anyone, I will kill Jacob. Do you understand?"

Jacob looked over his shoulder at Collin, who had the "deer in the headlight" look. He turned his attention back to the crazed woman in front of him.

"I asked you a question!"

"Yes…I understand," Collin answered.

"Good. Now you run along and wait outside. I need a few minutes alone with my man," she said.

Jacob looked back at Collin once more who shook his head from side to side.

"It's okay. Go wait outside. Do as she says. Call no one," Jacob instructed. Collin didn't move. He kept shaking his head.

Suddenly Jacob felt the cold steel of the gun poking into his cheek. "Collin, go now. I'll be fine. My woman and I are going to have a little talk. It'll be okay." The pressure of the gun eased off slightly.

Without a word, Collin slowly backed out the door and closed it behind him. Becca stepped away from Jacob, but kept the gun pointed at his head.

"What do you want, Becca? Why are you doing this?"

She kept the gun pointed at Jacob. "Why don't you want me? I love you so much."

"Becca, I hardly even know you."

Her green eyes flashed anger. She repositioned her grip on the handle of the gun. "You didn't take a chance to get to know me. What? I'm not good enough for you?"

"I never said that. You just came on so strong it scared me."

She stepped closer to Jacob and pressed the gun between his eyes. "I should kill you right now so you can't hurt another woman the way you've hurt me. No one deserves to be treated this way." Her eyes welled up with tears.

"Becca, please don't do this. We can work something out."

"Promises, empty promises!" she screamed. "The only reason you're even talking to me is because I have a gun."

She was right, but he wasn't going to tell her that. A breath slipped through his dry lips. His heart pounded in his chest. "That's not true. Becca, please lower the gun. You say that you love me, prove it."

The cold expression on her face was replaced with confusion. She started to lower the gun, but then her eyes narrowed, and she raised it back up.

"We can get through this, Becca. Let me help you. Just give me the gun and we will work this out," Jacob said.

Her facial expressions bounced between anger and confusion. "I'm so tired of falling in love and being treated like garbage. You don't understand what it feels like to put your heart into someone, only to have them reject you. Jacob, I love you."

He was no good at this. He hadn't taken any training on how to negotiate in a hostile situation. Nothing he was saying seemed to make a difference. He swallowed the nausea that boiled in his stomach.

"Becca, I don't know what to tell you. I don't love you, but I care what happens to you. You need help. Give me the gun and I will get you whatever help you need, I promise," he said reaching for the gun.

She took a few steps back. "Don't touch it!" Tears streamed down her cheeks. She reached up with her free hand, and wiped them away. Her eyes narrowed and filled with a rage he had never seen in a human before. "If I can't have you, I don't want to live," she said as she thrust the gun forward. Before he could react she shoved it under her chin. "Just remember… you did this to me." She pulled the trigger.

"No…don't!" Jacob screamed as he lunged for her.

Her limp body crashed to the floor. Jacob stood over her, gazing down in horror. The air sucked out of his lungs as the door behind him flew open.

"Jacob!" Collin screamed. "Are you all right?"

Jacob turned around and faced him with Becca's blood and brain matter running down his face.

Collin approached him and stood over Becca's body. Blood flowed out of an exit wound in the top of her head. Jacob stared at her lifeless body. His heart sank.

"I never wanted this to happen. All I wanted was for her to leave me alone," Jacob mumbled.

"We need to call the police," Collin said. He grabbed Jacob's arm. "Come on. There's nothing we can do for her. She's dead."

Jacob turned toward Collin. His eyes welled with tears. He followed

Collin out of the house toward the ambulance. While his partner called for police on the radio, Jacob leaned against the ambulance. Guilt rushed through his body. *Could I have done something different?*

Several police units showed up at the house, lights flashing, and sirens blaring. The detectives separated Collin and Jacob as they took their statements. Jacob leaned up against a police car answering the officer's questions, giving him the account of what happened. They'd already called the dispatch center confirming they were sent to the call. Detective Horowitz pulled up to the house and spoke with a few of the officers, bringing him up to speed on the incident. As he spoke with them, he glared at Jacob.

The news media arrived and set up across the perimeter, shooting film for the evening news. A few reporters shouted questions to Jacob from across the yellow tape; he ignored them. He was in the middle of a horrific nightmare. He was more confused than anything. Part of him felt relieved that Becca wouldn't be stalking him any longer. The other part of him felt sorry for her. It was obvious she had mental issues and didn't know what she was doing.

Detective Horowitz approached Jacob. "So, guess the case against you is over now. I bet you feel good about that."

Jacob shook his head. "There's nothing to feel good about right now. A disturbed woman just killed herself in front of me. What do you expect me to do, be happy?"

"Honestly, I could care less about what you feel. I think you raped her and pushed her over the edge. I've seen it before." Detective Horowitz straightened his necktie. "Forensics confirmed she had gunshot residue on her hands. So that alleviates the possibility of you killing her."

Jacob's eyes narrowed and his brow furrowed. "I didn't kill her and I didn't rape her either!"

Detective Horowitz sighed. "Guess we'll never know, will we?" He shook his head and walked toward the media.

A few moments later, Matthew arrived in his command vehicle. He spoke with an officer and they allowed him to cross the yellow tape. He walked over and talked with Collin for a few moments. Once he was done, he approached Jacob.

"You doing okay?"

"As good as can be expected," Jacob quietly answered.

"I'm not sure what to say, Jacob. This is terrible. I knew she was disturbed, but I never thought it would come to this."

Neither did Jacob. The last thing she said to him rang through his ears. Was it his fault? He shook off the doubt, reached into his wallet, and pulled out his company ID. He turned toward Matthew.

"Here," he said extending the ID toward Matthew.

"What are you doing?"

"I'm quitting. I'm sorry, but I can't give you the proper notice. Please accept my apologies for that."

"Jacob, you've just been through a horrible thing. I don't think…."

He pushed the ID in to Matthew's chest. "There's nothing you can say that will change my mind. I'm thankful you hired me and gave me a chance, but I can't stay. There's too much pain here. I can't do this anymore."

Matthew took Jacob's ID. "What are you going to do?"

Jacob sucked in a deep breath. "There's a question I have to get answered. I'm moving to Boise, Idaho."

More from Jerrid Edgington.

Resuscitation: The Reaper Series Book Two

Chapter One

James compressed the pregnant woman's chest who was splayed on the warm asphalt of the two-lane highway while Jacob called for a helicopter.

The volunteer fire fighters that freed her from the car stood around watching. Jacob was thankful for them, but he was agitated they weren't more aggressive in offering assistance. It was a matter of minutes before the baby the woman was carrying would also die.

They were on a highway in the middle of the woods. The road wasn't well-traveled. The sun peeked through the plush green trees that lined the curvy road, casting various shaped shadows on the asphalt.

Jacob glanced at the other vehicle. A man's body slumped over the steering wheel with the windshield caved in and the glass pierced into his skull. The steering wheel buckled from the impact of his body being flung into it—he hadn't been wearing a seat belt.

Jacob grabbed his cell phone. He couldn't control his trembling fingers as he tried to push the numbers on the keypad. Taking a deep breath, he tried to control his anxiety. Slowly he exhaled through pursed lips and dialed the emergency room at Magic County Hospital. After several rings, a woman answered the phone.

"ER," she said abruptly.

"This is Jacob, on Medic-57. I need to speak to the doctor, now!"

The clock was ticking and they didn't have long before they would lose the unborn child, too. Once a patient went into cardiac arrest from trauma, they had less than a one percent chance of survival unless they were on the operating table. If the mother wasn't breathing, neither was the baby. Jacob's primary concern was what could he do to save the baby? Would CPR be sufficient until they were able to get her to the hospital? They were forty-five minutes away from the closest facility and the helicopter wouldn't fly a patient in cardiac arrest because there wasn't enough room for them to be able to continue resuscitative measures. Their options were limited to only one and he needed the doctor on the phone. Jacob paced back and forth next to his partner, James. With each compression, the woman's head bobbed up and down.

The operator sighed. "Hold on."

A moment later, a man picked up the phone. "This is Doctor Young."

Jacob's throat constricted. "This is Jacob on Medic-57. We're on scene of a head on collision with one confirmed fatality. We have a pregnant female who is approximately eight months pregnant. We lost pulses a moment ago, and we're forty-five minutes from the nearest hospital. What do you want me to do?" Life or death calls brought out the best in him, but the added element of having a child's life in his hands terrified him. There was silence on the other end of the phone. "Hello? Are you there?" Jacob felt as though a vacuum had sucked the air from his lungs.

James pumped frantically on the woman's chest. Beads of sweat from his forehead slowly traced down his face and fell onto the lifeless woman's body.

"Yes. I'm here. How long has she been in cardiac arrest?"

"Less than a minute. My partner is doing CPR on her now."

Doctor Young cleared his throat. "You have two choices. I can talk you through a field C-section, or you can do nothing and the baby will die. There's nothing you can do for the mother. She's already dead."

The thought of cutting into the woman's abdomen horrified Jacob. "I'm not trained for that! I don't know the first thing about performing a C-section."

"Look, I know you're scared, but that baby will die if you do nothing. That is a guarantee. At least if you try, the baby has a chance at life."

Jacob sucked in a deep breath. He didn't have time to think. He had to get control of himself. *I should've called in sick today.*

"Do you have access to a scalpel?" Doctor Young asked.

Jacob grabbed the OB kit with shaking hands and ripped it open. The scalpel dropped to the ground. He reached down and picked it up. "Yes, right here," he said holding it. He wiped the sweat off his forehead with his arm. Seconds ticked away, lessening the chance for the baby's survival.

"Do you have any betadine on your ambulance?"

"Does it matter if we disinfect her stomach?"

Doctor Young sighed. "Good point. Now, take your scalpel and cut a vertical incision from her Xiphoid process down to her pubic region. Don't cut too deep. You don't want to perforate her bowel."

Jacob put the phone on speaker and laid it down on the ground next to him. He pushed the scalpel into her skin, being careful not to go too deep. Adrenaline surged through his body. Afraid of doing serious damage, he was careful how far he slid the scalpel into her stomach. The urge to slice her stomach open and pull the baby out was overwhelming. As the blade pierced the skin, a small trace of blood trickled from the entrance wound and down the side of her swollen abdomen.

"How is it going? Have you made it through the first layer of tissue yet?" Doctor Young asked.

"I'm trying," Jacob nervously answered. His hands trembled as he slid the scalpel down the woman's abdomen. A thin line of blood traced his incision. He concentrated on not allowing the CPR that James was performing to distract him. As long as her heart was being compressed, oxygen rich blood was making its way to the baby.

"You're doing fine. There is going to be quite a bit to cut through. But Jacob, you need to work fast."

As if there wasn't enough pressure, now I have to go faster?

The tone in Doctor Young's voice renewed the urgency that he needed to work faster. The only chance the baby had to survive rested solely on his shoulders. After making the initial pass, Jacob cut a little bit deeper. Blood pooled making it difficult to see where he was cutting. A wave of nausea rolled through his stomach. He choked down the urge to vomit and refocused on the task.

"There's a lot of blood."

"Get some gauze and wipe it away," Doctor Young instructed.

Jacob sat the scalpel down on the woman's abdomen, reached into the jump bag, and retrieved several small white packages of gauze. He ripped them open and blotted the blood clearing a visual path. The scalpel bounced on her stomach with each compression. Picking up the scalpel, Jacob continued cutting. After several passes, bowel and intestines came into view. Jacob grasped the organs, lifted them up, and pushed them to the side. Just underneath, a semi-pink mass appeared. A sigh of relief slipped through his lips.

"I think I've made it to the uterus."

"Good. You'll need to cut through that carefully. Remember, there's a baby inside of there."

Jacob's hands shook uncontrollably, making it difficult to hold onto the scalpel.

Calm down. You can do this.

Pushing the scalpel ever so lightly into the mass, he started to cut through. A moment later, a large gush of fluid flowed out of her abdomen.

Oh no! What have I done?

"A lot of fluid came out of her."

"What color is it, Jacob?"

"Clear."

"Okay, that's good. That's the amniotic fluid. Carefully continue your incision, but hurry. You're running out of time."

Cautiously he continued to cut through the uterus. A few moments later, dark hair from the top of the baby's head appeared. A momentary sigh of relief pushed his fear away; he was close.

"How are we doing, Jacob? Is the incision big enough for the baby to fit through?"

Jacob grabbed more gauze to soak up the remnants of the fluid. *How is Doctor Young able to stay so calm through this?*

"Yeah. I think so."

"Now you need to reach in, grab as much of the baby as you can, and pull it out."

"Am I going to hurt it if I pull too hard?" Jacob wouldn't be able to live with himself if he caused permanent damage to the small child. This life was innocent. He'd made it this far and didn't want to turn back now.

"Not any worse than if you do nothing and the baby dies."

Jacob sensed the urgency in the doctor's voice. He focused on what to do next. He reached in, grabbed the baby, and tugged on the small body. The baby wasn't budging—he panicked. "The baby won't come out!"

"Listen to me, Jacob. You have to pull that baby out and do it *now!*"

The baby was sliding off into certain death. With one last heave, he pulled as hard as he could. The limp and blue baby slid out of its mother's stomach. James stopped doing CPR, grabbed the umbilical cord clamps, placed them on the cord, and cut through it once it stopped pulsating.

"The baby is out!"

"Good. I don't hear it crying. Have you stimulated it?"

His greatest fear was lying lifeless in front of him—a baby that wasn't breathing. Jacob retrieved the bulb syringe and suctioned out the baby's mouth and nose—still no breathing. James grabbed the baby and with his large fingers, compressed its small chest. His hands were twice the size of the baby. It was so little and frail. Jacob had done the impossible and successfully performed a C-section. He couldn't bear the thought of losing the baby now.

Dust flew from their leather boots as the two men ran toward their ambulance. Jacob got inside first, reached down and helped James into the back. He placed the baby on the cot and continued to compress the chest. The silence in the ambulance was deafening. His chest constricted against his thumping heart. Vertigo hit him full force and he grabbed the cot in an effort to steady himself. He forced himself to suck in a deep breath.

Jacob grabbed a bag valve mask, hooked it up to oxygen, and ventilated the baby; it was a boy. With each squeeze of the bag, his chest expanded, filling with oxygen. While performing CPR with one hand, James placed the cardiac monitor leads onto the baby's bare chest; a green flat line scrolled across the screen; his heart wasn't beating. Grabbing the pediatric kit, Jacob pulled out the laryngoscope and an endotracheal tube. As he slid the straight blade of the scope into the tiny mouth, he couldn't see anything past the baby's large tongue. He repositioned the laryngoscope, lifted the tongue out of way and the white vocal chords appeared. With ease, he slid the tube past them and then secured it to the baby's ashen colored face with a tube holder.

After what seemed an eternity of performing CPR, a blip appeared on the cardiac monitor, then another one. Jacob's heart skipped a beat. He stared at the monitor and his breath quickened.

"Come on, little man. You can do it. Fight!" Jacob pleaded.

In rapid succession, the baby's heart rate scrolled across the screen. Jacob reached down, squeezed his brachial artery, and felt a strong heartbeat. The corners of his mouth tugged upward and a small smile traced across his face.

James stopped compressing the baby's chest.

The color of the baby's trunk changed from ashen to pink. His small arms moved intermittently, but he still wasn't breathing on his own. After a few minutes the baby's arms and legs also changed from ashen to pink.

The emotional workout almost brought Jacob to his knees. In the near distance he heard the familiar sound of the helicopter approached. This was music to their ears; if only they could've arrived sooner. James slid a needle into the baby's small arm. He was able to establish an IV on his first attempt, a rare accomplishment on a newborn child. After he secured the IV, he leaned back against the wall of the ambulance, his breathing slowing to a normal rate.

The flight crew, once on the ground, approached Jacob and James with their flight cot and equipment. After giving them a brief report, they whisked the baby away, and ran across the asphalt toward their air ambulance. Moments later, they were airborne.

James and Jacob sat down on the bumper of the ambulance. The emotional stress took a toll on their bodies. For several minutes, neither of them spoke. Several of the volunteer firefighters walked over and congratulated them. Jacob couldn't feel proud for what they'd done. They were able to save one life, but they also lost two others. The odds of the baby surviving were grim. He wasn't sure if the CPR was effective enough to keep blood blowing to baby's small body.

James placed a hand on Jacob's shoulder. "Great job, man. I couldn't have done it."

Jacob rested his elbows on his knees. He tried to be a macho man and not let his feelings get the best of him, but he couldn't hold back. The floodgates of emotions opened and unleashed their unforgiving fury upon him; he wept.

After a few minutes, Jacob peeled off the blood soaked gloves, and dropped them on the ground. He dried his eyes, walked over, picked up the cell phone, and pressed it against his ear.

"Hello? Can you hear me, Jacob?" asked Doctor Young.

Jacob dried off his eyes and cleared his throat. "Yes. I'm here. Sorry. We handed the baby off to the flight crew."

"Is he okay?"

"Yes. We got him back."

"They saved the baby!" Doctor Young yelled. He could hear shouts of joy and people clapping in the background. In the midst of the chaos, for a brief moment, Jacob was happy. Realizing they faced a grim situation, kept their composure, and were able to give the baby a chance, he smiled.

"You did a great job. I'm proud of you."

"I wish I could feel good about it, doc. Thank you for your help." Jacob hung up the cell phone and slid it back into his pants pocket.

James followed Jacob over to the mother's body. James pulled a sheet over her up to her head. Jacob knelt down next to her body, studying her face. Her face, pale and lifeless, yet so peaceful and angelic. Not more than an hour ago, she was driving down the road probably thinking about what color to paint her baby's room. Now, she was dead. It saddened him to think the child would never know his mother. He reached down and pulled a few strands of dark brown curls out of her eyes.

"You have a son. A beautiful little boy. I'm sure you'd be proud of him. I'm so sorry we couldn't do more to save you." A tear trickled out of the corner of Jacob's eye.

James took the sheet and pulled it over her head.

Jacob stood while looking down at the woman. "I'm in a lot of trouble now. I just did something paramedics aren't allowed to do and I may lose my license."

Catch *Resuscitation: The Reaper Series Book Two* for sale on Amazon now.

http://www.amazon.com/dp/B00KQSWPIG

Connect with the author on his blog:

http://www.authorjerridedgington.com

A note from the author:

I want to personally thank you all for reading my debut novel, *Racing the Reaper*, the first book in the Reaper Series. I would greatly appreciate it if you could take a moment to post a honest review on Amazon at this link: http://www.amzn.com/B00GQD9S94